BRANTFORD PUBLIC LIBRARY
39154901176107

D0563699

THE CANDLELIT MENAGERIE

THE CANDLELIT MENAGERIE

a novel

CARALINE BROWN

ARCADE PUBLISHING · New York

Copyright © 2020 by Caraline Brown

All rights reserved. No part of this book may be reproduced in any manner without the express written consent of the publisher, except in the case of brief excerpts in critical reviews or articles. All inquiries should be addressed to Arcade Publishing, 307 West 36th Street, 11th Floor, New York, NY 10018.

Arcade Publishing books may be purchased in bulk at special discounts for sales promotion, corporate gifts, fund-raising, or educational purposes. Special editions can also be created to specifications. For details, contact the Special Sales Department, Arcade Publishing, 307 West 36th Street, 11th Floor, New York, NY 10018 or arcade@skyhorsepublishing.com.

Arcade Publishing® is a registered trademark of Skyhorse Publishing, Inc.®, a Delaware corporation.

Visit our website at www.arcadepub.com.

10 9 8 7 6 5 4 3 2 1

Library of Congress Cataloging-in-Publication Data is available on file.

Cover design by Erin Seaward-Hiatt
Cover art by Gettyimages

Print ISBN: 978-1-950691-55-5
Ebook ISBN: 978-1-950691-57-9

Printed in the United States of America

For Dail Ambler, Beat Girl

Part One

Part One

One

LILLIAN COULD HEAR THE SOUND OF the lion as soon as she awoke. She knew it was roaring because it was hungry and she wondered, not for the first time, what on earth they fed it.

Through her thin curtains she could see the light breaking on London for another day. Instead of rising, Lillian rolled over and pulled the blanket up under her chin. The mornings were the coldest part of the day, and at this time of year she slept almost fully clothed, as the heat never seemed to reach her small room at the top of the house. She extended her legs, but her knees stayed bent as her feet hit the end of the bed. She'd never had a bed that was big enough for her.

In the rooms below, she could hear the call bells start to ring as the house roused itself from the night. At last she rose. A jug and a basin stood on the floor and she squatted down beside them, lifted her skirts, and splashed a little icy cold water around her groin with her hand. She wrung out the cloth alongside the basin, then fished inside her top half and sponged under her arms. Her mistress, the good Miss Mary Unsworth of Tottenham Court Road, had given her the remains of a bottle of lavender water and she carefully measured a few drops in her hands, rubbed them together, and smeared them under her armpits.

The lion roared again and Lillian smiled to herself as she brushed her hair, thinking of the handbill she had found. Her mistress often sent Lillian on errands to Covent Garden, and only last week she had been handed a piece of paper with pictures of the most strange and amazing of animals. The bill promised a place with dazzling birds of every size and colour; giant beasts with noses that hung to the floor; cold-blooded lizards with tongues as long as your arm; animals that carried their young in a belly pouch. Even birds that could talk! To own such a beast would surely denote your place in the world, the leaflet said.

Lillian was grateful for her work but knew she was not particularly good at being a lady's maid. Yes, she could put up her mistress's hair and ensure it stayed in place for the day, but her own was a different tale. Her dark hair had the texture of a horse's mane and simply refused to stay put, constantly escaping from the constraints of the pins and ribbons her mistress had given her in an attempt to dress Lillian as the position demanded.

As a child back in the country, Lillian had been allowed to wear breeches on account of her size. Now she yearned for the freedom such clothes had given her. She dreamed of cutting her hair short like a boy. She had heard of women who hacked off their hair and posed as boys to follow their lovers into battle, such as Phoebe Hessel, who'd fallen in love with a soldier and enlisted in the Fifth Regiment of Foot in the British army. Lillian had devoured the details of Phoebe's story in the newspaper, learning that she served five years as a private, even earning a small scar on the elbow as the result of a bayonet wound received in the Battle of Fontenoy. Oh, how she yearned to follow her into battle! But she would have settled for simply being able to wear breeches.

Lillian paused in her toilet and considered herself in the small looking glass that stood on her chest of drawers. She was not an unattractive woman, although she only ever received a second glance on account of her height. The tip of her nose, which was neither big nor petite, always seemed to catch the light. Her green eyes were framed by the fairest of eyelashes that made her eyes seem smaller than they were, but her lips were an acceptable colour of pink, especially when she squeezed them between her teeth. Her chin was neat and round as a small hen's egg. Specks of food remained on the front of her dress despite her constant attempts to keep it clean. Lillian's mistress was kind and she truly loved her for taking her in, despite not having the appearance of the average lady's maid. She was aware how folks tittered when she followed behind her mistress's petite figure. So be it. Lillian had been laughed at most of her life. She knew what she looked like in the required dresses and bonnets the other maids wore. They pinched at her waist and clung to her throat and itched at her wrists, as if the clothing were squeezing the life from her.

She squirmed as she remembered last week's visit with her mistress to Wedgwood's Rooms in Pall Mall. Miss Unsworth had given her strict instructions to stay three feet behind and keep her hands clasped at all times lest she knock into anything. Lillian had never felt so large and ungainly as in that shop, which was piled floor to ceiling with china so delicate you could almost see right through it. She had breathed in the smell of perfumed candles that filled the air as ladies wandered with their maids amongst huge tables laid out with the very best in Wedgwood designs, tantalising creations in blue, green, and lilac and others in yellow, black, and white. It was such a quiet and refined atmosphere, punctuated only by the sounds of cups being gently lifted and placed back on their saucers, that Lillian hardly dared breathe. But when her mistress dropped her handkerchief, she had moved forwards to pick it up so quickly that her cloak caught the handle of a gravy boat positioned at the edge of a fully laden table. She sent half a dozen teacups and saucers, along with a three-tiered cake stand, crashing to the floor in a cloud of white ceramic dust. The collective intake of breath quickly gave way to a fluttering of fans, then titters at

Lillian's obvious confusion and distress as the shop assistants flustered around her mistress with assurances that it was a mere accident, whilst casting black-eyed looks at the clumsy perpetrator.

She shook her head at the memory.

Lillian looked again at the advertisement in her hand. It boasted that if London led the world, then the greatest place in London to see such magnificent sights was at Grady's Menagerie on the Strand.

Grady's Menagerie!

The words rolled around her head and something inside her stirred. Almost twenty years of working and drudgery and orders, and never ever anything for herself. Her imagination was on fire, pictures forming in her head of what these creatures might look like. She needed to see these animals. To smell them, to get close to them. Yes, she *had* to see them.

And today was Sunday, her afternoon off. As soon as her work was done, she planned to set off for the Strand.

The winter sun was drooping in the sky by the time she finally got away. Fearing the place might be closed before she got there, Lillian quickly made her way up Fleet Street and across Holborn in ten minutes. Outside the Lyceum she caught the unfamiliar whiff of animal. Quickening her step, she walked past Andrews Medical Supplies, Daniel Steele's stationers, a few more steps beyond Neeles the engraver, and there it was. Grady's Menagerie.

Craning her neck, she read the grand title of Exeter Exchange Menagerie painted in bright letters at the very top of the building. Another sign declaring Edward Grady Dealer in Exotic Birds and Beasts sat above and between two Doric columns whilst a large window opened onto a balcony where images of all the animals that could be found therein were painted. Behind the window she could see half a dozen young women, their heads bent over pieces of cloth they held in their hands. Seamstresses, she presumed.

A SHILLING TO SEE ALL THE ANIMALS OF THE WORLD, the sign at the entrance proclaimed, and she duly laid down her two sixpences to the fat old lady in widow's weeds sitting in the booth.

It was dark as she entered, and she squeezed her eyes closed to help adjust to the gloom. When she opened them, she could see the room was lit by candles placed in small recesses cut into the walls all the way down both sides of a huge hall. Then the smell hit her, an overpowering stench of rancid meat and fetid straw, overlaid with animal excreta. The ceiling was so high it must be impossible to heat in winter, she thought. The cold from the cobbled floor reached up to her calves through her shoes. Lillian shivered and hugged herself, but quickly forgot the cold and the smell as her senses were overtaken by the sights of the strangest and yes, truly, the most amazing creatures.

Here was one that looked like a dog, covered in spots, and made the oddest sound as if it were laughing at her. THE HYENA, AFRICA, a small notice above its cage declared. Next to it was a pig with huge quills for hair. PORCUPINE, THE AMERICAS, she read. She recognised the creature in the next enclosure, a kangaroo from Australia. *That's where they send all the thieves and pickpockets*, she thought. A loud snorting sound made her turn to find a massive boar, bigger than anything she had ever seen on the farm. Then she became aware of the sounds of birds, seemingly hundreds and hundreds of birds, all singing and calling and flapping their wings in a blaze of colours, and in the distance, a variety of roars and screams and shouts.

The smell of pipe smoke reached her nostrils. Out of the corner of her eye she caught the silhouette of a stocky man standing in the shadows at the end of the corridor, puffing away. She continued to wander from one side of the Great Hall to the other, pausing to examine the creatures in their pens, stalls, and cages, noting their countries of origin. Where had these creatures come from? What did they eat? Did the sun shine in their home?

There were few other visitors as she stopped to stare at a pair of wolves occupying a corner pen with a painting of the Seven Hills of Rome set as a backdrop, forming a tableau of sorts. One wolf was gnawing at its front paw and she noticed its foot was tethered by an iron bracelet to a ring on the wall. Its water bowl was empty.

"They should take better care of you," she said aloud.

"Take better care?" said the man with the pipe, stepping forwards, one hand on his lapel. He was accompanied by a huge dog that leaned against him, its head reaching his waist.

Lillian looked at the man with curiosity, as if he were one of the exhibits. He was a short sturdy creature modelling the bushiest of sideburns, the colour of Seville oranges. He sported a double-breasted coat with a black velvet collar and a black and red checked waistcoat. The ensemble was completed by a shiny green cravat, pinned with a tiger's claw, about four inches long and set in a bed of silver. She thought he had a slight look of the paddywhack about him, like some of her father's friends when they had a drop too much and the colour rose in their cheeks.

"Sir, it seems that many of these creatures could do with a change of straw and the simple matter of their water bowls topping up," she said sternly.

"Ah," said the man, taking a deep bow. "What a pleasure and an honour it is to meet a fellow aficionado and expert of the world's great fauna."

"I . . . I'm no expert, sir," Lillian stammered.

The man took a puff on his pipe and squinted coldly at her.

"No," he said. "I don't suppose you are."

Before Lillian could reply, the man continued, "You like my charges, my dear?" His tone had abruptly changed. He was smiling now.

"Sir," she replied, "I've never seen the like. I . . . I am quite overwhelmed. I never knew such creatures could exist."

The man chuckled. "England rules the waves, my dear, and those ships we send bearing goods to the four corners of the globe are returning with a different cargo, creatures the like of which no one had ever imagined nor seen before."

Lillian's mouth fell open.

"Allow me to introduce myself," the man said, taking another bow. "My name is Edward Grady, the . . . ah . . . *eponymous* owner of this 'ere *humble* establishment."

He emphasised the second syllable of *eponymous* and the first in *humble*.

"And this is Teddy Diamond," he added, indicating the shaggy grey dog, who wagged his tail and gave a woof at the sound of his name. His tongue hung out of his mouth so that it looked like he was smiling.

"I've never seen such a large dog," said Lillian, stepping back.

"Wolfhound," said Grady. "From the old country. You'll never find a stronger or gentler canine."

The man held Lillian's gaze until she pulled her eyes away and smiled down at the dog, who gave her hand a lick.

Grady puffed on his pipe once more. "And what brings you to this wondrous emporium of the exotic?" He waved his hand to indicate the empire in which he stood.

"The lion, sir!" she replied, beaming. "I hear it in the morning when I wake, and at night when I retire. Why, it is like he and I feed at the same time, even sleep at the same time. I've been looking all over and I think I can hear him in the distance but I've not found him yet."

She dropped her eyes and her voice drifted away. She was suddenly aware that she might be talking nonsense to a complete stranger.

Grady stared at her. "Come with me," he said and took her by the wrist—not too roughly, but with a sense of urgency—and pulled her behind him.

He led her past the loitering families taking their last views before they left, past the exotic birds, around the corner and past the ram with the large horns, and finally to the end of the first-floor corridor. Slightly breathless, Grady stopped at the final cage.

"There," he commanded, pointing. "Look."

After so many nights hearing its roar, she was finally there in front of the beast. She watched as he took three paces, turned, then took three more, this being the limit of the size of his cage. Without thinking, she inched closer until she found herself gripping the iron bars with both hands.

"Careful!" Grady cautioned.

The smell of unkempt, mangled fur mingled with the damp urine-sodden straw as the lion paced around its cell. It stopped. Paused. And released a loud heavy stream of yellow piss that smelt both sweet and foul in the air. Lillian caught the tang of salt on her tongue.

"Meet Leonidas," said Grady.

Lillian whispered the unfamiliar syllables, "Lee . . . on . . . eye . . . das."

Her knuckles were white, the bars cold and damp. She went to wipe her nose and smelt iron and lion. The beast looked her right in the eye and they held each other's gaze. He opened his mouth and the heat and smell of his breath was warm on her face and the aroma of putrid meat filled her nostrils. But he didn't make a sound.

Grady grabbed her hand. "'Ere," he said. "Stick it out. Let 'im smell yer." He shoved her open palm through the cage right under the lion's nose. Lillian did not flinch. Grady moved back a few steps to watch. The lion looked at her and stared. Her fear fell away and Lillian fell powerfully in love. She wanted and needed to be near that animal.

"I think he likes me," she said.

"I think he does," Grady agreed.

But Lillian didn't need telling. She knew.

When she turned around, she blushed to see how closely Grady had been watching her and now stood there, grinning as if he had planned the entire encounter.

Two

GRADY COULD NOT GET THE STRANGE tall woman out of his head. That first day he had stood in the shadows watching her, and whispered to the dog, "Never seen a lass as big as that, Teddy Diamond. Wouldn't be surprised if there's a touch of *Digitus vel instrumentum magnum*, eh?" and had laughed to himself. The dog gave a single bark.

Grady was not averse to a big woman, and as he thought back to his encounter with Lillian, he grew a little hard. He sang a ditty to himself that he'd often heard at the Cock Tavern:

That one's a Man is false, they've both been felt,
Tho' Jolly swears, Bess is, or sh' has been gelt.
She bullies, whistles, sings, and rants and swears
Beyond the Plyers at St. Katern's Stairs;
She kisses all, but Jenny is her dear,
She feels her Bubbies, and she bites her ear:
They to the Garret or the Cellar sneak.

LILLIAN'S VISITS TO the Exchange became a regular Sunday afternoon event. As soon as she arrived at the entrance she would be greeted by Alfred, the hurdy-gurdy man's capuchin monkey, dressed in a waistcoat and red velvet tasselled hat. Alfred would run towards her waving his collecting tin, and Lillian would obligingly drop in her shilling entrance fee, after which Alfred would then run over to Mrs. Ogden, sitting in her widow's tweeds in the admission booth, and empty the contents on the counter.

Mrs. Ogden would then let out a loud bellow—"Grady, she's 'ere again"—and the owner would appear within seconds, as if he had been waiting for her, ready to accompany the young woman on the walk through the Great Hall, taking the opportunity to point out the little improvements he was starting to make. He was delighted when his efforts were rewarded with a smile. When they reached the lion's cage he would stand back and watch, intrigued, while she muttered endearments and Leonidas tossed his head, shook his mane, and gave one seductive, gentle growl after another.

It wasn't until her fifth visit that he asked, "You've never told me . . . how do ye earn thy crust, my dear?" He leaned in with what he thought was a winning smile but instead exposed the gaps in his yellowing teeth.

Lillian blinked. "Sir, I'm a maid in Tottenham Court Road and I'll thank you for not coming too close to me."

Grady held up his hands and took a step backwards. "Apologies, my dear. You've nowt to fear from me. Just being friendly."

"My mistress is Miss Mary Unsworth," she said, pulling her shawl around her shoulders to indicate the visit was drawing to a close.

Grady gave a hurried bow. "Miss Lillian. Your servant." He watched her go, thinking it best to not to chase after her, lest he make matters worse.

Seven days till she comes again, he thought, and gave a small sigh.

GRADY LIKED TO tell his customers that the larger animals each had their own boy to take charge of them, but this was far from the truth. A fleet of young hemps came and went, depending on the money they could make from the few buckets of dung they managed to scrape out of the stalls. Lillian's observations had made him realise he needed more. The stock needed more. It was no longer just a case of mucking out—the growing number of animals needed grooming and care and proper feeding to make them attractive enough for sale.

Grady was not the only keeper of a menagerie in London, or even in Covent Garden. Nor was his shop the biggest or the best. He considered his strongest rival to be a man called Polito, who operated a similar-sized establishment less than half a mile away. The competition between Polito and Grady was well known in the nearby drinking houses, and woe betide anyone who got in Grady's way on a day when Polito had been swifter than he in securing something new, unusual, and in demand. The gossip was that they had both been in love with the same woman once, but it was so long ago no one could remember who it might have been or who the lady eventually chose.

Grady was ambitious and he had plans. The demand for exotic creatures was on the rise and he needed to present an emporium that was cleaner and better kept than those of his competitors. He discovered that dirty animals did not live long and customers would soon stop coming if a Grady purchase did not last at least until the novelty of owning an animal wore off.

ON HER NEXT visit Lillian asked, "Who takes care of the lion? I thought he had his own boy but I've yet to see him."

"Now there's a thing," Grady replied, keeping his distance and starting to pace in front of the lion's cage. The dog stuck to his ankles, watching his master as if he expected a morsel of something tasty to fall from his hand at any moment. "It's difficult here with so many new animals each time the ships come in."

He stopped and took another puff on his pipe.

"In an ideal world, each creature would have its very own boy, of course. But these are difficult times, what with talk of war with France and taxes and the like. This lot are all here to be sold, you know?"

He played with the silver tiger claw on his cravat.

"I've been thinking," he said. "Got a proposition for you."

"Oh yes?" Lillian replied warily, continuing to stare at the lion.

"I need someone to help me, a housekeeper for the animals, if you like."

Now she turned towards him, a quizzical frown on her face.

Grady quickly continued. "Keep the boys in order as well. Tell 'em what needs to be done." He nodded at her. "Someone not afraid of their smell nor their roar nor their appetites." He took several puffs on his pipe in quick succession.

"Do you mean me?" she said, tapping her chest.

"Call it instinct," said Grady and held her gaze as he let his words sink in, watching her reaction.

"Work here?" Lillian murmured, her eyes widening.

"May I speak frankly?" Grady continued.

Lillian nodded, staring at him as she had previously stared at Leonidas.

"I see a woman trapped, caged if you like . . ."

She put her hand up to the high collar at her throat and ran her fingers around the inside.

"Come . . . tend the animals. Groom them. Care for them."

She raised a hand to her long hair.

Grady could read a signal a mile away. "You'll probably want to cut your hair, of course. Make it easier to manage."

He let the idea hang in the air and grow on its own.

"And breeches might be better too," he added.

"Where would I sleep?" Lillian asked, and Grady played his trump card.

"The fellow who had this place before me was a huge gent," he said with enthusiasm. "A big old jack of legs, a duke of limbs. He'd had a special bed made, he was so tall. It's all ready for you should you want it. And don't worry about me. I've got a couple of rooms above the Bell."

Teddy Diamond barked his encouragement. Lillian looked at Leonidas, then turned towards Grady. Her eyes were shining.

Grady melted. "And of course you'll be able to see this fella every day," he said, and Leonidas gave a delighted roar.

Three

HENRY FEATHERSTONE STROLLED BY THE RECENTLY built wall
alongside the Thames. Pulling his coat tighter around him,
he stopped to watch the small boats and barges scuttle back and
forth and to admire the construction work across the river. London
had long ago left the plague behind, and the Great Fire was not
even a memory for any living being. Now a million strong, each
day the city continued its inexorable march towards becoming the
greatest in the world. It already was, according to the seamen down
on the Woolwich docks.

He stopped at a bench and shook open his evening paper. Along
with the rest of the city, he had an insatiable appetite for news.
This was the third paper he had bought today. He did a quick cal-
culation in his head. With six daily newspapers, and around fifteen
tri-weeklies, it meant that at any one time there were forty to fifty
thousand papers in circulation.

"Forty thousand newspapers!" he chuckled to himself.

But despite such literacy, the baser instincts still ruled in the
alleyways, as men indulged in that human trait that takes great
satisfaction in watching physical supremacy exerted over another.

Whether by fist, tooth, or claw, London liked nothing more than to place its meagre earnings on the outcome of such encounters. Bear against bear, bear against dog, man versus man.

But the greatest of these fights was undoubtedly the pitching of cock against cock.

It was rumoured that Featherstone had been one of the "hangers-on" for the highwayman, Jack the Lad, when he finally went to meet his maker, many years ago now. But no one would ever dare ask him.

Jack had caused major humiliation to the City's gaolers, escaping his dungeon despite being fettered hand and foot, his legs padlocked to the floor. Freeing his wrists from his handcuffs, Jack had picked the padlock with a nail and somehow managed to climb the chimney, using the instruments of his own imprisonment to crack through the brickwork. Up through the ceiling, he found himself in a passage leading to the chapel where he broke through the wall. Two further gates standing in his way were easily negotiated. Finally, facing a door made of iron, Jack somehow got it off its hinges, only to find himself on the roof of Newgate itself—and no way to get down.

What could he do but return to his cell back the way he came, make a rope out of his blankets, and use them to lower himself off the roof and down into a side street? Jack was twenty-one and this was his fourth escape.

Sadly for Jack, the draw of the Strand proved too much and he was arrested in Drury Lane a mere two weeks later and hanged within the month. They said the execution of Jack Sheppard drew over a third of London as witness. Friends of the prisoner, "hangers-on," were employed to drag down on the body as it swung to speed up the inevitable process.

What on earth was Henry Featherstone, the animal doctor, doing with a man like that?

FEATHERSTONE DESCENDED THE steps, pushed open the door, put down his five shillings, and entered the small amphitheatre. He ignored the odour of unwashed man mixed with bird and turd and straw and smiled approvingly at the floor with its thick layer of knucklebones carpet, which enhanced the birds' grip. The Royal Cockpit on the south side of St. James Park was one of London's more fashionable venues. But Featherstone felt just at ease here as in the dives of Pickled Egg Walk or Horseshoe Alley.

The Cockpit drew the lowest of the low to the highest of the quality for what was said to be, at six thousand years old, the world's oldest spectator sport. There was something about the viciousness of the cock flying against its own that drew all types of men, regardless of birth.

Despite his profession, Featherstone enjoyed betting on animals. It wasn't the money that drew him in but the simple love of the cockfight. He only placed as much as he could afford to lose—five guineas, no more—although bets of up to one hundred guineas were not unusual at the Cockpit.

Tonight was a Welch Main event. Only one cock would emerge triumphant, having beaten up to sixteen opponents, each fitted with a set of silver spurs designed to inflict maximum damage. Anyone blinding a cock's eyes would be fined forty shillings; anyone sticking a pin in a cock would be fined twenty. All bets to be paid as soon as the fight was over, and "*any man who shall not pay his dues on one wager and maketh another wager to be put in a basket and be hung to the eaves of the pit that all men may see him and to remain there until the end of the session when he shall be cut down.*" So said the rules of engagement.

The spectators nodded as Featherstone strolled by, whilst the feeders invited him to take the once-over of their fighters.

"Here's Swallow Catcher, sir," said one. "You'll not see a finer Red Dun in all of London."

"Shouldn't you be resting him?" said Featherstone, shouting to reply above the noise. "He fought a hard battle at the Horseshoe the other week. You should set him on his walk for the rest of the season, man."

"Here's Hector," said another, offering his bird to Featherstone for inspection. He gave it a cursory glance as he looked for his favourite, who tonight would be facing the much-talked-about Ferenought.

"Where's Ding Darling?" Featherstone asked, and his handler appeared, carrying the bird. Darling sported a smattering of white over a set of black feathers, each feather looking like a wet bloody knife. His neck and head were stout as well as long; just as a good fighting cock should be built, giving great advantage in battle. His eyes were large and full and his beak crooked, the body short and compact, the breast rounded and the thighs thick and firm going all the way to the neck, a good indication of staying power. His feet were broad and thin with the longest of claws. He strutted like a champion. Even he knew he was a winner.

"He'll fuck any hen in the house, sure he would," said the man to Featherstone's left.

"Yes, and then finish off the rest of 'em," said his companion, laughing.

"My money's on the Darling!" said another.

Featherstone looked at the tall man holding Darling's opponent, noting his slight stoop and dirty yellow hair, uneven and sticking out in clumps and angles as if it had been hacked at with a knife. He thought he seemed agitated as he held the bird close to his chest, whispering in its ear.

"I've not seen him around before," Featherstone said, nudging the man on his left.

"New to London, sir, so I understand. Making a bit of name for himself with the birds, though. His Ferenought's won a number of battles. Master rates him anyway. Button's his name. John Button."

Featherstone took a step forwards and put out his hand to stroke Button's charge. "May I see your bird, sir?" he said.

Button licked his fingers and smoothed a clump of hair before holding the bird up for inspection. The comb and wattle had been cut off, as had Darling's, to save them being used against them in the battle to come.

Ferenought's legs were thinner than the Darling's, despite weighing the same at just over four and a half pounds, said to be the perfect weight for a fighting cock. His body was stout but the brown-black feathers seemed somehow softer. He was stringier and lacked his opponent's confidence.

"I thought we were going to have a contest, eh lads?" said Featherstone, and the crowd responded with a good-natured laugh.

"You might be surprised, sir," said Button, holding the bird tightly to his chest and tenderly stroking his head.

The officials assembled: the Master, two wardens, and the holder of the stakes. Cocks that weren't fighting stayed hooded. Ding Darling strutted around the pen, his short, hard feathers assuring the assembled of his good health.

The setters-to carried the cocks into the pit and the birds were examined to ensure they had the same marks and colours as noted on the match bill. The Master made a final check that the spurs of both fighters were the same size. The birds were held beak to beak, then let go with a flourish. The fight was on.

They fanned and puffed their chests, but Ding Darling wasted no time. With his feathers splayed, he strutted, then pounced. Peck followed vicious peck until Ferenought stumbled and fell back. A roar went up amongst the crowd.

Ferenought would not go on, and the two handlers jumped in to set the two birds against each other once more. The crowd roared again. Featherstone could feel the blood lust rise in the room. At first Ferenought refused once more, but then changed his mind and the birds set on each other, feathers flying as they fought in the air. Ferenought fell back again. Button jumped in the ring, grabbed his bird, and vigorously began to suck the blood from his head. Darling's man held onto his would-be victor, calming him and stroking him down, but blood was up for Darling, sensing victory and a weakened opponent.

Once more the birds went beak to beak. Gaining a second wind, Ferenought flew at Darling's eyes. Darling put up his claws and stuck into Ferenought's chest, but the blood was flowing from his eyes now; blinded, his confidence had gone. Both birds fell back. The dry bones on the floor were turning crimson. The room fell silent. One . . . two . . . maybe three seconds . . . then an eruption of sound as the audience came to a realisation at the same time. Neither fighter had survived the final onslaught. The Master rang the bell. The arena exploded. Both cocks dead, and the only way to decide the winner was on the single throw of the Master's die.

His word was final.

In the east the watchman could be heard calling: *"Two of the clock in the morning and all is well"*—which seemed to confirm the peace and stillness rather than breaking it. The City had settled and gone to sleep; the coffee shops and bawdy houses had long ago locked their doors. All the lights in the streets were extinguished.

Silence. No sound from man nor beast was heard. Any foot or hoof placed on cobble would be made carefully and quietly, respectful of the sleeping citizens and with no desire to disturb the night from its slumber.

"Two of the clock in the morning and all is well."

But all was not well with Featherstone, who made his slow way home by the river. The evening had unnerved him in a way he could not quite fathom. Instead of the usual belly full of wine and pocketful of guineas, he carried instead a melancholic heart.

"Why on earth would a man be so upset at the result of a fight?" he asked himself for the hundredth time.

He could still picture the young lad Button, standing head and shoulders above the rest of the crowd, fingers dragging at his hair and his face wet with tears. The lad's grief for the dead bird foxed him. Birds were coaxed into existence, fed, watered, trained, fought, and died. That was the way of the thing and that was what they were here for.

Besides, everything died. Featherstone remembered the frog in the glass on the desk in his study and recalled how he had walked in just the other morning to find it floating and lifeless. Had he cried? No, by god! He'd just get another. Yet he hadn't. Not yet.

His thoughts returned to young Button. Could he be what Featherstone was looking for?

Four

I T WAS A FRESH NEW MORNING as John Button made his way along the Tottenham Court Road. A light rain had washed the cobbles so they sparkled; as the horses clip-clopped past, even their dung smelled fresh and clean. The tang of citrus hung in the air. London loved its oranges, and it seemed wherever you went there was this smell of orange mixed with horse and a thousand other scents at the outer reaches of one's nose—fresh baked bread, cabbages, last night's ale, this morning's coffee, and the underlying stench of all the animals that shared the city, whether on two legs or four.

An hour earlier Button had received a message from the old man he'd met at the cockfight the previous night, asking him to pay a call. He had no idea what it meant, but neither was he going to refuse. He looked up at the sky and thought of his mother. "If there's enough blue in the sky to make a pair of sailor's trousers, then the day will get better," she would say. *Enough to make two pairs*, he thought, and smiled.

He never failed to be struck by the sheer noise of London, in marked contrast to his village in Dorset where there was barely a raised voice except on a Saturday night when the drinkers at the Shepherdess were thrown out. He paused to take in the sounds of street sellers crying their wares, horses and carriages thundering by, and shouts and screams and laughter hailing from the coffee houses. Women of all ages filled the streets offering services and wares: chair mending, knife grinding, pins, needles, mouse traps, brushes. Hawkers of meat and vegetables, oysters, crabs, and oranges filled the air with their cries of *"Hot pies! One pound fish! Mend the old bellows! Fat chickens!"*

When he reached the address to which he had been directed, he was shown to Henry Featherstone's study. Button pushed open the door to be greeted by a fat arse. The arse's head was lodged under a large armchair.

"Goo—good afternoon, Mr. Featherstone," said John. "Is something lost? Can I be of assistance?"

"Arthur. I've lost Arthur," a muffled voice replied. "Can't find him anywhere."

"Shall I lift the chair, sir?" said John.

"Yes, please," said Featherstone. "That would be splendid."

John duly lifted the chair to reveal a rather more dishevelled fellow than the gentleman he had met the previous night. Featherstone was a portly man of average height in his mid-fifties with knee-length breeches fitted into shoeless, stockinged feet. His shirt sported the longer cuffs of a fashion now past and was open to his waist, whilst his hair had come loose from the ribbon at the nape of his neck.

"Don't just stand there, man! We have got to find him!" said Featherstone.

John looked around the room and wrinkled his nose. There was a noxious odour hanging in the air, which he later learned was a formaldehyde preservative; it would become so familiar it no longer imposed on his nostrils. Books were piled on top of books, feathers used as markers in those that were closed, others left open with inky scratchings underscoring and marking various exclamations of a point that had struck the reader. Bright mounted butterflies rested quietly on the desk alongside various hard-shelled beetles with pins through their torsos. A microscope sat next to a frog, long bereft of all moisture, splayed out on a board, nailed and crucified with a white belly exposed. A large bunch of yellow daffodils made a splash of colour amongst the browns and blacks of the dead things.

"About six inches from head to toe, black and orange. Eight legs. Hairy. Got him off a sailor down the Cockpit one night," said Featherstone. "He's a hardy fellow—when he's in his box, that is. Bit of a lethal bite they tell me, though, and I don't want to try it."

"Bit of a rum do to have lost him then, sir," said John.

"You're not wrong, young Button. Ha! You're not wrong!"

Featherstone continued to move around the room, peering behind the piles of books, lifting jars with dubious floating contents, and pausing briefly to stroke the feathers of the stuffed black crow mounted on a tiny plinth that sat on the desk.

"It may look a mess but I know *exactly* where everything is," Featherstone said.

"Except Arthur, sir," said Button.

Ignoring this, Featherstone continued his search.

"Mrs. Tomkins is forbidden to touch anything in this room," he said.

"Too much rum! Too much rum!" said a voice, and for the first time John noticed a huge bird, bigger than anything he had ever seen, at least a foot tall, with the brightest of blue feathers and sporting a magnificent red crown. It sat on a perch in a huge cage in the corner of the room.

"Oh my goodness," said John, amazed. So it was true! There really were birds that could speak. "But I don't drink," he said, addressing the bird.

"Too much rum! Too much rum!"

Featherstone smiled and shook his head. "That's Silver. He's a parrot and doesn't understand a word you say. Merely a learning process. A repetitive action, if you like. Talk to him enough times, he will learn what you say and simply repeat it."

The parrot interrupted. "I don't drink," it said.

"God's nails," said Featherstone. "You only said that once!"

"A talking bird," said John.

"A talking bird," said Silver.

"Goodness," said John.

"Goodness," Silver repeated.

Featherstone looked at John with astonishment. "Well now, I've owned that bloody bird for three years and never got a word out of him, bar the painful reminder of having drunk too much. Rum! Which I never drink! And I call him a 'him' but truth is I couldn't tell you if he is a she or whatever."

John smiled at Featherstone. "It's simple, sir. You just blow up his arse."

"You do what?"

"Gently blow around the nether regions and all is revealed. The secret of bird keeping is all in the nether regions."

"A ha, there he is!" said Featherstone and dropped to his knees. "Quickly! Pass me that cage."

John sprang to attention and grabbed the box on the study desk, sliding the lid up as Featherstone deposited the errant occupant back in his cage. Featherstone held it up to his eyes and John looked the tarantula in the face.

"I used to make boxes like these," he said, staring at the little cage. "I'd take a log of pine and chop it into little pieces, then whittle and smooth each one till I had enough sticks to bind them all together to make a box. Used to take hours."

"What did you keep inside?" Featherstone asked as he poked a finger through the bars to stroke Arthur's back. Arthur jumped and the finger was quickly withdrawn and the cage placed back on the desk.

"Canaries, mostly," John replied.

"I saw you had a way with birds the other night, young man.

Been making quite a name for yourself down at the Cockpit. What's this about their nether regions, then?" Featherstone indicated that Button should sit in one of the two chairs in front of the fire.

"Do you mind if I take the other chair, sir? I'm deaf in the left ear and would rather you addressed your words to my right."

"Of course, my boy. How come you cannot hear in your left?"

Button grinned. "I fell into a pond as a child trying to catch a frog," he said, sweeping some bits of dirt from the chair and taking his seat. "Caught a bad cold which settled in my ear and never could hear in it again."

Featherstone clapped his hands. "I knew you were an animal lover!" he exclaimed. "Come, what's this about bird care?"

"It's simple. If they're healthy, then their shit is hard and white and dries real quick, but when it's thin and watery that's no good."

Featherstone made a face. "There's a lot of call for knowledge of parrots and the like around here, you know."

"Been taking care of all sorts of birds since I was a lad. Bird seller passing through our village taught me. He had a handcart full of cages with birds from all over the countryside—bullfinches, chaffinches, thrushes. I'd heard them sing but never been so up close." John smiled. "I think he could see he had me like a fly in a tar box."

Featherstone looked intrigued. "Tell me more, boy."

John spoke faster, warming to his tale. "My eye was caught by a little bird with a pink breast and cheeks and a blue-grey crown, nape and bill. He told me it was a chaffinch and would cost me a coupla benders." John paused and looked up at Featherstone. "That's a shilling," he said.

Featherstone smiled and nodded.

"Said he was giving up the bird-selling game and moving to London to make cages. Told me that if I liked birds then that's the place to be. Talked about a shop in London where they have over a hundred . . . or maybe nearer two hundred . . . different types of birds. All sorts of sizes and colours, he said, some that can even speak! I didn't believe him but of course I know different now I've met Silver."

"And last night?" Featherstone said quietly.

"When Ferenought was defeated." Button let out a heavy sigh. "He was the very first cock I had ever reared. His death was—" He did not complete the sentence.

After a few moments Featherstone gently asked. "What about other animals? The four-legged variety. Are they of interest?"

"That's why I'm here," John said brightly. "I've heard there are some magnificent specimens brought back from our ships overseas in the colonies. Animals with necks six feet long, beasts that can roar louder than a musket, and birds that can speak, of course!"

"How long have you been in London? Been up the Strand? Grady's Emporium?"

John shook his head.

Featherstone continued, "They have all the creatures you describe, the largest and wildest of animals from the five continents." He rose from his chair and opened his arms wide. "Lions! Tigers! Huge animals that can eat an entire goat in twenty minutes. Bigger than anything you have ever seen in your short country life, I'll wager," he said, wagging his forefinger at John before taking his seat once more. "I know the owner, Grady. Can't say I am a friend, but when his charges need servicing, he calls on me because he knows I'm the best."

"Is that so?" said Button.

"Heavens! There is no one else in London who knows those exotics like me, boy! They get their coughs and colds, bellyaches and snots, just like we do. I am a doctor to the animals. That's what I do."

Button nodded his head, impressed.

"Well what do you think?"

"What do I think about what, sir?"

"Why do you think I asked you to come here? I need someone to help me. An apprentice."

"An apprentice?" Button repeated, looking around the room as if Featherstone could be talking to someone else.

"I've been building a good practise with a wealthy clientele. Everyone seems to want their monkey or talking bird. Why, Lady Maresfield keeps two black swans, a flamingo, and an ostrich on her estate. The Prince himself has a zebra. There's so much demand I can't do it on my own anymore."

He paused.

"I need to pass on my knowledge to an apprentice. And I think you might be just the man."

He smiled and looked at Button. "Well?" he said.

Five

LILLIAN FELT THAT MISS MARY UNSWORTH was only pretending to be sorry to see her go. It took a strong heart to ignore the behind-the-hands laughter at the discrepancy in their sizes when they were out walking. Whilst she had been very generous to Lillian, on the day she left Miss Unsworth wished her well, shut the door, and, Lillian suspected, rarely thought of her again.

Lillian quickly settled into the apartments on the top floor of the Exchange. In truth, she had not been so comfortable since she was a child. Her room had a small fireplace that ensured the nights were generally warm. The bed was as large as Grady had promised, and she could still hear the lion's roaring at night. She loved to stretch both arms as wide as she could without touching the opposite walls, and her feet never reached the end of the bed.

The first thing she did was cut off her hair. She admired the result in the handheld mirror her mistress had given as a parting gift, checking her appearance from the left and then the right, enjoying the lack of weight on her head when she shook it. She found a pair of trousers hanging in the wardrobe, left behind by Grady's predecessor, the so-called Jack the Beanstalk, and was delighted to find they fitted well.

Each day she supervised the boys who arrived at sunrise to muck out the stalls. A fleet of young unkempt lads in scraps of cloth, some with boots if lucky, would turn up with their own bucket and broom and proceed to sweep the dung into a corner, then fill their pails with water and scrub out the cells. Despite the bedding being changed once a week, the place permanently stank of sodden hay and animal excreta. The smell of urine had found a permanent home in the wooden floor and had no effect on Lillian, but it infuriated Grady, who was desperate to provide the perfect environment for the growing numbers of paying visitors.

No sooner were the stalls cleaned out than the boys would disappear, each with their own buckets of dung, which they would later sell to the Vauxhall Pleasure Gardens and other places enjoyed by the gentry. Such places had call for a never-ending supply of fertiliser to keep the gardens attractive.

Some of the boys loved to wait behind to watch the animals being fed, and if Grady was in a good mood he would let them stay. The event they most enjoyed—and the most gruesome—was the feeding of a live goat to Leonidas the lion. After hours, Lillian would creep into his den unseen and sit grooming him and crooning to him.

The Exchange had to be swept and ready for customers by ten each morning. The Great Hall housed animals on both sides, with the more ordinary exhibits, such as the possum and the porcupines, kept closer to the front entrance. The deeper one walked into the menagerie, the more interesting the creatures became. The animals that Londoners were willing to pay good money to see were housed around the right-hand corner.

Lillian had spent the last two hours bent over, sweeping in the bird enclosure. She put down her broom and pulled herself up to her full six feet and stood with her legs wide apart, hands on her hips and reaching backwards, letting out a satisfied sigh. She pulled out a cloth from the pocket of her breeches and wiped her face, wrinkling her nose at the smell on the rag.

Her back hurt, she was forever scratching at the fleas that bit her ankles, and she stank of unwashed animal and straw.

She had never been happier.

Just then she heard a yelp above the usual cacophony of noise, followed by a howl of anger.

"Charlie!" she shouted. A scrap of a boy who only came up to just above her waist, trousers finishing at his knees, turned to look at her.

"I've told you before. Don't poke the wolves with that stick. You'd regret it if he was quicker than you. And if he wasn't chained to that wall then he would be!"

The boy, with his mane of black hair, grinned and turned away from her. "I'll see you tomorrow, Miss."

"See you tomorrow, Charlie," she replied, and waved to the others as they took their leave.

"All mopped out and shipshape, Miss Lill?" asked Grady as he appeared at the entrance.

"As well as can be expected, sir," replied Lillian. "I can't seem to stop that wretched brat Charlie from poking the animals. They'll turn on him one day, I know they will."

"Well, one less brat in the world, then," said Grady, unbothered.

"I think you should take a look at Leonidas, Mr. Grady," said Lillian. "He's not his usual self, keeps shaking his head, pushes me away if I stroke his head."

"Hmm," said Grady, rolling his eyes and pushing up his sleeves. "Let's take a look."

"Better get Featherstone in," he said ten minutes later when he'd examined him. "I'll send one of the boys."

Six

WHEN THE INSTRUCTION TO ATTEND THE Exchange reached the men, Featherstone and Button made haste to leave the house, the old vet chattering about what to take, what might be needed, and what he might see.

"You never know till you get there, boy," said Featherstone.

Button did not know whether to be more frightened or excited. During the few short weeks he had been at 23 Neal Street, he'd heard much about Grady's Menagerie but had not yet visited. During this time he had formed a strong bond with the parrot, who never failed to admonish him with cries of "Too much rum!" each time he saw him. Somehow Button understood that the talking bird was being slightly cheeky—tongue in beak you might say, he said, laughing to himself. Most days he would visit Featherstone's study and chat to the parrot, whose vocabulary was starting to expand considerably.

"Slippy outside. Slippy outside," Silver now cried as the pair gathered their instruments.

"Come, Button, come," said Featherstone. "We will take our tools and see what's needed when we get there." Waving a bottle of brandy aloft he said, "Sometimes the greatest tool of all."

Button had not quite learned the London art of avoiding the ten types of shit that were there to be trodden in. He stopped as they reached the corner of Haymarket to scrape an unfortunate lump from the bottom of his shoe. As Featherstone marched on, Button could not help but notice people pointing at the doctor as he walked past, sharing exchanges with their neighbours behind hands. Since his arrival in the city, he had heard stories about Featherstone and his past dealings with those born on Newgate's steps, but had rarely witnessed firsthand the fascination he appeared to generate.

He trotted behind Featherstone, his lanky body bent in an effort to avoid attention whilst the vet strode ahead, his belly leading the way. When Button caught up, he asked about the Exchange and its eponymous owner.

"Truth is, there's little love lost between me and Grady," said Featherstone. "But we need each other."

"How so?" asked the apprentice.

"Grady needs an animal doctor like me—like you will be—but he hates the cost. And as much as I despise the way he keeps these beasts, the work is good and I believe it *is* important that ordinary people can see with their own eyes that we share the earth with extraordinary creatures that live and breathe. When new crates land at the docks, then it's down to me—to us—to dispense care and succour to the new arrivals. Many have spent days at sea, locked in wooden crates in which they can barely turn, surviving on the scraps of nuts and rotten vegetables poked through the slats."

Button listened intently.

"I'm an old man and I've seen many things, but the sight of an animal falling out of a crate, parched with thirst and with iron mangles around its feet truly breaks my heart. And that Grady is happy to make profit from such creatures—" Featherstone curled his lip.

As THEY NEARED the Strand, Button saw the flower merchant sweeping up the rejected blooms that lay bruised on the floor. The paper boy, already hawking the third edition of the day, cried, "Mornee stannart!" Suddenly a dog cut across his path, immediately followed by a man chasing it with a stick.

"You little fuck," said the pursuer, belting the animal around the snout. It yelped out in pain and received another kick in reply. Button looked away.

Up Fleet Street they walked, past the stationers, the engravers, pawnbroker, and silversmiths, until they reached the Exchange, where they could see Grady waiting for them at the entrance, puffing his pipe.

He gave the pair a brief nod of acknowledgement and said, "Thanks for coming, Featherstone."

The vet nodded back, shifted the bag from his left hand to his right, and indicated his companion. "This is Button," he said. "My new apprentice."

Grady took a step back and looked the young man up and down, then held out his hand.

"Pleased to meet you, Button," he said.

"And yourself, sir," said Button, giving the hand an enthusiastic shake. "I've heard much about you."

"And all bad, I'm sure, if it was delivered by this one here," cackled Grady, cocking his thumb at Featherstone.

Button licked his lips and began to reply, looking towards his master for direction. "I'm sure that's not—"

Featherstone interrupted with a dismissive wave. "Ignore him, Button. Come then, what have we got here?" he asked.

"It's Leonidas," Grady replied, now serious. "I think it might be the toothache again. Keeps shaking his head and rubbing his face along the floor."

"Let's take a look, shall we?"

Grady led the way with Featherstone and Button following behind. When Grady was sufficiently ahead of the pair to be out of earshot, Featherstone turned to his apprentice and whispered,

"Problem we have, of course, is taking a look inside his mouth. Lions are very independent creatures and don't take kindly to being messed with—especially with a toothache. Ha!"

Button nodded.

Featherstone continued, "Interestingly, I must say it's unusual to find a lion with any teeth at all. They're usually all removed to make the cat a safer pet."

The three men walked deeper into the menagerie, passing stalls on either side, each around twelve feet wide and secured with vertical iron bars. Candle flames flickered as they walked briskly past. Painted on the walls at the back of the pens were scenarios of an imagined life in faraway places, designed to place the specimens in the context of their native lands. About waist high, at a slight distance from the cages, a wooden bar was installed to enable visitors to lean on and observe the creatures on the other side.

"Keep up, Button," said Featherstone to his companion, who had stopped to stare openmouthed at a huge pair of porcupines.

"Don't worry about this lot," said Grady. "I keep the good stuff 'round the corner. Otherwise you'd see it from the street and then who'd be paying to come in, eh?"

Turning to the vet, he continued, "I have a new helper, too, Featherstone."

"Oh yes?" he replied, but with little interest.

"A woman," Grady said smugly.

Featherstone stopped and turned to look at Grady. "Really? What on earth would a woman want to be doing in a place like this?" he asked.

"I have my charms!" said the menagerie owner.

Featherstone sniffed. "Quite," he said with disdain, and continued walking.

Grady quickened his step until he was matching Featherstone's stride once more.

"Well, yes, she's a bit of a strange one, but the animals like her—particularly the lion."

"Can't wait to meet her," Featherstone replied. Calling back over his shoulder to his companion, he said, "Hear that, Button? Looks like you're not the only new boy around here."

Button gave a weak smile, unsure of the reaction expected of him.

"She's with Leonidas now," said Grady, carefully watching his companions. "Come see."

Grady stood back to let Featherstone and Button go in front of him. "Last stall on the left," he called. "Step quietly now."

Button could not have predicted the sight in the cage in front of them.

A woman with closely shorn hair, wearing brown leather breeches, lay on the straw-covered floor, eyes closed and arms draped around a large creature eight feet long. It sprawled on its side, lying on a large wooden platform with half a dozen leather buckled straps, as yet unfastened. Her fingers played with the mane of long, reddish-brown fur, which was clumped and matted. The creature's eyes were dull and the whiskers drooped. It swished its tail from side to side, clearing a patch in the straw where the cold floor had become visible, all the while emitting a low guttural rumble. The three men watched silently from the safety of the cage exterior as the woman crooned in low tones to the animal, seemingly oblivious to her audience.

Button stood mesmerised, staring at the scene in front of him, looking from the woman to the lion then back again to the woman.

Grady said quietly, "Lillian. Animal doctor's here."

Startled, the young woman made to get up, but the lion lifted its head and gave a growl, the meaning of which was quite clear. "He doesn't want me to go," she said.

"You stay there then, girl," said Featherstone, opening his bag and starting to rummage inside. Button said nothing.

"We are going to need some strong brew," Featherstone told the menagerie owner.

"We've given him as much brandy as we could find," said Grady. "And I've brought some myself, but we are going to need more.

It's the only way he is going to let me near him. And laudanum. A great deal of laudanum. The two mix well."

"How will we make an observation of its mouth?" asked Button.

The woman looked up at Button for the first time and smiled. "It's fine," she said. "He understands me and I can tell him what happening. I'm sure he'll let me open his jaw long enough for you to see which is the bad tooth."

"Are you sure?" said Featherstone to Grady, who was turning a heavy iron ring full of keys around and around in his hands.

He shrugged. "Trust her," he said without raising his head. "She has a way with that big cat I've not seen before."

Grady finally selected the right key, put it in the lock, and turned it. The cage door sprang inwards. Cautiously, Grady and Featherstone stepped forwards into the lion's den, making sure they stayed close to the door. Button remained outside. None of them took their eyes off Lillian and the lion as she whispered in its ear and the beast rolled over on its back, exposing its barbed cock and balls whilst making a quiet mewling sound.

Lillian pressed her hand down firmly on the lion's chest, crooning all the while, and gently prised open its mouth. Featherstone made a cautious move towards the lion and gestured to his apprentice. "Smell that, Button?" he whispered urgently. "Something's definitely not right in the mouth."

Button nodded. He could catch the whiff of putrid breath from where he was standing.

Slightly irritated with his reluctant companion, Featherstone snapped, "Get in here, man. Come in. You're not going to learn anything standing out there, are you?"

Button caught a fleeting smirk on Grady's face, which galvanised his courage. He tentatively entered the cage.

Turning to Lillian, Featherstone said a little more softly, "I need to get a good look at these teeth. Do you think he would let me do that, Missie?"

Without taking her eyes off the lion, she shook her head.

"Probably not, sir. He is in immense discomfort and is only letting you look as a favour to me."

The old vet nodded.

"Right. More brandy it is, then," he said to Grady. "And laudanum. We will have to get him inebriated so I can check these teeth."

Grady made a "puh" noise with his lips. "That's a great deal of brandy, Featherstone."

"And that's a great deal of lion to have howling in pain at your customers if we don't sort it."

Grady rolled his eyes.

Featherstone indicated the leather holdall he had left in the corner. "Get the bag, Button," he said. "You'll find a blue bottle in there marked LAUDANUM."

Button quickly found the bottle and passed it to Featherstone, who held it up for Lillian to see. "My lady, this is laudanum. It will not hurt your precious beast, but will send him to sleep so he will not feel any pain whilst we open that mouth and remove whatever is that's troubling him."

Lillian nodded.

"I have your permission, Grady?"

"Go ahead," he replied.

"And yours, my dear?" he said to Lillian, who nodded once more and smiled.

"Thank you." Turning to Button, Featherstone said, "Take that tube and let me have five measures."

And then to Grady, "Now, let's gets this lion strapped down." Between the four of them, they each took a leather strap and buckled it securely around the increasingly groggy lion.

Grady gave the creature a tentative kick in the rear, much to Lillian's admonishment and a black look from Featherstone.

"Best be careful, gel," he said with a grin.

"Looks like he is asleep," said Featherstone. "Let's take a look inside his mouth." Once the jaw was open the vet inserted a rolled-up leather tube, which kept the mouth exposed. It was immediately apparent which was the errant tooth. One of the lower molars was cracked and the gum surrounding it was red and puffy. The vet gently touched the area and a green-yellow liquid oozed over his finger, which he wiped on the straw.

"Shouldn't be too much of a problem," he said. "Pass me those pliers in my bag, Button." The apprentice rooted around the holdall until he found the largest pair of steel extractors he had ever seen.

Lillian continued to stroke the lion's head whilst Featherstone manipulated the instrument into the right position, then—with one quick tugging gesture—extracted the offending article from the mouth in a gush of pus and blood. He was holding the tooth high in the air in victory when Grady leaned forwards and grabbed it.

"I'll take that," he said.

Button had retreated to the corner of the stall once more, and now his eyes followed the woman as she came out of the enclosure and looked him square in the eyes.

"Hello," she said with confidence, holding out her hand, which Button took. "My name is Lillian."

"John Button," the apprentice replied.

The two held each other's hands and eyes for a few seconds, saying nothing. Featherstone and Grady exchanged glances. Grady clapped his hands and the spell was broken.

"Undo those straps and let's get out of here before he wakes up."

HOURS LATER, JOHN lay in his bed thinking about Lillian. Lillian! Lillian! He had never met a woman as tall as himself. Small girls made him uncomfortable. They reminded him of his birds. Small little arms and tiny bones that he feared he might crush in his enthusiasm, but this woman was solid—no reed in the wind. Women had previously held little fascination for him and he guessed the same was true of them, with his tendency to bend down to their height, which only resulted in his looming over them in a gloomy way, which only made them laugh.

"You're a lanky streak of piss," his mother would say. The girls in his village had gazed up at him and said, "Ooh, you make me neck hurt, John."

But the girl at Grady's place had looked him right in the eye and she had been so . . . what? Solid? Strong? Capable!

And the way she talked to that lion.

Seven

L ATER THAT NIGHT, A BIG GIRL in a big bed stretched her legs
out as far as they would go, took a deep breath, pulled her
knees to her chest, hugged them, and smiled. She had never met a
man so tall that he didn't seem to mind her own size. And what
brown eyes! She put the palm of her hand to her nose and breathed
in the smell of him, which still lingered from when they had shaken
hands. She smiled again.

Lillian had little experience of men. Most looked up at her and
then ran off with some dainty little specimen with curls and gig-
gles. Not that she was bothered much. She had never understood
why the girls at Miss Unsworth's had spent so much time talking
and gossiping about the male servants. It seemed faintly point-
less. She far preferred the company of animals. But something had
stirred inside her when Button met her eye, and now she wanted
to examine this unbidden emotion, keep it close, it, turn it over
in her mind, try on these new feelings, and see how they sat in her
head. Would she even feel the same when she saw him again?

Lillian would not have to wait long. Following the professional
visit of Featherstone and Button the day before, Grady had invited
the young apprentice back to the Exchange to take a more leisurely

view of the rest of the fifty or so animals he kept in the three rooms that made up the menagerie.

On the day of the visit, Lillian got up with the sun on a bright March morning and by eight o'clock had already supervised her army of small boys on the cleaning and turning over of the straw and the removal of the previous night's excretions. Having satisfied herself that all was as it should be, she returned to her bedroom and washed her hands in the basin. She fussed with her fringe, which was starting to grow past her eyebrows, licked her fingers, and swept them through the short hairs on her head in an attempt to keep them in place. She did this every morning and every night and but still specks of dirt and straw were left behind.

Lillian pinched her cheeks and stretched her mouth wide to check her teeth for any remains of the morning's egg and turtalong rolls. She reached for a small round porcelain jar that sat on the dresser alongside a small brush no bigger than then size of her forefinger and a glass of water. Written on top of the jar were the words HEMET'S ESSENCE OF PEARL AND PEARL DENTIFRICE.

First she dipped the brush into the water, then the powder, making sure to carefully shake any residue back into the pot, and proceeded to gently rub her teeth, spitting out the chalky liquid as she went.

Hemet's Powder was newly available in the capital, declaring that it was fit for the King and promising to render teeth *White and beautiful without in the least impairing. Fasten such as are loose; keep such as are decayed from becoming worse; perfectly cure the scurvy in the gums and make them grow firm and close to the teeth; they will likewise render the breath delicately sweet and remedy almost all those disorders that are the consequence of scorbutic gums.*

Lillian did not devote much time to her appearance, but having worked with the animals for the past few weeks, she could see that the problem that occurred most frequently amongst her charges were issues with rotten teeth. She was determined to hang on to hers for as long as possible. She shuddered when she thought of the yellow wooden teeth that sat in Mrs. Ogden's mouth and how she would spit them out and wipe them with the hanky she kept in her apron before popping them back in her mouth. A wedding gift from her late husband, she'd said. A visit to the tooth surgeon was the last thing she wanted. Hemet's Powder was worth every penny of the shilling it had cost her, despite earning ten bob less than she had at the Unsworths'.

She placed the toothbrush beside the hairbrush and hand mirror that sat on her dresser, carefully positioning them just the right distance apart. Her finger lightly traced the rim of the porcelain basin. She smiled at her good fortune.

Lillian made a final check of her appearance in the hand mirror and then hurried downstairs.

GRADY WAS WAITING at the entrance dressed in his customary red waistcoat, topped off with the tiger claw set in a silver pin.

"Ready for our visitors, Miss Lill?" he asked without looking at her, taking out his pocket watch to check the time and then looking up at the sky. There was not a cloud to be seen nor to keep in the heat, and the day was bright, crisp, and cool.

"God is in his heaven," Grady said, patting his belly, "and all is right with the world."

"Certainly, sir," Lillian replied, giving her trousers a couple of brisk strokes with the backs of her hands and straightening the clean white shirt she had put on that morning.

"Before we start our day," Grady suddenly said, "I have a little present for you." He produced the lion's tooth that had been extracted a few days before. Three inches in length, it had been cleaned and bleached, a hole drilled through, and threaded on a leather thong.

"Bend yer head," he said. Lillian duly obliged as he slipped the gift over her neck.

"Bring yer luck," he said.

Lillian gripped the tooth in her hand, feeling its smoothness. "Thank you, Mr. Grady. Now I can always be with Leonidas."

The Exchange was open from ten in the morning until dusk. Visitors were greeted by liveried doormen decked out in the style of the beefeaters from the Tower of London itself. Ever the showman, Grady never missed an opportunity to create a spectacle.

"Told him to get here as soon as we open," he said to Lillian, then turned to address the visitors who were starting to gather in a long line at the ticket booth.

"Come one, come all!" shouted Grady, spreading his arms wide to the guests as he walked down the line of children with their mothers and nannies. The excited chitter-chatter of the small children mingled with the admonitions of their carers to "sssh" and "keep calm" as the little ones bounced up and down, all the while tightly holding onto a hand. The older ones, refusing to hold any hand at all, resolutely kept theirs in their pockets.

Grady strolled up and down the line, making sure to catch the eyes of young visitors. He stopped in front of a fair-haired little boy, aged about twelve and dressed in a black coat with a green waistcoat and white stockings, his boots half laced.

"And what have you come to see, young man?" he asked in a loud voice that caught the attention of those in the queue.

"Look, there's the owner," said one of the nannies. "He'll put *you* in a cage if he sees you jumping around like that."

"The polar bear, sir," the boy replied brightly.

"Ah, the polar bear," Grady repeated. "Yes indeed. One of our largest and most frightening exhibits, if I may say so. Caught by a whaling ship in the North Sea. They killed his mother and then transported him back to land in a barrel. Wouldn't fit in it now, mind, the size of him! Make sure you keep your hands in your pockets, young man—he's very hungry today and he loves the taste of little boys."

The boy's eyes grew wider and he took a step back behind his nanny's skirts.

"Ha ha! I'm only funning with yer. 'Ere." He flicked something at the boy, who upon catching and examining it found it to be a coin about the size of a sixpence but made of copper.

"Look closely, boy," Grady said. The boy squinted. "You can see my famous lion on one side. And see what it says along the top? GRADY. That's me, see? And EXCHANGE, that's the name of my emporium!"

The boy gazed at the coin in his hand. "Thank you, sir," he said.

"You're welcome. Enjoy your visit. Tell your friends." Grady strode away, leaving the lucky visitor surrounded by a small gaggle of kids shouting, "Let *me* see. Let *me* see," as they jostled to get their mitts on the coin. Then, with a half-considered afterthought, Grady looked back over his shoulder and said, "And don't miss the two-headed sheep on the top floor."

"Ooooh," said the boys, their eyes widening even further.

Turning to Lillian, he said, "Now where do you think this young man has got to?"

As he spoke, the man in question appeared at the end of the queue, hair freshly shorn from a visit to the barbers, his brown jacket matching his breeches, and his stockings clean and white. The ensemble was completed with his neckerchief tied in one of the fashionable knots of the day.

"Looks a little more presentable than his last visit," Grady said to Lillian with a wink.

Marching to the end of the line, he grabbed Button by his arm and pulled him forwards. "Come. Come. *You* don't need to queue."

"Your servant," Button replied, giving a small bow. "And Miss Lillian, I believe?"

Lillian smiled and, to her annoyance, felt her face grow hot.

"Sir," she said, lowering her eyes.

"Let's get this show on the road," said Grady. "Give me ten minutes, Mrs. Ogden," he said to the woman in the booth, "and then start taking their money. Follow me!" He guided Lillian and his guest past the growing queue and into the menagerie.

The pair left the bright morning behind them as they entered the gloomy dankness, their eyes slowly becoming accustomed to the large room. The only daylight came from a large window way above, with additional light supplied by the occasional sconce filled with whale oil. Individual stalls about eight feet wide lined both sides of the large hall, and inside each was an animal of some kind. Despite it being first thing in the morning, and all the animals' stalls only recently cleaned and made ready for the day ahead, there was still an underlying smell of straw and urine interspersed with the previous night's spent candles. Grady and Lillian were used to it, of course, but it was still quite new to Button, who took out a hanky and held it to his nose. And the noise! Just as his ears picked out the roar of a lion, he heard another sound. Was that the famous polar bear? And what was that mewling? As if in expectation of the stage on which they were about to make their appearance, the animal cacophony grew louder as the opening hour got nearer.

"I love this time of the day," said Grady. "You can feel the excitement in the room."

Indeed, the animals now seemed to be standing in anticipation and starting to pace their stalls. The three strolled down the left side of the Hall, admiring the occupants of each enclosure, Grady regaling them with tales of their origins and clever dealings. When he stood still, Button could feel the cold from the stone floor creep up through his shoes. He looked into a stall marked HYENA and noticed a manacle at least four inches wide attached to a chain, which was secured to a large bolt that had been hammered into the ground. A rat ran in front of him.

They reached the end of the room, where Grady paused before a huge aviary at least ten feet tall and six feet wide. Numberless birds of every size and colour flew around the cage, all competing in their chirping and cheeping and not one keeping still for a single moment.

"They call me the Terrestrial and Aerial Fascinator," Grady

said, with a flourish of his hands, "the truly modern Noah." He cocked his head and paused to determine the effect of his words on his audience and from his pocket produced a much thumbed and folded piece of paper.

"The *London Chronicle*," he said grandly. "The twenty ninth of January seventeen eight seven."

Button and Lillian held out their hands to take the newspaper cutting. They touched briefly and Lillian blushed again.

"Now now," said Grady, whisking it out of their grasp. "No one touches this piece of paper but me." He held it out of their reach. "Suffice to say, it contains some very positive comments about myself and our charges here. Listen . . .

"This noble lion strikes every beholder with surprise, has been largely shown to multitudes of admiring spectators and has met with the approbation of all. He is now exhibited with many other curious and uncommon animals at the Grady's Grand Menagerie at the Exchange. The truly Terrestrial and Aerial Fascinator et cetera et cetera," he said, carefully folding the piece of paper and putting back in his waistcoat.

"But before I became the custodian of this very modern ark, I was on the road with my creatures. One in particular." As the trio turned the corner, they were greeted by the biggest bird they had ever seen.

"Oh my dear lord," exclaimed Button, taking a step back, eyes as wide as coach wheels, only to realise the bird was not moving.

Never tiring of the surprise, Grady laughed. "Stuffed," he said. "Taxidermy, it's called. A new way of preserving the creatures in such a way that you can still enjoy 'em but don't have to feed 'em or care for 'em. The scientists love it—they can get quite up close and no need to worry! This one was stuffed by the very greatest of all London's taxidermists, Mr. Thomas Hall himself."

Grady stood back, crossed his arms, and regarded the bird with pride whilst Button took a step closer. Truly, it was as tall as he and looked a bit like an emu. Its mouth was set for all time in the widest of angry squawks and the orange eyes, straining with fury, were surrounded by the most feminine of long eyelashes. The head, with a large bony protuberance on top, sat on a bright blue feathered neck at least a foot long, from which hung what could only be described as a long orange fleshy bib. The entire ensemble rested on an oval-shaped black ball of feathers perched upon two long legs, which ended in three-toed razor-sharp claws at least five inches long.

"Meet my famous cassowary bird. The biggest in the world. The eye of a lion with the defense of a porcupine. The most vicious of all birds," said Grady. "Hails from southeast of Asia and brought to Europe by the Dutch."

He paused.

"Can't fly, of course."

"Can't fly?" queried Button.

"No, but it can fight," Grady replied. "And her voice! My god, you could hear her voice from across London. A loud rasping screech of a sound as if Drake himself was setting off to fight the Spanish but with added braying donkey to put the fear of the Lord in them."

"Female?" said Button.

"Of course, man, look at the eggs!" Button looked down at the cluster of three mottled green and white eggs that had been set out around the cassowary's feet to form a tableau of the doomed bird's life.

"My golden goose, she was," said Grady with a theatrical sigh. "We toured the country together. Warwick, Oxford, Cambridge, Reading, Abingdon. I'd set us up in a public house and charge a shilling a time to see her. Even went inside the gentry's houses when the ladies could not be seen in some of the less salubrious of places we had to pitch up. Bit of a dinner entertainment."

He turned and gave Lillian a mock bow. Lillian was no stranger to the cassowary, passing it each day as she went about her business, but was only now hearing the story for the first time.

"And how much would you charge for such an event?" she asked.

"An entire guinea, my dear—and often a very nice dinner as well."

Lillian smiled.

"Everything came to a head in Oxford, of course," he continued.

"Oxford?" said Button.

Grady paused for effect, looked down, and shook his head with a dramatic flourish. "Just before our arrival at the Crown where we were due to go on display, our Cassie here"—he crooked his thumb at the stuffed bird—"gave birth to the most amazing egg! Three times as large as a chicken's or even a duck's, and four times as tall. Shell as tough as a tortoise. The so-called 'learned collegians' of the town had heard of our impending arrival and, being scholar-like, were keen to see bird and egg for themselves before anyone else. Of course they wouldn't believe a humble travelling showman such as myself and presumed the egg to be a fake."

A small crowd of visitors had gathered and were listening to Grady's story. He paused for effect, then raised his voice a notch. "A mob of these so-called scholar types turned up with the sole purpose of taking my egg and proving it to be real! And of course, to show it to be true, they would have to kill the very thing they were trying to prove!"

The assembled visitors looked at each other and raised eyebrows.

"I can see, my friends, that you find this story to be quite ridiculous as well! The first cassowary egg that had ever been laid in this country and they insisted on taking it from me. In the name of science!"

Grady then lowered his voice and the audience drew in closer to hear him. "There were about thirty of these so-called gentlemen in the room."

A vigorous nodding of heads.

"First, they took the measurements of the egg, a young clerk writing it all down in a huge leather-bound ledger. Then, having satisfied themselves thus, they called for a drill. 'No, no, my good sirs,' I said as their plan finally made itself clear to me. 'Not my Cassie egg. No.'"

An intake of breath from the visitors.

Grady looked at those gathered around him, making brief eye contact with each one, then shook his head. "I am sorry to report they were determined to have their way. What could a poor fellow like me do but go along with their plan, a plan to blow out the yolk like a common chicken egg to show it fer real."

The crowd gave a collective "Oh!"

Grady held out his hands and shrugged, then his speech grew more earnest. "Of course I couldn't let them see how furious I was, and so, the deed was done and a very nice omelette was served at the Crown that night."

He laughed. "Around this time I thought it pertinent to lay my claim as the greatest living authority on the subject of the casso-wary, and I published my pamphlet: *The History and Anatomical Description of the East Indian Cassowar, the Greatest Rarity Now in Europe.* Just a few pages, mind, but it contained the sum of all knowledge of the English cassowary bird. Before we reached a new town, I would send a young boy ahead of me with a couple of dozen copies of the pamphlet to soften up the audience, so to speak, and it did the job. When we got there, we were welcomed with open arms. They could not wait to see my bird and—of course—every-one had heard of the egg."

Abruptly he turned and indicated to Button. "Now this young fellow here . . ."

Button looked startled to be singled out for attention.

"This young man knows all there is to know about birds, don't you, Button?" said Grady.

Button opened and closed his mouth a few times.

"And he is to be our new bird doctor!"

Button blinked again.

"So if any of your polly parrots are in need of attention, just bring them to us! Only a shilling for a consultation. Satisfaction guaranteed."

Button nodded and gave a semblance of a smile as he shuffled from foot to foot.

Now Grady sensed that something else had taken the attention of the crowd. Marching towards them was a short man in his early forties, reaching no higher than Button's waist. A fat chubby ginger bewhiskered little thing, dressed all in green with a bright yellow belt around his middle and leaning on a staff as he walked.

"Top of the morning to you, Owen," said Grady cheerily. "How is my favourite leprechaun today?" He added under his breath, "and why are you not sitting in your stall chatting to the visitors like I pay yer for?"

"Stop yer blathery babbling, ye eejit," said the dwarf. "Thought you'd want to know that ridiculous Jack Slack kangaroo is getting all excited again."

And off he waddled.

Grady's erstwhile crowd of listeners looked at each other and uttered a collective "ooh!" at the promise of drama.

Never one to miss an opportunity, but still none too pleased at having his oratory interrupted, Grady said, with just a little irritation in his voice, "Next floor. Up the stairs. Round the corner on the left." A few of the crowd broke off and quickly made for the stairs.

"Who was that little man?" asked Button.

"Young Owen O'Brien," Grady replied. "A paddywhack, of course. They're all deficient over there. Been with me years. People like to see a little man. I don't own him, though. He's his own man. I pay him a wage and he sits in his stall. Lazy little mopus. Used to be more of a draw, but no one's interested now. It's the animals people come to see."

"I've not seen anyone like that before," said Button, not taking his eyes off the retreating dwarf, who was now being followed by half a dozen of the children.

"Grumpy as well. I'd introduce you but there's no point. He hates everyone. I'm sure it would be a different story if he had the bellyache. He'd want to know you then. A few years back I had more of the human curiosities than the animal kind. People would come from all over to see my fat lady. Weighed the same as that black sow we just passed, I'll swear. Cost a small fortune to feed and she was always hungry, hungry, hungry all the time. Five loaves a day, at least three gallons of milk, and you didn't dare put your lunch anywhere near her. Ate at least four chickens a day. I seemed to spend my entire time feeding her. Little Lizzie Large we called her. Her belly hung down to her knees, I swear. And her legs were as wide as an elephant's. The fat on her legs lay in swaths of skin like pleated curtains. She had a special boy to lift all the folds around her body and wipe them clean to save them from going red and sore.

"And the complaining. My god, she was never satisfied. '*This chair is too small for me. This chair is too big for me. My bed's not big enough. Why is there not more food?*' On and on. We were in Devon when this farmer seemed to fall for her ample charms—if you get my drift." Grady tapped his nose and then cupped his hands under his chest. "And I sold her on for five gold crowns. To be honest, I was at the point where I would have given *him* the five gold crowns to have that Little Lizzie Large taken away."

Lillian squirmed, Button looked away, and Grady laughed.

"Ah, but my beautiful white negress was another story. Tall and thin. Not like you, my dear. You have good strong thick bones. This one's were made of green twigs that would bend in the wind. You've seen a black man, Button? Well, this one had all the attributes of a black man, the thick lips, flat nose, and tight curly hair, but the amazing thing was she was white! Skin white and cool like alabaster. Some defect I'm sure, but she had a certain elegance about her. Rarely spoke. Sadly, her heart was as cold as her skin and she would never return my advances. Lives with the taxidermist I told you about earlier. But she does not exhibit herself any

more. I think he may have had better luck with her than me."
Grady seemed to drift off for a moment.

"Now where was I?"

"You were telling us about the egg, Mr. Grady," said Button.
"And how I'm to be your new bird doctor," he muttered under his
breath.

Looking at each of them to ensure he had their full attention
once more, Grady continued. "To my very good fortune, as we
arrived in Abingdon, not far from the Queen's Windsor residence as it happens, the good Cassie laid herself yet another egg. I
wrapped it in straw and bundled it up as fast as I could and sent it
off forthwith to our very own Queen Charlotte."

He stopped to smile and observe the effect of his words on his
audience of two.

"I am told she spared no time in displaying the egg in her very
own menagerie in Richmond," he concluded.

"But what went wrong?" asked Button.

"Wrong? Wrong? Why would anything go wrong?"

"Well . . ." said Button, indicating the dead stuffed bird.

"Alas, the dreadful winters of the late '70s proved too much for
my bird from Java, and winter in the north of England is particularly harsh. I am sad to report to you good people that the poor
thing finally keeled over in northernmost Durham. I could find
no reason for her death. I had her stuffed and here she is now.
My darling Cassie. The cassowary that laid the golden egg—well,
the green and white egg! And to her I owe my good fortune. The
money I earned from her enabled me to put the payments down on
the Exchange, and here we find ourselves today."

Grady paused for dramatic effect, putting his thumbs in the side
pockets of his waistcoat and looking from one to the other.

As Button and Lillian patiently waited to hear where the story
would go next, they became aware of a commotion in the room
upstairs that seemed to get louder and louder.

One of Lillian's young helpers suddenly rushed around the corner. "Sir. Sir. Quickly, sir. There's trouble with the kangaroo, sir," he shouted.

"What is it, boy? What is it?"

"Sir! Sir! He is jumping around all over the shop, sir. That boxer, Birmingham Bill, was in and he squared right up to him, sir, and next thing you know the kangaroo's given him such a swipe that—"

Loud cheers came from the direction of the kangaroo's stall, interrupting the boy.

"—that Birmingham Bill is on the floor and the kanga's above him and won't let him get up!"

"For god's sake, is there no peace?" said Grady. "You'll have to do something, Button."

"Me?" said Button. "Why me? I know nothing of kangaroos."

"You're the flamin' vet, aren't yer?"

"Just the apprentice, sir!"

"Well, apprentice your way out of this then!"

"While you two stand arguing, someone could be getting hurt!" said Lillian, who headed off in the direction of the kangaroo. "Come with me, Charlie," she said, gesturing to the messenger.

"Lillian, wait!" said Button and set off after her whilst Grady followed at a brisk pace.

The crowd of twenty or so mothers, nannies, and children parted as Lillian arrived and shouted "Stop!" The scene that greeted them would have been worthy of an illustration by Gillray or Cruikshank himself.

The famous boxer lay flat on his back, arms and legs spread akimbo. The dwarf was standing above him, a leg either side of his head and his hands raised in imitation of the prize fighter. Just a few feet away a red animal at least three feet bigger than the dwarf with short fur and long, V-shaped pointed ears was bouncing around on large feet, balancing like a tripod on a huge muscular tail at least three feet long. The kangaroo kept darting his head in at the dwarf as if to butt him but not quite touching him. The kids were screaming, "Kill the leprechaun. Go on. Kill the leprechaun!"

"Mothers. Control your children," shouted Lillian, drawing herself up to her full height. Button ran up behind her.

A groan was heard from beneath the dwarf as Birmingham Bill began to stir.

"Oh, shut up," said the dwarf as he sat back on the fighter's face and the children screamed with laughter. Button seized the moment to pick up the large net he had noticed on the floor and quickly slipped it over the head and forearms of the kangaroo, who continued to stamp its large feet in frustration.

"Got ya!" he said.

"Oh, well done, Mr. Button," said Lillian, clapping her hands.

"Get off me," said Bill, pushing the dwarf aside and dusting himself down as he got to his feet.

"Suit yourself," said the dwarf.

Trying to bring matters to order, Grady addressed the crowd once more. "A very interesting animal, the kangaroo," he said.

The children groaned.

"Can I have a ride on the camel now, Mother?" asked one.

"Brought to these shores by our very own Captain James Cook himself when he returned from New South Wales, having exchanged our charges here for the thieves and cutpurses he left behind in the Australias. From a standing start it can jump twenty-five feet in front of him and even jump ten feet in the sky. Notice his short front arms? Well, they might box with these, but it's the back legs your need to watch out for and their very vicious toenails."

The children had grown restless and bored with Grady's pontificating. Resigned to the lack of any further exhibitions of boxing, the crowd began to look for other amusement.

"How long do they live?" asked the boy to whom Grady had given one of his tokens an hour or so before.

"Not long enough," said Grady. "Now, who wants to see a tiger come all the way from the Indias?"

Half a dozen hands shot up. "Me! Me!"

"Follow me, then," said Grady. Turning to Lillian and Button, he added, "I'll leave you two to sort out this mess."

"This way, children." Grady turned the corner and was gone, leaving Lillian and Button alone for the first time. Neither said a word and then both spoke at the same time.

"I—"

"You—"

They laughed.

Lillian beamed at Button. "You were so brave," she said.

Button shrugged his shoulders. "Didn't know what to do, really."

"Oh, you definitely did the right thing. That's why we keep that net there." She put her hand to her head and smoothed down her hair.

"Well, it's certainly an exciting place to work, that's for sure."

"I love it here," said Lillian.

"All the animals," said Button.

"Lions . . . tigers . . ."

Button could not take his eyes from hers. "I was wondering what you did with your Sunday afternoons?" he asked.

"Well, that's often the busiest time of the week," she replied.

"Ah." Button looked away from her, but then they both turned at a noise behind them. There, on the straw, was a foot-high miniature version of the six-foot red fighting kanga.

"It's a baby kangaroo!" said Lillian.

"My goodness," said Button.

"Mr. Grady needs to see this!" Lillian said. "Mr. Grady! Come quick!" she shouted.

Suddenly the baby kangaroo made a jump in the direction of its mother and vanished. Button and Lillian looked at each other in surprise but before either could comment, a head appeared out of what looked to be a small pouch in front of the mother's belly.

"Good lord!" said Button, leaning forwards.

"Mondays," said Lillian.

"What's that?" said Button as he continued to stare at the baby kangaroo.

"I'm free on Monday afternoons," said Lillian.

Grady reappeared. "Ha! So he is really a she, eh! No wonder she was putting up her fists," he said. "Thought our pugilist friend there was threatening her boy and went to defend it. I am betting this must be the first baby kangaroo in London."

"I'd love to see Vauxhall Gardens," said Lillian, quietly.

"And so we shall," said Button.

"Self-renewing stock!" said Grady. "People will want to see this. I need new handbills! London will know of this and everyone will want to visit Grady's Exchange—the greatest menagerie in all of England."

Eight

ONE BRIGHT MORNING IN LATE MARCH, Lillian arrived at the menagerie to find young Charlie leading two of the ostriches away. Two be-feathered arses sat on four long lanky legs that swayed in unison as they slowly disappeared up the Strand. Grady stood with his hands on his hips, watching them go.

Lillian put down the pail of water she had been carrying. "Where are they going?" she asked.

Grady turned his head towards her, noting her arrival, then back to the ostriches. "Taking your advice, Lill," he said. "Making some space. More animals than we need or can afford to feed, and something has to go, what with the crowds coming to see the young joey jumping in and out of his mother's pouch every five minutes."

Lillian couldn't say she was sorry. She had always found the ostriches to be spiteful beasts, just as likely to give you a vicious nip or peck as soon as your back was turned.

"I know what you're thinking," said Grady. "Don't worry. That collector down in Chelsea, Old Man Manners, has taken them. Sold him an emu last summer. Now wants to 'explore the genus' as 'e calls it."

"I am always happy to hear you have made a sale to a place

where they might be better cared for," said Lillian primly, picking up the pail and turning back to the entrance.

"Manners was telling me that you can feed iron to an ostrich and they can digest it . . . Keen to try it for himself," Grady called after her, the sound of amusement in his voice.

"Mr. Grady!" said Lillian, horrified.

"Forget it," he said with a laugh, clapping his hands. "Besides, we have something new coming today."

"Oh yes? What have your dock rats managed to find now?" Grady had eyes and ears all over the Woolwich docks and prided himself on having his pick when something exotic arrived from far away.

The boys who had overheard Grady and Lillian talking were stopping to earwig the conversation and whispering to each other in excitement. It was always an occasion when a new exhibit arrived.

"Well I hope it's not *too* big," said Lillian, playing with the lion's tooth hanging around her neck. "Those wretched ostriches did not take up a lot of space."

Grady tapped his nose. "Just you wait and see. You'll not have seen its like before, I wager, and as far as I know this will be only the second one ever seen in this country!"

The boys started to clamber around the Exchange owner, jumping around in excitement and tugging at his shirt, which stuck out at the back. Teddy Diamond stood barking at the commotion. "Mr. Grady! What is it? What is it? Do tell!"

"You'll see soon enough," he said to them all, turning abruptly and giving one of the smaller ones a cursory cuff on the ear. "Get that stall cleaned out and run to the grocers and get plenty of milk! It's only a baby, so it's going to need milk."

"A baby," said Lillian and smiled to herself. She had always dreamed of having a child of her own, but had long ago allowed her mother to convince her that it was never likely to occur. The younger visitors were naturally attracted to their counterparts in the animal kingdom, and since the baby kangaroo had arrived, Grady had been forced to create a separate queue just for the children wanting to see the joey, charging an additional fee, of course.

Over the last couple of months, Grady and Lillian had settled into a tolerable working relationship. Each day her love of the Exchange creatures—those on four legs and two—continued to grow. She was loved by the boys, many of whom had never known a family life, having been dismissed at a young age as simply another mouth to feed.

But Lillian still remained wary of Grady and, whilst her instinct told her that there was nothing to fear, she made sure never to be alone with him. However, he was starting to listen to what she had to say, she noticed, and more often than not do what she wanted. Slowly it began to dawn on her that she had become an object of fascination for the menagerie owner, though she had no idea why this might be so or what it might mean.

She was also aware of Grady's seemingly relentless search for riches and glory and how he would relish every opportunity to take centre stage in his own empire. And while their ambitions would often complement each other, still Lillian would find herself asking for collars or chains to be loosened, or extra straw and water to be provided. She had spent quite some time persuading Grady that it would be bad for business if the boxing match between Birmingham Bill and the kangaroo went ahead and the kangaroo was hurt, and Grady had eventually, reluctantly, backed down. But this only led to more threats to sell the joey to one of the estates out in Chelsea, where there was plenty of farmland and they had the money to invest in the unusual.

"We are not here solely for the amusement of the lords and ladies of London, you know," Grady would tell her at least once a day. "It's an em—por—ee—um," he said, emphasising each syllable. "We are here to make money."

Lillian learned to hold her tongue and keep her head down when he spoke so.

A few hours after the departure of the ostriches, Lillian was wandering between the stalls, checking on her charges and letting her thoughts stray back to last week's trip to Vauxhall Gardens on the south bank of the River Thames. She remembered how Button had gently taken her hand to help her into the little boat that ferried the visitors from one bank to the other, and smiled when she recalled the tightrope walkers and tumblers they had watched as dusk fell, standing side by side, their shoulders touching, as the musicians played. He regaled her with tales of the gentry he was meeting and how popular he was with some of the old ladies and their parrots.

Taking a moment's breather from the stale air of the menagerie (though in truth, the smell rarely imposed on her senses anymore), she walked outside to take in the unusually hot spring morning. As she leaned against the wall, staring down the road where the ostriches had been led earlier, her reverie was interrupted by the noise of the trundle of a barrow as it was pushed over cobbles. Teddy Diamond began to bark. She listened as the sound got louder and the source of the noise slowly came into view: two men, each with a grip on a hand barrow that held a large square wooden crate about three feet high and wide, pushing it towards the Exchange.

Guessing it must be their new arrival, she went outside to find Grady already there, thumbs hooked in his waistcoat pockets as usual, standing in front of two men. Both were dressed virtually the same in big ankle boots, leather gaskins, shirts, and waistcoats, the ensemble topped off with flat hats. Hanging from each of their belts was a billhook, a distinctive flat-bladed knife with a curved edge and a wooden handle. Dockworkers, she guessed.

She watched as Grady looked the men up and down, then side to side, then held up his forefinger.

"One," he said, pointing his index finger up at the sky, then at the men, then wagging his finger and repeating, "One. I was only expecting one of you."

"We've pushed this all the way up from Blackwall, squire, and all the time the crying inside," complained one of the young men, taking a hanky out of his pocket and wiping his brow. "And it must weigh about a hundred pounds at least. Not easy work on a hot day like today."

The other one chimed in indignantly. "We was nearly assaulted in Fleet Street from a woman asking me if I had a baby locked in the box," he said. "It's a two-man job, squire. We want a bob each and we ain't going nowhere till we get it."

Suddenly a cry, not dissimilar to a human baby's, came from within the crate.

Lillian ran towards the cart and peered through the slats of the wooden box, but all she could see were two big eyes blinking in the darkness.

"Oh Grady, you've got to let it out—now—oh please," she implored, appealing to that part of him that seemed to pay attention to her.

"Now, now. Let's have a bit of calm," he said and pointed at the box. "Go on. Do as she says. Get that crate down off the barrow."

The two men moved quickly to stand in front of the cart, legs apart and arms crossed.

"Ain't going nowhere till we getting paid."

"Oh Grady, pay them, please," said Lillian, begging Grady with her eyes.

Grady heaved a sigh. "Nip around and see Mrs. Ogden. Get her to give you a bullseye for each of these bacon-faced bagpipes. And get 'em a drop of the old author as well. I have a feeling this is going to be thirsty work."

He rubbed his hands together, his greed and excitement there for all to see. "Now, let's see what we have in here . . ."

When Lillian returned a few minutes later with cups, money, and drink, Grady and the two men had managed to get the crate off the barrow and all three were now leaning against it, beads of sweat catching the light on their exposed forearms. Teddy

Diamond was running around and around the crate, barking all the while.

"Ah good, three cups," said Grady, licking his lips and quickly setting the cups out on top of the crate. The other two men watched as he pulled the stopper from the bottle with his teeth, poured a draft into one of the cups, put it to his lips, and drained it down.

"Ahhhh," said Grady. "That hit the spot."

"Oi," said the men. "Don't forget the workers."

The mewling inside grew louder.

"Don't just stand there, you pair of mopus," said Grady, waving his hand at the crate.

"Drink first," said the younger man, his eyes fastened on the bottle.

"Drink first," said the other more sternly, crossing his arms. widening his stance, and lowering his chin.

Grady sniffed and poured three more drafts; the dockers lifted their cups. Knocking them against each other, they threw back the liquid, then both let out satisfied sighs.

"Another?" said Grady.

"Another!" said the men.

Thirst satisfied, the younger one pushed up his sleeves "Right then," he said, pulled the billhook from his belt, and started to work at the crate, sticking the sharp end of the blade into the gap between the slats and leveraging until the wood began to crack and splinter. It took only five minutes for the crate to fall open and reveal its contents.

Sitting on its bottom and back legs—and looking very sorry for itself—was a little grey creature no bigger than two feet high. A square chin jutted from its oblong head, with two eyes set lower than its nose and two large incongruous ears pointing upwards on their own, marking eleven and one o'clock.

"What is it, Mr. Grady?" the boys shouted. "What is it?"

"It's a rhinoceros," Grady informed them and was greeted by a knowing "Oh," though in truth none of them knew what that was. "From the Greek 'rhino' for nose and 'ceros' for horn."

"Where's its horn, then? I thought they had horns," said Lillian. "Like that one in that book of yours."

"Indeed they do, Miss Lill, only this one's got no horn yet," he said with a stiff smile and false patience. "It's a baby, see?"

The dog began to growl at the new arrival and crouched down on its haunches, creeping slowly forwards on its belly, watching Lillian with one eye and the baby rhino with the other.

"There's nothing to worry about, Teddy Diamond," said Lillian, resting one hand on the dog's head to reassure him and reaching towards the baby with the other. The rhino flinched and backed away and the dog immediately stood up and advanced on him, barking at the strange creature.

"Teddy Diamond, shame on you!" Lillian scolded and returned to making a series of cooing noises, offering her hand palm side up towards the baby rhino so it could smell her. The dog withdrew, resting his head on his front paws and making a low uncertain rumbling sound. The little creature raised its big eyes to look at Lillian, blinked, then leaned forwards and gave a tentative sniff of the proffered palm. Lillian grinned and clucked once more.

"There there," she said.

"Watch out, might be dangerous," said one of the men, stepping backwards and treading on Teddy Diamond's paw. Teddy jumped up, hackles raised, and stood, teeth bared, snarling at the docker.

"The only thing dangerous around here is you," said Lillian. Turning back to the baby, she continued to mew. "You're only a baby, aren't you," she cooed.

"Two hundred pounds this has cost me," said Grady, standing back to admire his purchase.

Tentatively, Lillian reached out her hand. Her fingertips found small coarse hairs just starting to poke through a thick tough hide, making the skin quite rough. Her hand was drawn to the strange ears, shaped like grey conch shells, which appeared to wiggle independently of each other. She stroked behind the left ear and the skin seemed much softer and thinner; the baby bent his head towards her hand, then mewled.

"This little beauty is going to grow to at least five thousand pounds in weight. That's the size of an elephant, you know," said Grady.

The dockers nodded their admiration for the expensive purchase and its potential. "The only rhinoceros in town," Grady continued. Then, in a more contemplative tone, he added, "They hate each other, you know? Elephants and rhinos. They go mad if they see each other. Imagine the fight that would be. Eh, Lill?"

"Well, it's a good job we don't have any elephants, then," said Lillian. She was surprised to catch a faraway look in Grady's eye.

"Right, let's get him into his stall," he said.

There was a thick three-inch-wide leather collar around the baby's neck, to which Grady now hitched a heavy chain. He gave it a tug. When nothing happened, he gave a sharper pull to get the rhino to its feet, but still the baby would not move and instead began to moan in a voice that sounded a little like singing. The men joined Grady and all began to pull at the rhino, but it simply refused to budge.

"Never heard that sound before," said the darker of the two men. "What do you think he wants?"

The other shook his head. "No idea," he said.

The three men continued to tug at the rhino, but still it remained resolutely on its backside. Despite Teddy Diamond barking his encouragement to get moving, the rhino seemed to have quickly become used to the dog and simply ignored him.

"Don't fancy your luck when it's a ten-ton monster," said the taller of the two dockers, dropping the chain and stepping back, taking out his hanky and mopping his brow once more.

"I didn't sign up for this," said the other, accepting the hanky proffered by his partner.

"Wait!" said Lillian. "I know!" She dashed off. The men all looked at each other and shook their heads.

She returned in less than five minutes with a bowl of pears. "Hello baby," she said, holding a pear in front of the rhino. For the first time the baby stopped its mewling and started on a new higher, more insistent note. It opened its mouth and Lillian dropped in the pear. With its eyes closed, the baby rhino appeared to smile as it sang, *"Num a num a num a num,"* in a high voice.

"I think he likes fruit," said Lillian, laughing and holding a second pear in front of its nose.

"So it would appear," said a slightly grumpy Grady. He gave another tug on the lead and this time the baby did not resist, getting to its feet and padding after Lillian, who led the way. Lillian soon found herself mimicking the baby's sound and the baby then followed Lillian's song, so that both appeared to be singing together as they made their strange procession down the corridor of the menagerie. All the visitors stopped to stare as they passed by the other stalls, the singing of the woman and rhino complemented by a cacophony of barks, yips, yelps, screeches, and roars.

"I'll be putting you in the stall with it," Grady shouted after her. Lillian just smiled and sang the rhino song even louder.

LILLIAN NAMED THE baby rhino Keebar, and as the days passed, she became increasingly enamoured of the strange, hard-skinned, singing creature. His stall became her first stop every morning, and she noticed that whenever she put down a pail of water, the rhino would nudge at it repeatedly until he knocked it over on the brick floor. Then he would lie down in the puddle and drive himself forwards with his muzzle, rolling over and over in the wet and showing off his soft white underbelly. When Lillian tried rubbing the exposed area, she was greeted with the song once more. *"Num a num a num a num."*

One morning she tried emptying a pail of water directly over Keebar and was rewarded with a loud squeal.

"Ha! I thought so," said Lillian. "Go get more water, Charlie, as many buckets as you can, and rags. Get lots of rags."

"Yes, Miss," said Charlie and was gone.

"Now, how watertight can we get this stall?" she wondered aloud.

Two hours later Lillian was filthy and wet, having plugged most of the gaps between the bricks in the enclosure with as many old cloth rags as she could find. Keebar was up to his ankles in two inches of water, lying down and rolling over and over, singing all the time.

"You're going to give that kangaroo a run for its money, Keebar," said Lillian.

NEW HANDBILLS WERE printed and given out all over London. COME SEE THE SINGING BABY RHINO—THE ONLY ONE IN LONDON! they declared. More coins were struck, featuring the rhino on one side and GRADY'S EMPORIUM on the other. These would be given to those who visited the rhino more than twice in a week.

And so the crowds of visitors and potential customers flocked to the menagerie on the Strand. Some simply lay down their shilling and wandered the stalls to marvel at the strange and exotic creatures from around the world whilst others—the more well-off— would make the occasional purchase. But it seemed that everyone would take the time to watch the baby rhino roll over and over in the water and listen to his singing.

Each morning Keebar greeted Lillian with a song. She made sure to always have a small piece of fruit ready, which she would drop into his mouth while he rolled over on his back with his eyes closed and she rubbed his belly. Keebar could never get enough of whatever treat was on hand. If he saw anyone with food, he would immediately start to bleat, and few could resist his calling for whatever sweetmeat they might be enjoying, despite Lillian's entreaties not to overfeed him. It didn't take long for the boys who mopped out the stalls in the morning to discover that Keebar's favourite drink was sweet wine. Careful not to let Lillian see them, the boys would steal a draft from the flagon Mrs. Ogden kept in the not-so-secret compartment in her admission booth and feed it to the baby so that he quickly became tipsy and staggered around his stall, banging into the sides, accompanied by peals of laughter from the boys.

About four weeks after Keebar's arrival, Lillian, in the company of young Charlie, was making her customary morning round of the animals before opening the Emporium. As she approached the rhino stall, she was greeted with a low groan rather than the usual *"num a num"* singing sound.

Lillian quickened her pace. "Keebar?" she queried, peering over the wall of his enclosure.

The baby rhino, now almost doubled in size from the day he had arrived, was lying on the floor on his back, all four legs stretched out, his white tummy exposed and distended to three times its usual dimension.

"Oh Keebar," said Lillian, climbing over the low wall and kneeling down beside him. She quickly ran her hands over his body to check for the source of the pain.

"Ooowww . . . oooowwww," moaned the baby rhino.

She frowned. Turning to Charlie she said, "Fetch Grady . . . and the animal doctor. Both of them. Quickly."

"Yes, Miss." Charlie nodded and was off.

"Is it your belly?" Lillian asked the baby and began to rub as it writhed in pain. "Owwwww . . ." it would cry every few seconds or so.

Within fifteen minutes, Charlie reappeared, out of breath from running. "Sent Dick to get the doctor," he panted, "but can't find Mr. Grady nowhere."

"Well, let's hope John Button can get here faster," she sighed.

It only took another ten minutes for John Button to appear. "I ran all the way," he said. "What happened?"

"I keep telling people not to give him scraps," she said, explaining how Keebar was so greedy that he would eat anything the visitors threw at him. She now felt sure he had eaten something that disagreed with him. "What do you think we should do?"

Button stroked his chin. "Let's move him to a dry spot," he said, grabbing the rhino's back legs. "It will be easier to treat him. Charlie, take one arm. Lill, take the other. One . . . two . . . three. There we go, that's it."

Between them they moved the baby rhino's groaning form to a raised corner of the pen with fresh straw. Lillian sat down beside him, taking the huge head in her lap. Button opened the large leather holdall he had brought with him and pulled out a funnel about six inches long and made of leather.

"Now, let's see what happening here," he said as he knelt down and put the cone to the baby's belly and his ear to the cone.

After a few moments, he straightened up and looked down at Lillian. "He has certainly eaten something that does not agree with him. That distention of the belly is due to a buildup of gas which is gurgling away in there. Now, if this was you"—he paused and blushed, not quite looking her in the eye—"I'd advise you to take plenty of peppermint, but I doubt there is enough peppermint in the whole of London to cure a baby rhino. Ha!" He laughed nervously.

He continued, "We can either massage the belly to release the gas or we can try puncturing the stomach, although that might be a bit drastic. We certainly can't leave him in this state for very long."

"Puncture his stomach?" Lillian asked. "Sounds dangerous."

"Indeed," Button said, nodding vigorously. "Where's Grady?"

"I've no idea," said Lillian, continuing to rub all the time. "But I couldn't possibly take a risk with his prize specimen without his say-so."

"Then massage it is, Miss Lill," said Button as he rolled up his sleeves. "May I show you?" Button knelt and put his arms around Lillian from behind, laying his hands over hers and starting to work the rhino's belly with firm, round strokes, all the time maintaining a steady rhythm. "Like this," he said, a strand of his yellow hair coming loose from the black ribbon that held it in place. "Nice and firm and steady."

Lillian had not been in such close proximity to another human being since she had sought cuddles from her disinterested mother when she was a child. She immediately felt her temperature rise and flushed as the blood rushed to her cheeks. Her pulse raced a little faster and she wondered if he was aware of the effect this intimacy was having.

But Button appeared oblivious to Lillian's discomfort. "Charlie, are you watching this? Note the pressure I am applying while I work my hands around the belly. Watch so you can take over from Miss Lill when she tires."

Charlie had been leaning against the wall of the stall, picking the last bit of Mrs. Ogden's mutton pie from his back teeth with a bit of straw, watching the exchange between the man and the woman and grinning to himself.

"Yes, sir," he said and gave a mock salute.

"Owwww," cried Keebar. Button pulled away and stood up. Immediately Lillian felt the loss of his heat as he withdrew and knew she wanted it back again.

She gave a little shudder. "I've got it," she said and continued to maintain the pressure Button had put on her hands, all the time singing the baby rhino song. Somehow she could still feel his hands on top of hers. She wondered if she would be able to smell him on her hands and if anyone would notice if she stopped the massage—just for a second—to check.

Button stood and watched. "You certainly have a way with you, if I may be so bold, Miss Lillian," he said. Lillian looked up at him, knowing she was blushing inside, but hoping she had adopted enough of a nonchalant demeanour.

The three continued with the task, each taking a turn to massage the belly, no one saying a word, the silence broken only by the exotic birds screeching from the aviary at the back of the hall, the lion giving a desultory roar from the next floor up, and the baby rhino continuing to mewl in pain at their feet.

When it was time for Charlie to take his turn, Button turned to Lillian and said quietly, "They say, it's an ill wind that blows nobody any good."

"How so?" Lillian replied, rubbing her upper arms to relieve her muscles.

"I really wanted to talk to you once more," Button said quickly. The words tumbled from his mouth. "It's a new book I've been reading. On the development of society. The role of money, and other things as well, of course. I'd be most keen to learn your opinion and . . . and . . . following our most excellent walk the other day, I think you too might be intrigued by some of the ideas the author espouses."

"Yes, yes of course," she replied. She'd enjoyed watching him wave his hands in the air as he described some new idea that had fired his imagination as they'd walked in the Vauxhall Gardens.

"What's it called?" she asked.

"*The Wealth of Nations.*"

"Yes, I've heard of that," she said, picking up on his enthusiasm.

His eyes grew large with enthusiasm. "Some very basic simple ideas but written with great clarity. The power of money! Did you know that the only way to become rich is to manage matters so as to make one's income exceed one's expenses?"

Lillian laughed. "Ha ha! Tell that to Mr. Grady." Then she adopted what she hoped would be a more serious face. "Obvious, but so very true when you put it like that," she added.

"Your turn, sir," said Charlie, and Button knelt down beside the rhino once more. Lillian followed him.

Button continued in a whisper, "Of course, the man is totally opposed to the trafficking of other human beings—which I know you feel strongly about. As do I."

"Of course, of course!" she said. "Wouldn't it be wonderful to hear him speak in person?"

"And he talks about the division of labour, how the right job of work should go to the right man—or woman, of course," he said, glancing at Lillian, "to ensure the job is done to the very best that it can be. One day I shall have the most magnificent animal practise London has ever seen," he declared. They'd touched on some of these ideas during their stroll.

Lillian remembered how excited she had been to walk in the Vauxhall Gardens with this tall young man who shared so many of her own thoughts and beliefs; how they had interrupted each other's words with "yes . . . yes . . . and . . . and," until they were both saying virtually the same thing at the same time and had burst out laughing. As she took her turn with the belly rubbing once more, she wondered if he remembered the afternoon in the same way. Lillian paused and wiped her forehead with the back of her hand.

"What am I thinking! Charlie, take over from the lady," Button said. Lillian pulled herself to her feet and flapped her hands to get the blood flowing once more.

Lillian and Button stood together watching Charlie in silence. She could feel the warmth of his body beside her once more and realised, when he spoke, that she had been holding her breath.

"I have brought you something. A present. I hope you will not think me too forward."

Lillian blinked in anticipation as Button reached into his bag and produced a small leather-bound book. On the dark cover, in gold embossed letters, were the words AN INQUIRY INTO THE NATURE AND CAUSES OF THE WEALTH OF NATIONS. The author's name, Adam Smith, below.

"Wait, let me clean my hands," she said, dipping them into one of the buckets of water lined up against the back of the stall, rubbing them together, shaking off the excess water, then wiping them dry on her apron. Her face lit up as her forefinger traced the outline of the title's gold embossing.

"Why, thank you, Mr. Button," she said. "I do not have many books of my own and certainly none as grand as this. I shall read it and treasure it and—"

"—and discuss the contents with me, please. That is why I have given it to you."

Lillian pulled herself up to her full height and, looking Button in the eye, smiled and nodded. "Thank you. I appreciate it."

"Is it always so hot in here?" said Button, looking down at Charlie, who had kept up the massaging through the exchange. Charlie smiled. Button ran his finger around his collar to loosen it and blushed.

He continued, "There is a wonderful diorama planned at Kensington Gardens next week. It's probably not quite your sort of thing—"

"I'd love to," Lillian interrupted.

"The . . . the . . . Battle of Montreal . . ." Button continued. "May . . . may I request . . ."

"Yes, that would be lovely," said Lillian.

"May I request the pleasure of your company?" he finally finished.

But before Lillian could say any more there was an almighty noise, as if a pig's bladder had been emptied of air.

"Little bugger," cried Charlie, pinching his nostrils.

The gas trapped inside the rhino's belly had finally found its way to freedom, along with other detritus of the digestive system.

"Urgh," said Lillian and Button in unison. All three turned their backs and tried to move away as fast as they could to avoid the flying excreta accompanying the emission of gas. Daring to glance over her shoulder, she could see Keebar lying on his back, now with a smile on his face.

"*Num a num a num,*" he was singing.

Lillian laughed.

"Thank goodness," she said. She turned to Button, hugging the book to her chest. "Thank you so much. I'm not sure if I will have read all this by then, but I would be delighted to accompany you and discuss what I have managed to get through."

"Thank you, Miss Lillian," said Button and seemed to give a little hop of joy.

As the weather grew warmer, the couple began to spend almost all their spare hours together, visiting the Bell and other taverns. It was a time of great change; long-accepted ideas and beliefs were regularly being questioned and reexamined, and Button and Lillian found mutual interest in the new scientific discoveries and inventions of the age. Both were passionate readers and would frequently walk and talk and discuss the ideas in the books they read. They fervently believed in the abolition of the slave trade and having exhausted the *Wealth of Nations*, had moved on to the poems and writing of Hannah More and frequently attended public talks and demonstrations from other great London thinkers of the time.

A favourite commentator of theirs was Ignatius Sancho, the first African known to have cast a vote as a resident of Westminster, and one who also frequently wrote to the newspapers under the pseudonym "Africanus." Even though Sancho had died over a decade earlier, Button and Lillian loved to chat to each other about what it must have been like to visit his Westminster grocer's shop.

"Some of the greatest commentators of our age must have visited that shop," said Button. "Just imagine."

"Oh yes," said Lillian. "I read in *The Lady* that the artist Gainsborough was a frequent visitor."

Lillian was a regular reader of *The Lady* magazine and would often seek Button's thoughts on articles she had read.

"Can it really be true that some desperate criminals would put out the eyes of children in order to use them as beggars?" she asked. "Could such wickedness truly exist?"

"Indeed, I have heard it to be so," said Button. "And the perpetrators mainly women, I understand, which makes it even worse somehow. These beggars may not be as poor as they look, you know. Featherstone assures me that it is well documented that some leave behind a very tasty sum when they die. Why, he told me about a certain Mary Jones, a beggar for forty years in Charing Cross whose cat he had attended. Died just a few months ago and left ninety half crowns in a mug in her lodgings!"

"No!" said Lillian.

"And a further six thousand invested in funds!" added Button.

But nothing consumed the pair's conversation as much as the care of animals and how best to ensure the beasts at Grady's Menagerie could live as well as possible. How might they be fed and watered? What tricks and skills should be employed to keep them healthy? How to help them nest and rear their young? Lillian frequently came into contact with other animal owners who would visit Grady's Menagerie to make a purchase. And whilst it frustrated her that the animals for whom she had cared so lovingly would disappear to some far-flung country house, she used it as an opportunity to question the new owners as to the circumstances her charges would find themselves in, to see if she might learn something new.

"I am certain that the animals benefit from being able to stretch their legs and to have an actual run. I know how awful I used to feel when my bed was too small," Lillian worried.

"They have so much more space on these country estates," Button assured her. "I have seen for myself how the animals thrive when they are away from those cages that Grady keeps them in."

"It's the one thing that makes their departure so much more bearable," she replied.

LILLIAN AND BUTTON also speculated about the quality of care in some of the other establishments and travelling menageries, and Button would reassure her that no animal was better kept than by her at Grady's and that Grady could not take any of the credit at all.

"Not even at the Tower?" she asked.

The Tower of London had been home to many different animals since the long-ago days of Henry III and included lions from the Barbary Coast, tigers, leopards, and many different types of bear, including a white polar bear. There was even a monkey house. Neither Button nor Lillian had visited the Tower Menagerie but both were keen to do so.

"Why, at the Tower the entrance price is a cat or a dog which can be fed to the lions," said Button. He did not know this to be true, but had been assured by Featherstone that it was the case.

EVER SINCE BUTTON'S encounter with Fred, one of the many street entertainers stationed outside St. Clement Danes church, he had been determined that they visit the Tower. Fred owned a pair of performing poodle dogs called Castor and Pollux, which he dressed up in matching frilly tutus, Castor in pink and Pollux in blue. Button often stopped to admire the animals' antics, the most favourite being Pollux walking on his hind legs pushing a small child's pram with Castor inside wearing a pink bonnet to match her tutu. Both dogs could deliver an extraordinary display of somersaults, cartwheels, and kiss-chase. Gradually Button and Fred had begun to exchange civilities and when Button had revealed his profession, Fred had been most insistent that he see the sight of the lions for himself.

Fred told him that each year, on the first day of April, the royal lions of the King's own Menagerie at the Tower of London were led down by their keepers into the moat for their annual bath.

"It is the most amazing sight, sir," Fred had said. "I've been to see it myself many times, so I have. All of London seems to be there. The majestic procession of the lions—ten, twenty, even thirty of the magnificent beasts—being led on golden chains as the drawbridge is lowered. It's as if these Kings of the Wild are aware of the very nobleness of the occasion as they walk down with their heads held high and their manes blowing in the breeze; down into the moat where they play and frolic like the big cats they are. They say they keep dogs on shore for the sole purpose of receiving the fleas that jump from the lions. The event is always attended by their Majesties who—with great ceremony—invite the young ladies from the crowd to step down into the moat to throw water over the royal lions."

Royal lions! Button had thought. How Lillian might enjoy such a thing! And indeed, both had laughed with anticipation at such a spectacle. He could barely contain his excitement and thought what a wonderful outing it would prove to be for himself and Lillian.

And the perfect setting for something he had been thinking he might ask her.

Nine

LILLIAN JUMPED OUT OF HER WARM bed and eagerly pulled back the curtains, keen to see the colour of the dawn and what it might promise for the day ahead. But even the grey wet drizzle she discovered outside her window, over the rooftops and beyond, could not dampen her spirits. She splashed her face, brushed her teeth, and carefully removed the dress she saved for special occasions from its cardboard hanger. Her old mistress had given her the garment just a few short months ago but it might as well have been years, so much had passed since she had left that employ. She had spent many an evening unpicking the seams and to let them out and it now fitted as well as Lillian might ever fit a dress, albeit a bit tight around the bosom.

Last night she had hung the dark navy flannel dress over her little kettle as it boiled to steam away the crumples and creases. Now she carefully pulled the costume on over her head and smoothed the material down over her curves with her hands. It was still a few inches short due to her exceptional height, but at least that meant it did not attract too much of the detritus of London, she thought. She grabbed the green silk scarf one of the Exchange visitors had left behind a few months ago and tied it round her neck. She had refused to accept it at first, but Grady had insisted. It had been there a month or so and no one had claimed it and she should

have it as her own, he said. "Besides," he added in a low voice as
he cleared his throat, "it brings out the colour of your eyes."

She picked up the small drawstring bag she used to carry her
handkerchief, some pennies, and the odd sixpence. It was made
of a light blue silk with gold-coloured strings and she was pleased
with the way it complemented her navy dress and scarf. She took
one last look in the mirror and, satisfied with what she saw, closed
the door behind her and went down the small stairs that connected
her room with the menagerie and into the Great Hall itself.

"Good morning, everybody," she greeted the creatures and proceeded to walk down the hall, peering into the various cages and
enclosures to check on her charges. The animals replied to the
familiar sound of her voice with a collection of yips, barks, and
growls.

She stopped for a moment to peer into the kangaroo enclosure.
"Hello, young joey," she said. Joey, of course, was nowhere to be
seen.

"Hello, Mum," she said. "Are you looking forward to your
visitors today?" But she did not wait for an answer as she lightly
stepped on past the huge aviary, which sprang to life with vivid
song and colour. The flapping of the birds' wings wafted the smell
of the cage across the Hall, and she could catch the reassuring
odour of the large room which she had grown to look on as her
own domain.

"*Num a num a num*," Lillian sang as she skipped on towards the
rhino stall. "Morning, Keebar, and how's your belly today?" she
asked. Keebar replied with his own song, "*Num a num a num.*"
She peered over the stall to make sure it was still watertight and
checked that pails were filled with water and ready for the day
ahead. Running her hands through her hair, she made a mental
note that the baby was growing fast and that his time in a stall
without bars would soon end—and then what would happen if
a buyer had not been found? Not for the first time she queried
Grady's consideration of their charges, reminding herself that he

was first and foremost a showman and one that knew the price of everything.

But today, though, she preferred to think about what the day had in store for her—and for Button.

On then to the lion's cage, where she paused to watched him pace, all the while fondling the tooth on a chain hanging around her neck. She gripped the iron bars with both hands and pressed her face between the gap. The lion padded over to greet her and pushed his face towards hers.

"Leonidas," she said, not flinching at the smell of his breath. "I shall report back tonight, of course, and will be sure to make a note of everything—what they eat, how they are cared for, and the very chains they use to lead them by."

Seemingly satisfied, the lion turned and padded away.

WHEN SHE REACHED the front door of the Exchange, Grady was standing guard as usual, gossiping with his beefeaters at the entrance.

"Don't know where she thinks she's going," he proclaimed in a loud voice, cocking his thumb at Lillian. "Thinks she might learn something, she says. Thinks others know better than we how to keep our lions."

The beefeaters tittered.

"Don't be silly, Grady," she said. "You're just jealous. I've told you. Mr. Button has said no one in London looks after their lions as well as at Grady's Emporium."

The beefeaters looked at Grady and snickered again.

Grady said nothing but jutted out his chin and pushed his hands deep into his trouser pockets.

"These are *royal* lions, Grady," said Lillian, emphasising the word *royal*. "Who knows what I might learn!" She gave a little twirl.

"And I suppose you are going with that little mopus Button,

eh?" Grady replied, pulling himself back up to his full height again and grinning in a way that slightly unsettled her.

"And what if I am?" she said, turning on her heel and losing her good humour for a few moments. "I work hard enough on your behalf the whole week through."

"Go!" said Grady. "Go!" He waved her away. "But don't come back with any more of those clever-dick ideas of yours. Besides, I've got Birmingham Bill coming over for a drop today and he's still keen to fight the kanga, so I've got a busy day ahead and plans to make."

Knowing he was simply trying to goad her, Lillian ignored him and busied herself in preparation to leave for the day ahead. She walked back down the line of cages on her left as far as the aviary and then back again on her right, glancing about her as she went to ensure all was it should be, stopping every now and then to pick up something that was out of place, and all the while brushing down her dress and smoothing her hands over her hair.

"Keep an eye on Keebar for me," she said to Charlie, who had been quietly standing by throughout the exchange between Grady and Lillian. "Make sure the water doesn't run out again."

As she made to leave the building, Grady took a step in front of her. "Ah. There's just one thing," he said, waving her back and taking a sly look at the beefeaters, who were nudging each other and grinning. "I wouldn't want you to be too disappointed, like . . ."

Lillian stopped and turned, suddenly aware of the smirking beefeaters. "What?" she said. "What is it?" Grady and the beefeaters looked at each other and collapsed with laughter.

Twenty minutes later Lillian was on the Strand, her previous good humour replaced with an unhappy anxiety. She walked quickly, weaving her way through the typical London hubbub. Here were the purveyors of brushes and brooms, mouse traps and rat traps, nosegays and flowers, matches and stockings. And over there hurdy-gurdy players and mountebanks, dancing dogs and quack doctors, acrobats, jugglers, and clowns, street sellers, ballad singers, knife grinders, and more. "Mew!" cried the women who had carried their milk in tubs and pails all the way from the cow keepers in Islington. Vendors and menders all shouted their wares, their cries forcing their way into her head and fighting with the news Grady had just delivered.

What on earth was she going to tell Button?

ARRIVING AT THE Tower of London first, Lillian anxiously searched for a sign of her companion, her former anticipation and excitement replaced by a sense of self-consciousness as she stood, on her own, unaccompanied. They had agreed to meet on the corner of Tower Street at ten in the morning, and here she stood as the London workers went about their business, each intent on their own agendas and purposes. To her right the Tower loomed large and magnificent, taking up the full picture frame of her vision. A bright red curtain had escaped from a small window at the top and she briefly wondered if the occupant of the room could feel the draft. To her left the river was nowhere to be seen, although she knew it was there. The Tower sat in the quiet of the grey London day like a great cat waiting to play with any who would come near. Nowadays, all were allowed—common or royal—but whether they were welcome was another matter. None who stood in the shadow of this beast could feign ignorance of the history of the place, its role in the story of the city in which they lived, and its dark insistence: "*abandon hope all ye who enter here.*" In the distance Lillian could see the red of the Yeoman Warders' uniforms as they patrolled the drawbridge entrance of the Lion Gate. Somehow, despite the murky day, the sun managed to catch the light from the hilt on their swords. So these were the figures upon which Grady based the guardians of his Emporium, she thought, remembering the snivelling caricatures she had left behind an hour before.

She looked up at the sky and the gathering clouds and shuddered, hoping the rain would hold off. The smell of the river drifted up towards her. Unlike Paris, where the Seine simply sat there all day every day (the smell of which would eventually drive half the population away), relatively fresh water arrived in the Thames twice daily to wash away the excesses of the city's unnecessaries and done-withs. But still, it stank. And it was this she could taste on her lips, the rejected effluent of ten thousand hardworking souls, and the by-products thereof. All mixed with the smell of wet horse, of course.

AND THEN HE was standing in front of her.

"Mr. Button," said Lillian, taking his hand with the briefest of curtseys, dropping her head and careful to avoid his eye.

"M'lady," he said, taking both her hands and beaming at her with his usual enthusiasm. "So wonderful to see you as always and looking so . . . so . . . very lovely."

She gave a brief smile in reply. *How on earth am I going to tell him?* she wondered as they turned towards the Tower's entrance.

Button looked up at the darkening sky. "Are you warm enough, Miss Lill?" he asked, patting his pocket.

"Yes, thank you."

"And your charges? How is Keebar? Following a better diet now, one hopes?"

"Indeed, sir. Yes, sir. No more belly aches."

"And the joey? Still pulling in the crowds?" Button continued, patting his trouser pocket once more.

"Yes sir, all is perfectly fine," she replied with growing irritation. "But there is something I need to tell you."

"And I you."

They both stopped and turned to face each other.

"I—" they both said at the same time. The sky above them grumbled.

Lillian nodded at him. "After you." Without knowing, she held her breath.

Button took her hands in his once more. "Lillian . . . I am really sorry but . . . there are no royal lions."

Before she could reply he rushed on, "Featherstone told me I was a fool, that I'd been in London long enough to know when my leg is being pulled. It's one of the tallest tales in town, apparently . . . and I . . . I fell for it."

Lillian stammered. "I—I—" but before she could say any more, Button fell to one knee.

"Miss Lillian, I wonder if—"

"Get up! Get up! What on earth are you doing?" she said, suddenly self-conscious as to how she might look, the big tall girl in an ill-fitting dress with short rough-cut hair and the man at her feet. Out of the corner of her eye she saw a young couple passing by hold their hands to their mouths, nudging each other and snickering.

Button did not notice the couple but instead was trying to extract whatever it was he had in his pocket. Finally he freed a small black box, which he opened and held out to her.

"Miss Lillian, these past few weeks have changed me, even more so than meeting with Mr. Featherstone at the Cock Inn all those months ago. Our walks. Our talks. Why, each morning I wake up with thoughts of you in my head, and each night I cannot sleep for tossing and turning when I think of you."

Lillian pulled at his jacket. "Don't be ridiculous, Mr. Button," she said, aware that a small crowd had gathered around them. The sky thundered once more.

"Miss Lillian. I . . . will you do me the honour of being my wife?"

A FEW HOURS later Lillian was back in her room, restlessly pacing like her lion in its cage, all the time saying, "Oh . . . oh," to herself, over and over, as she played with the tooth on the thong hanging around her neck. The outfit she had so carefully chosen just a few hours before now lay abandoned on the floor like a wet dead thing. She picked up her hairbrush and ran it through her hair, once, twice, then threw it at the wall. It bounced back and knocked into her porcelain jar of dental powder, which fell off her dresser and broke in two.

"Ow!" she shouted at no one. "How dare he!"

The clouds that had been threatening to send rain all morning had finally emptied, and she had run nearly all the way home from the Tower. When she got to the Exchange, she walked briskly past Mrs. Ogden in the ticket box, keeping her head down with sheer relief that Grady wasn't there to see her.

Lillian finally lay down on the bed but was unable to settle as she rolled this way and that. She squirmed with embarrassment at the memory of them all laughing at her.

Button had got to his feet and led her towards the privacy of a small doorway. She noticed that somehow he held her green scarf in his hands. The small box he had thrust at her was nowhere to be seen.

"What have I done? What have I said?" Button asked, taking her elbow.

She shook his hand off her arm and took a step backwards. "I can't possibly marry you, Mr. Button."

He held his arms wide and palms open. "Tell me why on earth not? We share so many of the same interests, a love of books, the animals—"

She shook her head. "I never thought I would marry. I could not leave the Exchange."

Button floundered. "I thought we might set up our own place. We wouldn't need to *sell* animals. We would take care of them. The gentry are crying out for animal doctors of quality."

"What would Grady do if I was not there to take care of them? Why, you know how he is always promising to set up a fight between the kangaroo and Birmingham Bill?"

Lillian was becoming increasingly agitated at the thought of what might happen at the Exchange if she were not there. "What if anything happened to her, then who would look after the joey? Why—why—he would sell him!"

Button took her by the elbows. "Miss Lill . . . Miss Lill, please do not distress yourself."

"Besides, I like it at the menagerie. I'm happy there. I have a bed that fits and I am needed. The animals need me. Grady needs me."

"Oh, Grady," said Button, dismissing him with a wave of his hand. "That charlatan. Grady will manage. He will find someone else—"

"Find someone else!" Lillian exploded. "You think I am so replaceable? Disposable? So ripe for substitution? That *you* are the only professional? I may not mix with the gentry offering advice on their constipated parrots, but I warrant I have just as much ability with the animals as yourself, sir!"

And not knowing what else to do, she had turned on her heel and walked away, leaving Button still holding her green scarf.

BUTTON WATCHED LILLIAN'S back as she disappeared into the crowd. He could not understand what he had done to offend her so. Then the heavens opened. The rain fell on the happy and the sad and the small crowd dispersed just as quickly as it had gathered. No one was interested in his misery. He made his way home, both hands deep in his pockets, one wrapped around the scarf and the other holding tight to the little box.

Mrs. Tomkins opened the door to the wet and bedraggled apprentice and hurried him in.

"I am presuming it didn't go well then, young sir," she said as she bustled and fussed. Button shook his head.

"Oh dear," she said, flapping around him. "Come inside and let's get you dry. Silly girl don't know what she's missing. Still got that ring?"

Button nodded.

"Good, well, go and tell Mr. Featherstone all about it and I'll fix you a hot chocolate. He could do with the distraction. He's had one eye down that microscope of his and the other eye on the bird, been arguing all afternoon."

Button knocked on the door of Featherstone's study.

"Come in, come in," said the voice from inside.

Button entered Featherstone's study to find the aging gentleman bent over his desk, one hand on the microscope and the other making notes. The room made no more sense than it normally did—books piled everywhere, the parrot squawking in its cage, and the shelves lined with jars full of strange things bobbing about in liquid, their labels yellowed and peeling or lost completely. A small occasional table was placed between two red velvet armchairs set a couple of feet apart in front of a blazing fire. A giant boar's head hung above the fireplace, a fox head at one side and a deer head at the other.

"Too much rum! Too much rum!" shrieked the bird.

"Shut up about the rum unless we have something to celebrate. Do we, Button?" asked Featherstone, looking up briefly to catch Button's eye before returning to the microscope. The young apprentice remained in the doorway and shook his head without making a sound. The steam started to rise from Button's wet clothes and he loosened his collar.

"Not a great day then, young Button? Did you see the royal procession?" Featherstone laughed to himself.

"You know there was no procession, sir," replied the apprentice, removing his jacket and looking around for somewhere to hang it.

"No! Ha! Indeed!" said Featherstone, using his left hand to support his back as he straightened up and making a slight noise of discomfort with the effort. He gestured towards the microscope. "Take a look at this, my boy. It's a rat with two hearts, I'll swear. One of those young Exchange boys found it on the floor and brought it here. Ripped open by one of those animals and abandoned as a not too tasty morsel. Have you ever seen anything like that?"

Before Button could answer, there was a knock and Mrs. Tomkins pushed open the door with her ample bottom, her hands full with a tray holding two cups of chocolate.

"Ah, Mrs. Tomkins," Featherstone said. "Come in come in. And one for me, I see! Please set them down there."

"Only me," she said and went to place the tray down on his desk. "Chocolate for the young man."

"No! No! Not on top of that manuscript! That's my treatise on the African bullfrog. It's promised to the veterinary college by the end of the week." He grabbed his papers, shuffling them into some sort of order, and placed them on his desk, clearing the table in front of the fireplace to make space for the chocolate. "Let's get in by the fire. We can all get a bit comfy then. Button, go and pull up that stool."

Button glanced around for a seat and found a small grey stool about eighteen inches high covered in black-and-white striped animal skin. The base was decorated in ivory, which looked like . . .

"Yes, yes, it's an elephant's foot," said Featherstone. "Most ingenious."

Mrs. Tomkins glanced at the elephant stool and then the dead stuffed creatures on the wall and gave a slight shake of her head.

"Don't purse your mouth like that, Mrs. Tomkins, and take that seat over there," said Featherstone, indicating the armchair furthest away from his desk. Button pulled up the stool and sat with his hands clasped between his legs, his head hanging low.

"Now, Button, tell us both at the same time, so you don't have to repeat yourself twice. What happened at the Tower?"

Button composed himself and told them what had happened at the Tower. How he had kept the ring safe and sound until the right moment, how he had dropped to one knee and asked Lillian to marry him, how the crowd had gathered and the conversation that followed.

"And? We know she said no, but why on earth?" said Mrs. Tomkins.

"I think I may have insinuated that she was dispensable," said Button in a low voice.

"Indispensable?" asked his audience.

"Dispensable," Button repeated, putting the emphasis on the first syllable. "That she might simply leave Grady and the Exchange to its own devices and—and that—no one would notice."

"No one would notice?" exclaimed Mrs. Tomkins. "Why, that woman is a living saint by all accounts. The way she cares for those boys, those animals."

"You bloody fool," said Featherstone. "You're asking her to be your wife, for god's sake! You're meant to not be able to live without her! Not tell her she is dispensable!"

"No one wants to feel like that, Mr. Button," said Mrs. Tomkins, shaking her head.

"And she won't leave the animals," said Button.

"Well, what would she want with the animals if she was a married woman?" asked Featherstone.

"That's what I thought," said Button.

"Well, you didn't think hard enough, did you?" said Mrs. Tomkins. "You two with all your fancy lectures and book reading. 'Modern times' you tell me. You think a woman like that is just going to give up her life and come and live here? With us? And do what? Clean? Look after him?" she said, indicating the old vet with a backflip of her thumb. Featherstone sat with his mouth slightly open, surprised at Mrs. Tomkins's strength of reaction. "Mop up after you?" she asked, nodding at Button. "I don't think so, somehow," she said, shaking her head, articulating each word, and finishing off the outburst by crossing her arms and sealing it with a "Hmph."

"I'd never stop her doing what she loves," said Button, slightly surprised.

"I'm sure," said Featherstone, leaning over to pat the young apprentice on his knee. "And what's that you've got there?"

Button realised he was still holding Lillian's scarf in his hand. He sighed and lifted the scarf to his nose to smell her scent.

"What am I going to do? I don't want to lose her," he said.

"Come on, Mrs. Tomkins," said Featherstone. "You're the expert in matters of the heart, I'm sure. What should the poor boy do now?"

Mrs. Tomkins frowned, stared up at the fox head, and plucked at one of the hairs on her chin. A spark from a wet log on the fire made a bang and the parrot jumped into life again.

"Fire in the hold! Fire in the hold!" it squawked.

"I think I may have an idea," said Mrs. Tomkins.

"Oh yes?" said Button hopefully.

"A question for you both. Mr. Button," she said, turning to the young apprentice. "There's no reason why she couldn't continue to work at the Exchange, is there?"

"Of course not," said Button.

"So I thought." Turning to Featherstone, she said, "And could your professional business not carry more than one apprentice?"

"Well, when you put it like that, Mrs. Tomkins—" Featherstone replied and slapped his thighs. "Two apprentices! Now there's a thought."

"Good," said Mrs. Tomkins and clapped her hands. "Let the matter lie with the poor girl for a few days. It must have been such a shock for her, out of the blue like that. Leave it for now. You never know. She might even change her mind."

Ten

THE DAY AFTER THE VISIT TO the Tower dawned grey and miserable, much like the rest, and Lillian went about her work with heaviness in her heart, unaware of the conversation that had taken place a few hundred yards away in Neal Street. Downstairs, the sound of the rain beating on the roof of the Exchange mixed with the noise from the hurdy-gurdy man who was taking shelter in the doorway. When he saw her, the musician's monkey ran into the hall and tugged at her skirt, making his demanding screeching noise.

"Not today, Alfred," she said. But still he tugged on her skirts until she deigned to pick him up and set him on her shoulder while she went about the fussing and sweeping of the Great Hall, glancing into the various cages and enclosures to check all was well. By the time she had reached Keebar's enclosure at the end of the Hall, she needed to sit. She gave a deep sigh, shooed the monkey from her shoulder, and sat on the edge of the low wall.

"Oh, Keebar. What to do?"

And that was where Grady found her, a sorry sight of cropped dark hair on a head hung so low the face could not be seen, hands on knees. A snuffling sound rose above the noise of the baby rhino's protestations at the teasing by the monkey.

"Penny for them, my dear," said Grady brusquely as he approached. "This is not like you. Disappointed with the lion show? Not what you were expecting, eh?" He laughed.

But instead of the usual flippant response, there was a huge wet snuffle. A thought appeared to strike Grady and his eyes widened with anger. "Why, that young mopus! If he has touched you then I'll—I'll—" he blustered, clenching his fist.

"Don't be an idiot, Grady," said Lillian, shaking her head. "Of course he hasn't."

"Well, what is it then, my dear? You can tell old Grady," he said gently, kneeling down beside her.

Continuing to snuffle, Lillian replied, "John has asked me to marry him!"

Grady stood up immediately. "Marry? *Marry!* What right has he to—why, you're too young to—you can't marry, you live *here!* You can't leave here!"

A red-eyed, red-nosed Lillian looked up at him, snot and tears running down her face, and cried just as loudly, "I *know!*"

"Oh my giddy aunt, that's put the devil amongst the dandelions, for sure. What to do? What to do?" Grady exclaimed, starting to pace and casting his gaze around him as if the answer might suddenly appear. Now it was his turn to drop to his knees as he grabbed Lillian's hands and pulled a thin piece of grey cloth out of his pocket and handed it to her.

"There, there. Don't cry. I can't bear to see a woman cry."

Lillian took the handkerchief, checking it briefly before blowing her nose. The two sat in silence for a few moments.

Finally, Grady plucked up the nerve to ask, "And what did you tell him?"

Avoiding his eye, Lillian said, "I told him no, of course," picking at her shirt and wiping the back of her hand on her trousers.

Grady gave a barely concealed sigh of relief as he used the cane to heft his bulk to his feet. "Right, well, thank the devil good sense prevailed," he said, forgetting his momentary lapse into sentimentality. Lillian stood up, blew her nose once more, and gave the handkerchief back to Grady, who put it straight in his pocket and brushed himself down as if sweeping away the incident, puffing himself up and reverting to his usual arrogant demeanour.

"Yes," she said, nodding weakly.

"Well," said Grady, casting around for something to say. "Come and see that new horse tableau me and Charlie been working on. The corner is completely cleared out now and we've painted it on both sides so you'd swear you were in the Macedonian mountains themselves. Ha! The horse loves it. But I want to know what *you* think."

Lillian nodded and sniffed and together they set off to look at the new display.

GRADY KNEW MOST of the theatre owners in the vicinity of Covent Garden and the Strand. The Lyceum, Theatre Royal, and the Royal Opera House were all within spitting distance of the Exchange. He was particularly close friends with Richard Sheridan, proprietor of the Drury's Lane Theatre and a playwright himself, and had promised to supply a horse for the forthcoming performance of his new play, *Bucephalus*. Bucephalus was the famously temperamental black stallion that had been won and tamed by Alexander the Great. Legend said that it stood taller than any man and was known for the white star on its forehead, such as a bull might have—hence the name Bucephalus. Sheridan needed an animal to take on the eponymous role and somehow Grady had convinced the playwright that he had just the animal for the job. In return, Grady promised to have new Emporium tokens minted, which would feature the horse on one side and the Exchange on the other. Presentation of a token would give access to the new tableau where the horse would be stabled when not performing.

There was much excitement in London about the forthcoming play, the star of which was billed as *"None other than the very best horse in the Great Grady's Emporium and a descendent of the noble Bucephalus himself."* And indeed, the publicity for the play promised much to theatregoers. Sheridan had created a fantastic story of gods, goddesses, and oracles, the great adventurer Alexander the Great, and his horse, all delivered alongside some of the best stage effects Drury's Lane Theatre had to offer.

Between them Grady and Charlie had created the most marvellous tableau, with green rocky hills rising up into a snow-capped mountain range against a light blue sky dotted with clouds. When they arrived, Charlie was on his knees by the horse, rubbing him down with a strong brush, which he was dipping into a bucket of something dark. The horse gave a whinny and tossed its mane as the pair approached and Charlie stood to greet them, resting a hand on his hip and pulling back his shoulders to give them a stretch.

"Nearly done, Mr. Grady," he said. "He'll be as black as the ace of spades by the time I've finished."

Grady stood back to admire the almost black horse in its new home. "You'd swear Alexander himself was about to walk in. Well done, lad."

Lillian rolled her eyes when she saw the old nag that Grady had procured for the role. She put out a finger and wiped it along the horse's flank. It came away blue-black. "You're dyeing him?" she said with disgust. "Surely Bucephalus was much taller than that?"

"Ah, but who will be able to tell how tall any beast might be, when you're sitting looking up at the stage?" Grady replied. "Why, that mopus Jimmy Gray is only five feet high, but to hear the ladies swoon you'd swear he was six foot at least—and all the rest." Grady grabbed his crotch and laughed.

Lillian ignored the crude comment, walking around the horse and looking him up and down. "And didn't he have one blue eye and a white patch on his muzzle?" she asked.

"Who can tell the colour of a man's eye, let alone that of a horse, from way back in the stalls?" Grady replied. "We can sort that white star easy enough and add some more hair to the tail so it hangs further to the ground. Yup, I reckon Caesar here is just the horse for the job."

"Well, he certainly seems docile enough, Grady," said Lillian.

"Sure he is, yes indeed. And that's essential in a performer. The beauty of this 'orse 'ere is that he will do what he is told. Watch this. Make some space."

Grady waved Charlie and Lillian to the side of the enclosure, puffed himself, and commanded, "Get down!" To Lillian's amazement, the horse dropped to his knees.

"Play dead!" The horse rolled over on his side, gathering straw, which stuck to its still-wet sides and turned black.

Grady tapped the side of his nose. "Got him from my old animal touring mate," he said. Lillian gave a dismissive snort.

"Take Caesar over to Drury's Lane for the dress rehearsal," Grady told her. "Watch him go through his paces. You'll be amongst the first in London. That'll put the smile back on your mush."

HAVING PREPARED THE horse for his turn on the boards, Lillian, Charlie, and Caesar left the Exchange and turned right into Exeter Street, oblivious to both admiring glances and pointing fingers. Instead, her ears burned to the onomatopoeic sound of "Bucephalus" resounding in the background, which seemed to descend into the familiar hiss of disapproval she was so used to—most recently just yesterday at the Tower—

"Just ignore them, Miss," said Charlie to Lillian, who stuck out her chin and walked on with her cropped head held high. As they turned the corner into Wellington Street, she saw the bay window of the Bell Tavern and could hear the creaking of the sign as it swayed above her head. She recalled the winter evenings when she and Button had visited the upstairs room at the Bell to listen to various speakers on the Rights of Man and other philosophical discourse, which stressed the superiority of reason over the dictatorial nature of religion and superstition. They had often enjoyed a bread and cheese supper, sometimes a glass of porter, while hotly debating the evening's lecture. The memory pricked her eyes, but she brushed it away.

As soon as she arrived at the stuccoed portico of the theatre in Bridges Street, she was greeted by a swarm of young boys, some of whom she recognised from the morning muck-out at the Exchange. "Hello, Miss," they said. "What you doing here, Miss?"

"We'll take him for you, Miss," said one, whisking Caesar away. She had heard that Sheridan often used children as extras in his plays, which would explain why there were so many of them around, eager to look after the horse.

"This way, Miss," said another, a dark-skinned boy with the tightest of black curls mostly hidden under an oversized peaked cap. He sported a brass-buttoned waistcoat covering a once-white dress shirt and baggy beige canvas trousers. Lillian noticed he was wearing a solid pair of leather boots, unlike many of the other ragamuffins, and guessed his age to be around twelve years, slightly older than the other kids. "Charlie!" he shouted.

"Wotcha, Harry!" was the cheerful reply as both boys greeted each other with enthusiastic whoops and slaps on the back.

"Miss, this is Harry," said Charlie, giving his mate a shove forwards between the shoulders. "Old pal of mine from way back. Worked as mudlarks together for a while. Harry here found a gold coin once, dintya, Harry? That's where he got his posh clobber from. Harry, meet Miss Lillian of Grady's Emporium."

Harry pulled his cap off his head and nodded. "'Eard all about your animal place," he said. "You're famous round here, you are."

Lillian gave a little snort. "Don't be daft," she said, looking towards Charlie, who gave a small nod as if to say "true."

Harry went on, holding his cap and turning it in his hands as he spoke. "We've all heard the way you stand up to that old tripe-head. How's you look out for the young 'uns, takes care of the animals and all that."

"Well, that's very kind, thank you," said Lillian. "Although I am sure you must be exaggerating."

Harry ignored her reply. "Are you two hanging around for a while? Want to come and see inside?"

"Can we, miss?" said Charlie, just as Harry grabbed her hand. Lillian nodded, as excited as Charlie.

"Follow me," said Harry. Lillian and Charlie trailed him down the hallway, which opened up into the largest room Lillian had ever seen. She gasped. The ceiling here was even taller and higher than the Great Hall at the Exchange. Above and around her the seating was arranged in the shape of a horseshoe going up three, four tiers at least. Each one was divided into what looked like individual boxes, all the better to see the stage in front. The theatre was lit by spermaceti wax candles, the smell of which filled the air—mixed with something else?—as their wicks flickered brightly and reflected in the mirrored sconces, which appeared set against every spare inch of wall.

Lillian sniffed the air. "What's that other smell?" she asked.

"Oranges, Miss. Mr. Sheridan insists the boys cut them up and spread the juices all over the wooden benches. The smell covers a multitude of sins, so it does."

TEN WOODEN BENCHES were set in front of the stage. "That's for the orchestra," Harry informed them with pride. "We can get twenty-four fellows sitting and playing in there."

Charlie and Lillian nodded and looked from left to right and up and down. "My goodness. I hadn't realised how big it was from the outside," said Lillian, laughing with delight. "What a wonderful place."

Harry nodded but then added a little sadly, "I keep overhearing the bosses say they are going to tear it down or do it up or something."

"Why on earth would they change a thing?" said Lillian, continuing to look around, taking it all in.

Again he shrugged. "Modern times for London, Miss. Everywhere you go they are knocking things down and building things up. Now, you must both stay, of course, and watch your Caesar go through his paces."

"Oh, shall we?" said Lillian, looking at Charlie. "I should like that very much."

"Sure you can. You're lucky, it's our full dress rehearsal this afternoon, so choose any seats you like. Make sure you sit in the middle. Mr. Sheridan has the whole play down pat, but he is keen to see how it works with the actual star himself!"

A half hour later Lillian found herself in what she hoped was the best seat in the house, right in the middle and five rows from the front, Charlie on her left. The room was lit so she could not see the faces of any other spectators, although there certainly were various participants scattered throughout the room. Right at the very back, she could make out a shadowy figure with a large mountain of papers on his lap. *The great playwright himself?* she wondered. *Has he ever strayed into* my *domain?* The various members of the orchestra were starting to take their places and begin the discordant tuning of instruments. She looked to Charlie, gave him an excited smile, then wiggled her trousered bottom further down into the horsehair seat and waited for the red velvet and gold braided curtains to rise. Harry slipped noiselessly into the unoccupied seat beside her and slumped down.

"Awright?" said the youth, grinning from ear to ear, then leaning forwards to tip his cap at Charlie, who raised his eyebrows and nodded vigorously.

Lillian took in the stale gin and smell of old clothes that clung to him and filled her nostrils and could only nod and hold her breath. *I'll get no peace now*, she thought.

Then the music built to a crescendo and the curtains rose to reveal a giant gold disc hung in the centre of the stage against a painted backdrop of clouds and blue sky. Ten half-naked female nymphs wrapped in white sheets, each sporting laurel leaf crowns, formed a semicircle. In the distance horse's hooves could be heard, which seemed to be getting nearer and nearer as a huge voice proclaimed: "Whosoever should tame this horse would become King of the World."

Harry nudged her. "Them's coconut shells," he said. Lillian put a finger to her lips to shush him and turned back to the stage.

And then Alexander himself appeared, leading Bucephalus behind him. Lillian leaned forwards in her seat. She'd never seen such a handsome man, such a pronounced and regal chin and the most perfect Roman nose. Alexander sported gold breastplate armour over a naked chest which had been shaved and oiled, his defined pectoral muscles catching the light of the theatre. A short skirt made of bright red material, covered in vertical two-inch-wide slats of brown leather, reached a few inches above his knee whilst his sandals were laced with leather thongs to just below it. The whole ensemble was topped off with a gold helmet, out of which sprouted a red plume hanging jauntily over one shoulder. When he stood still, he placed both hands on his hips and the horse stood placidly beside him.

"I shall tame this horse and claim him for my own," declared the actor in a voice that would easily reach the back of the theatre. Clever lighting created a shadow of the horse at the front of the stage from which Bucephalus backed away. Alexander made a great fuss about leading him around the boards until the shadow fell behind him, as the legend had told.

"And I shall name him Bucephalus for the mark on his forehead. And we will fight many battles together."

Suddenly, loud thunderclaps broke out above the stage.

"You'll never guess how we got that to work," whispered Harry, leaning forwards to talk to Charlie.

"Sssh," said Lillian, as Alexander's mother Olympias took the stage and proclaimed that her son would one day rule the world.

"It's a large wooden gulley set high in the rafters and all we do is throw different size balls down it to make the effect. Works, eh?"

Then the nymphs walked on together, each singing a progressively higher and higher pitched set of "Ahs" and "Las."

The play went on to tell how Alexander and Bucephalus fought many successful battles together. How one would not leave without the other, and how each had shielded his companion against both their enemies and the elements. By the time the story got to the Battle of Thebes and Alexander was weeping over his wounded horse, the events of the last day or so began to overwhelm her and Lillian could no longer keep her emotions in check. She began to cry as well. Rain could be heard in the distance ("a large box containing barley seed, turned slowly," said Harry) as the horse moved from his forelegs to lie down on his side. A streak of blood stained the horse's flank, as well as Alexander's cheeks, as he lay down to comfort the beast in his final hours.

As the music played, Lillian pondered Button's question once more. *Sometimes I hate being a woman*, she thought, fondling the lion's tooth that hung around her neck, stroking the enamel with her forefinger.

Why can't I be more like Olympias? No one told her what to do, she thought with a sigh. *Would I really have to leave the Exchange if I married? Why? Why shouldn't I continue to work there? Go home to my husband at night? I am just as much an apprentice as he . . .*

As the heavenly chorus was bellowed by the nymphs who stood at the back of the stage, the thought grew and grew in her head while the voices rose to reach their crescendo. A small pair of wings—representing the soul of the horse, Lillian guessed—rose into the rafters of the stage, and Alexander stood to give his great final soliloquy.

"No greater horse had I than Bucephalus,
He was my Brother, my Father, my Beginning, my End
And I shall build a great city to remember him by
On the banks of the Hydaspes and name it Bucephala.
In honour of my friend."

And with that the curtain dropped and Lillian sprang to her feet. "Bravo! Bravo!" she cried, weeping and clapping and laughing all at the same time.

IT WAS DUSK by the time Lillian and Charlie emerged from the Drury's Lane Theatre. Charlie said he would stay back to chat with his mates awhile and Lillian decided to take the long way home, back through Covent Garden, so she could think.

It was an uncommonly warm evening for the time of the year, and the streets were filled with early evening revellers taking advantage of the unexpected sunshine. The area was well known for its coffee shops, frequented by artists and prostitutes, but Lillian rarely encountered any trouble on account of being so tall and generally mistaken for a man. As she strolled she watched the men throwing back their flagons of beer and the women laughing and giggling as they flirted with whomever they would, snatching the pitchers and flasks from the men and taking a cheeky swig or leaning their chests forwards as they played with their hair or adjusted their wigs, just long enough for a nose to linger between breasts and take in the female scent.

One of the women suddenly broke away from the melee and swung round, knocking into Lillian. Laughing she said, "Gardy loo!" her cheeks red and damp with sweat and her bosom hoisted so high that the rosy pink of the tops of her areola could be seen. But then she turned and looked again. "Lillian?" she asked.

"Millie?" Lillian blinked.

"Look at you dressed up like a feller . . . and you really have cut your hair like you said you would!"

Millie took a step back and put her hands on her hips as she took in all of Lillian's appearance from top to toe. Lillian grabbed both her hands and pulled her friend towards her. "Oh, Millie, is it really you?" She gave her a hug. "Are you still at the Unsworths'?"

"Still there for my sins," said Millie. "Somehow! Not the same since you left. No one to keep me warm at night." She winked and began to sing, "*She kisses all, but Jenny is her dear, she feels her bubbies and she bites her ear.*"

Lillian blushed, glancing around to see who might be listening.

Millie took a swig from the flask she was holding and staggered a little. "Everyone talks about you, though, Lillian . . ."

"Me? Why, what on earth would they say?"

Millie laughed again, a happy lighthearted sound like a fingernail flicking the rim of a crystal glass. "How you've gone to work at that animal place and started dressing like a feller. And you letting him sink his dagger, too?" she said, pointing at Lillian's crutch. "Prefer the boys now you look like one?" She slapped her thigh at the joke.

"Don't be so crude. As a matter of fact, I have a young man and he has just asked me to marry him."

"Well, ain't you the smart one," Millie huffed but with obvious admiration. "Mistress of the place, eh? Getting your *re-spec-ta-bull* hat on, eh?" she drawled, emphasising each of the syllables. "Well, that's the way to do it. You're over twenty-one! Get yourself a husband and *you* can be in charge. Ha! The abbess of a house of ill repute—only it's for animals!" She laughed at her own joke.

One of the men with whom Millie had been drinking shouted over at her, "Leave that feller alone and come back to us, Millie."

"See?" said Millie, revealing both her dimples in a broad smile. "Save some for me," she called back over her shoulder at her companions.

"It's been lovely to see you, Millie, but I really must go."

Millie held on to her hand. "What? Now? Come and share a jar with me before you're an old married lady."

"Another time, Millie," said Lillian, shaking Millie's arm from her sleeve. "But thank you. It's done my heart good to see you."

"Always was a deep one," said Millie. "Little kiss for old times?"

Lillian leaned forwards and kissed her on her forehead. "Good night, Millie darling."

Millie turned and waved as Lillian walked away and started to sing with great good humour. *"That one's a man is false, they've both been felt. Tho' Jolly swears Bess is or she's been gelt."*

Lillian took a deep breath, her decision finally made, and started to walk towards the Exchange.

WHEN LILLIAN ARRIVED back at the Exchange, she found the beef-eaters gone and Mrs. Ogden's ticket booth closed for the night. But the bars to the entrance had not yet been put in place and she supposed that either Grady or visitors must still be inside.

She entered the hall and immediately smelt smoke. Picking up her pace and sniffing all the time, she followed the trail towards the aviary, which sprang to life with flapping wings and screeches, and turned the corner to see Grady slumped in a chair, his usually immaculate waistcoat hanging open to the top of his breeches, stockings fallen down to the tops of his boots, laces undone. An empty stone jar lay on its side by his chair. His eyes were half open and he seemed to be mumbling some song to himself while puffing on a pipe and staring at his stuffed cassowary bird.

"Grady!" said Lillian, picking up the heavy ring of keys which had fallen, abandoned, on the floor. "How many times have I got to tell you? You can *not* smoke in here! There's dry straw all over the floor and this place could go up like a tinderbox."

"They call me the Terrestrial and Aerial Fascinator, the truly modern Noah," he muttered, staring hard at the bird as if willing it alive.

"Yes, yes, so you've told us many a time," said Lillian, waving a hand in front of her face and blowing the smoke away. "We've all seen the newspaper piece. But that doesn't mean you can smoke in here. The animals do not like it."

"I've been thinking, Lill," said Grady, beginning to struggle to his feet.

Lillian pushed him back, gently but firmly, into his chair. "You're as drunk as a sow, you old brandy face."

"I've been thinking," he repeated, slurring his words. "I've looked after yer, fed yer, cared fer yer—"

"Yes, and I've run this place for *you* and kept the animals fit and healthy so you can *sell* them and not a word of thanks do I get."

Grady began getting to his feet once more. This time Lillian took a step backwards. "And I'm a man," he said pointing at himself. "An impresario. I've travelled the country. Bought and sold all the animals in this place."

He cast his arms wildly around him, glaring at her all the while. He stopped, pointed at Lillian, and slowly and clearly said through gritted teeth, "Then that young mopus comes in here and wants to take you for his wife when I thought that . . ."

Lillian stood silently.

"What?" she said, though she knew full well.

"Why not *me*!" Grady shouted. Lillian flinched. "Me!" he said again and lunged towards her, grabbing her by the throat and pushing her up against the wall. His whole body seemed to be pressed against her and she could smell the stale brandy breath mixed with tobacco from his upturned face. She tried to move her head to avoid the fumes but the grip of his thumb and forefinger tightened further.

On the next floor the lion gave out the most almighty roar.

With as much strength as she could muster, she declared, "Let.

Me. Go. You *idiot!*" She looked him steadily in the eye and showed no fear.

From around the corner came a voice. "Miss Lill? Are you all right? What's happening? I smelled smoke."

Grady loosened his grip with a *bah!* He spat on the floor and slumped back in his chair as Charlie appeared.

Lillian soothed her throat with her hand. "I'm fine, Charlie. Thank you," she said without taking her eyes off of Grady.

Charlie looked at the dishevelled woman leaning against the wall and the drunken menagerie owner two sheets to the wind. He saw the pipe on the floor and immediately went and stamped it out. "You sure, Miss?"

"Yes I'm sure," she said, smoothing herself down. "Grady, there's no need for Charlie to stay, is there?"

"No. No," said Grady, shaking his head and looking away. "You go home," he said, and Charlie raised his eyebrows and left.

"Grady, what's this about?" said Lillian.

All the strength seemed to drain from the menagerie owner as he slumped back in his chair. "I can't have that mopus take you away from me," he whimpered.

She sat down beside him. "No one is going to make me leave the Exchange," she said gently. "I love these animals and they need me too."

"Marry *me*, Lill," Grady begged.

"I can't marry you, Grady. I don't love you and besides, I've made up my mind to marry Button."

"But—but—"

"Don't worry, I'm not leaving you. I'm going to marry him, but on the condition that I can still come to work. Can you see me as a wife sitting home with her embroidery? I don't think so. I belong here."

PART TWO

Part Two

Eleven

LILLIAN HAD BARELY TAKEN A FEW awkward steps through the Emporium entrance when the smell of urine-sodden straw caught the back of her throat. Her chin jutted forwards and her head pulled back as she retched and a blanket of sweat beads sprang up all her body. Clamping her hand over her mouth, she turned and waddled out of the building as fast as she could, somehow keeping down the pudding and sweet wine that Mrs. Tomkins had prepared for her breakfast just an hour before. The air in the Exchange no longer smelled to her as it did when she first arrived all those months ago. Instead of the sweet smell of fresh straw and freedom, now it was the smell of excrement that reached her first.

Outside in the crisp December air, she leaned against Mrs. Ogden's ticket booth and gave a sigh of relief whilst the discordant sound of the hurdy-gurdy man tuning up his instrument for the day ahead cut through the quiet of the early morning. She ran a damp hand through her hair, fanning her face with the palm of the other. The hurdy-gurdy man's monkey ran towards her and began pulling at her apron for attention. Sporting a red tasselled velvet fez and matching waistcoat, it reached as high as her knees and looked like a small child trapped in an old man's fur-covered body. The monkey began its familiar screeching through big yellow gritted teeth and she pushed him away with an irritated, "Get off, Albert."

Young Charlie had been feeding the porcupines in the stall near the front door when Lillian arrived and had watched her run out. Now he hurried after her carrying the small milking stool he'd been sitting on.

"Get out of it," he said, giving the monkey a shove with his foot. "How are you, Miss Lill?" He placed the stool beside her, gently taking her hand and pulling her to sit down.

"Yes, yes," she replied, shaking her head. "Please don't fuss, Charlie. I'm just a bit tired, that's all," but nevertheless she accepted the seat and sank into it. A fat black rat dodged around Charlie's legs and darted back into the menagerie. The monkey set off after it still screeching, given chase by Teddy Diamond. A voice came from inside the ticket booth. "Well, you would be tired in your state," it said. "Surprised your husband lets you leave the house, if you ask me."

"And no one did ask you, Mrs. Ogden," said Lillian, holding her huge belly, as she continued to take a series of steady deep breaths in an attempt to settle her stomach. She became aware of a metallic taste in the back of her throat.

"Oh! Look at your nose, Miss," said Charlie, letting go of her hand and casting his eye around for something to stop the flow.

"Oh, not again," she said, patting her apron pockets and searching in vain for a handkerchief.

The last few months had not been easy. She had got used to the horrible taste in her throat and the heartburn in her chest, a frequent evening visitor, and she was no stranger to the back pain; even the daily sickness which had plagued her in the early days had been manageable, not that she wanted to eat that much anyway, but the nosebleeds were the worst.

Swearing Lillian to secrecy, Mrs. Tomkins had produced a powder: GUARANTEED TO CURE AND RESTORE ANY AND EVERY FEMALE

SPECIFIC PROBLEM. Neither Featherstone nor Button could know of it, of course, being the modern medicine men they were. But Mrs. Tomkins swore on the efficacy of the potion and declared with great conviction that her sister had taken it for the first three months of her situation and the sickness had simply disappeared and that, indeed, many ladies of quality took the preparation each and every day and into the latter period of their life. "*And only three shillings and sixpence a pot!*" she concluded.

Lillian knew what her husband would say about the expense of such an item, but she hated the nosebleeds more than anything else. They would catch her when she least expected and the first she would be aware was when the red drops stained the floor.

It drove the lion wild.

Mrs. Ogden emerged from her tiny ticket box like an overfed blackbird, brushing down her widow's clothing where the chips of old navy paint had caught on her dark shawl. She produced a grey hanky from her pocket.

"Head back, please," she said, taking charge and pinching Lillian's nose in a face that had gone quite pale. Lillian did as she was told. Her pale green eyes stared up at Mrs. Ogden as the old woman gently wiped her cheeks and brow, pushing back the short hair from her forehead.

"I'm just saying you got to be careful," she said, dropping her voice an octave, emphasising the first syllable of "careful" (as was her wont) and leaning in towards Lillian's ear—all without letting go of the nose.

"You're with these animals all day long and everybody knows what might happen. What will this baby look like?"

"Please, Mrs. Ogden," said Lillian with some irritation, breaking away from her hold to spit blood on the floor.

"Why, my sister knows a woman from her village who was six months into her quickening and there she was, stirring the pot in her kitchen, when a billy goat suddenly appeared at the window and gave her the fright of her life. And sure enough, she gave birth to a little baby with white hair all over its body complete with pointy ears and a beard. And before you ask, yes, of course it could jump. Husband didn't want to know, of course. Destitute she was. Everyone knew what had happened."

Lillian had grown up listening to such fables but had attended enough lectures with her husband to know it to be pigswill. Nevertheless, the old wives' tale pulled her back to her childhood when all manner of terrible things were discussed behind turned shoulders and cupped hands and the story had the power to stir a feeling of apprehension in her bones.

Mrs. Ogden, hands on her hips, stood back to stare down at Lillian. "There will be some mark," she said. "That's for sure."

The beefeaters at the entrance, drawn by the commotion of Lillian's nosebleed and the opportunity to swing the lead for half an hour, were chatting in various groups with workers form the nearby shops, lighting pipes, taking some liquid refreshment, gossiping and spitting. A strong believer in the old adage that "where there's a crowd there's money to be made," the hurdy-gurdy man sent the monkey (by now returned, licking its lips and waving a stolen banana in its hand) into the crowd with its little red collecting hat.

Lillian took another swig of water from the tin mug some-one had placed in her hands whilst the men leaned against Mrs. Ogden's booth and gossiped in loud voices.

"I know of a woman who was frightened by a one-legged beg-gar and sure enough the baby only had one leg when it made its appearance," said one of the beefeaters with great assurance, giv-ing the monkey a sharp kick as it passed by. The monkey yelped and dropped its banana.

"And that woman with the rabbits," said another.

"I read about that in the paper," his pal replied. "Seventeen of them!"

Lillian overheard someone say in a stage whisper, "Maybe the lion is the father," followed by a snicker. She felt for the talisman hanging round her neck on its leather lace and stroked her belly.

Mrs. Ogden bent down towards her and Lillian caught the whiff of her sweaty armpits, vainly disguised by rosewater. "Just you ignore them," she whispered. "It's just that no one understands why you keep coming in here. You're part of a quality household now. Everyone says no good will come of it."

Lillian spat pink saliva on the floor. "I can't trust Grady. You know what he's like. He can't wait for me to go. And as soon as my back is turned he'll have the kangaroo fighting with Bungalow Bill, or setting Teddy Diamond against the wolf or—"

The dog barked at mention of his name.

"Now, now, you should be thinking bew-ti-ful thoughts," Mrs. Ogden said, wagging her finger and giving her arse an unconscious scratch. "Old Grady's more interested in finding what's lurking at the bottom of that stone flagon of his. He still can't believe you actually went ahead and married that young apprentice of Featherstone's. All that silly nonsense back in the spring—"

Lillian looked up sharply and Charlie turned his head away.

"Yes, Charlie told me all about it. Not a lot goes on round here that I don't know about," she said and snapped her wooden teeth twice.

"Make no mistake. He's delighted you're still here. See the way he keeps asking you questions about this and that?"

Charlie piped up. "He gave me strict instructions that you were not to be stressed, Miss. No heavy lifting of those buckets, and no dragging those goats into the lion's cage in case you has one of those bloomin' nosebleeds."

Charlie puffed up his chest and pretended to stick one thumb in his waistcoat while pulling on some imaginary sideburns with the other.

"And no running round with that bloomin' broom after the fricking rats neither. Leave her take care of the birds."

Mrs. Ogden rolled her eyes and gave a "tut" with her tongue while Lillian burst out laughing at Charlie's impersonation. Then she clacked her teeth once more and returned to her booth.

Lillian slowly rose to her feet, supporting her back with her left hand and pulling her trousers up with the right. "There's nothing to see here," she said, spitting on the floor, brushing herself down, and assuming authority once more. "Charlie, get everyone back to work. We open in twenty minutes."

She let out her belt an extra notch. The casual onlooker would be surprised to know Lillian was with child, her height ensuring the additional weight at the front was somewhat concealed. In an attempt at discretion, Lillian had taken to wearing a long brown leather apron over her regular outfit of worsted breeches and cambric shirt. A regular acquaintance, however, might be surprised to see how drawn she had become, her cheekbones casting a shadow on her face.

She pushed her hand into the pocket of her apron and felt for the piece of coal, the size of a small hen's egg, that she kept there. She liked to gnaw at the lump with one side of her back teeth when no one was looking, mixing the residue with her saliva to make a paste that she would roll around her mouth for hours on end, constantly licking the front of her teeth with her tongue to release the grit until the whole sorry—but immensely satisfying— snack had disappeared.

The show over, the workers began to disperse, setting down their mugs and pipes wherever they could find a surface and talking to each other all the while in low voices, their mumblings interspersed with occasional loud bursts of laugher.

When everyone had gone, Charlie said, "Miss, will you take a look at Caesar? He's been a bit restless this morning."

"A life on the stage going to his head, eh?" she said with a weak smile. "You go ahead. I'll be right behind you."

Lillian dawdled, in no rush to make her way past the animals calling out for her attention. The excited yips and yowls which had once greeted her now felt like a suspicious set of shrieks and caterwauls and the place seemed both melancholic and damp. The crisp fresh air of the winter sunshine was far more inviting.

Taking another swig of water, she thought about her forthcoming confinement in just a few weeks' time. She was not unfamiliar with the process of childbirth and only a little scared. Time and again she had been assured that she would have an easy time, thanks to her size and wide hips, but still something did not feel quite right—not least her husband's behaviour. Maybe it was her imagination, but he seemed so distant, spending hour after hour in Featherstone's library, nose deep in huge books full of drawings of animals and humans, stripped bare of skin, their muscles and ligaments exposed in all their glory.

Whereas once they had agreed on everything, it now seemed they could decide on nothing. Evenings were no longer filled with excited chatterings about this idea or that new author, nor comparing notes on their views or sharing talks of the animals sold or treated during the day.

And only two nights ago he had slept in a separate room, "so as not to disturb her," he said.

Working with her husband, she had assisted at the birth of many of the animals at the menagerie, most recently a she-wolf that had kept the pair up most of the night as they coaxed her litter into the world. Extinct for two hundred years in England, the wolves held a fascination for many of the visitors who were attracted to the corner stall, painted to evoke the Seven Hills of Rome where Romulus and Remus were kept. When the third cub of the litter appeared to get stuck, she and Button had disagreed about the approach to take. Button had been most insistent that he should extract the runt from its mother's belly and that he had the right instruments to do so. Lillian, on the other hand, had wanted to let nature take its course a little while longer and preferred to manipulate the prospective arrival into its correct position.

She remembered the look of disgust on his face as he watched her tear open the amniotic sac, which had failed to open, with her teeth. Button's irritated response had been to pull his bag together and leave. "For god's sake, woman, it's only a wolf," he'd said and left her there in the middle of the night.

FEATHERSTONE, OF COURSE, did not help.

"Don't be silly, girl," said Featherstone, leaning over his desk, wig askew as he squinted through his microscope. "Nothing to worry about. Not like the old days any more. My mother was always saying how they used a crochet hook to get *me* out. Ha! Ha!"

Lillian squirmed but stayed silent and continued to feed the parrot scraps of lettuce and seeds from a small bowl as it ran up and down its perch, spreading its blue wings every now and then and squawking but never letting its red beady little eye stray far from Lillian's hand.

"My wife will have a surgeon, of course," her husband declared, head deep in his newspaper in a chair by the window, one leg crossed over the other.

Looking up from his microscope, Featherstone replied, "Of course, Button, of course!"

Button put down his paper, folded his arms, and leaned back. Lillian was starting to realise that this usually meant he was about to pontificate on something.

"I have just read the most interesting treatise on the delivery of babies, a new type of forceps that's been developed. Did you see it, Featherstone?"

"No . . . no can't say that I have yet. Good, is it?"

"Important not to crush the head, you see."

"Well, of course." Featherstone nodded in agreement. "I've seen those old women tug babies from the womb just to speed up the delivery. Usually end up doing more harm than good. Ha!"

"Thank god, today we have some decent trained men to manage the process, men with rational and scientific expertise. Men who—"

"Men who know their science from their herbs and potions!"

"Men who know how these things actually *work*, for god's sake."

"Men who are *trained*!"

"Men who can read!"

"Educated men!"

Lillian shook her head and mumbled, "I am not going to that lying-in hospital," but she was ignored.

Featherstone stood up and was now leaning against the mantelpiece above the fire. "I was talking to one of the Fellows up at the Society a few days ago. Written something on internal manipulation techniques. Most enlightening, I must say."

"Makes you wonder how the human race has survived so long," Lillian said quietly.

"Thank god for modern medicine!" Featherstone exclaimed. Turning to Lillian, he gave her a wink. "You shall have the best, my dear. Nothing's too good for our girl."

"I'm not going to that hospital," Lillian said once more.

"My dear, my dearest Lillian," said Button, putting down his paper and reaching for the pipe he had taken to smoking. "We only want the best for you."

Featherstone held up his hands. "Now now, my dears."

Mrs. Tomkins walked in carrying a tray with the afternoon tea things.

"Then, she will have the baby here at home with us, won't she, Mrs. T?" he asked her.

Mrs. Tomkins shrugged, put down the tray, and began to lay out the cup and saucers.

"And a woman to attend me?"

Button took in a deep breath.

"And I will breastfeed myself."

Button gave his paper a shake, uncrossed his legs, and crossed them once more.

Featherstone put a hand on Button's shoulder as if to calm his apprentice. He clapped his hands. "And we will find a wet nurse to come and stay. Everything will be wonderful."

BREATHING THROUGH HER mouth as much as possible to avoid taking in the smell, Lillian made her way through the Great Hall to

Caesar's stall. She turned the corner and saw that her husband was already there, fussing over his preparations. Something made her pause rather than greet him and she retraced a few steps to conceal herself in such a position that she could watch quietly. The vet was leaning over a small table, neatly laying out his surgical instruments one by one on a metal tray. "The finest cast steel," Featherstone had pronounced when he presented Button with the set for his twenty-fifth birthday a few months before. Lillian watched from the shadows as he carefully wiped each instrument with a cloth, then offered it up to the light that streamed in from the window at the end of the Great Hall, each one glinting like a fish on a line. Then, oblivious to his audience, he lay each item down in an order made of his own devising and that only he would know if transgressed. It reminded her of a priest preparing for Holy Communion.

Am I really spying on my husband? she thought with dismay.

The noise of the tools took her back many years to when her mother had been in labour with her fifth. With a shudder, she recalled the candlelight glistening on the surgeon's instruments, the moans as she lay on her back, legs wide open, a small wet and bloody arm with a fist thrusting for freedom from between her legs, her mother in a sea of red, eyes and mouth wide open in a silent grimace of pure horror. Just for a moment their eyes had met. Lillian blinked, then caught the look between her father and the midwife in attendance, saw the minutest shaking of heads, and could hear words exchanged but without their making sense. She remembered the sound the instruments made as they were jumbled together on the steel tray, shuffled together like a metal version of the pick-up sticks the Exchange boys liked to play. Lillian had stood still, eyes and mouth wide open, as the door was closed in her face.

An hour or so later when she was summoned to help, she was instructed to take away a container covered in a white muslin cloth, streaked with blood. "Don't look in the bowl," she was told.

Carefully she carried the basin to the end of the hall, holding it out in front of her, arms outstretched, head slightly averted, an aroma reaching her nostrils, of what? It reminded her of the cloth strips she used once a month. She didn't want to look. She really didn't. But then, of course, she had to.

The picture would be forever etched on her brain—the red mess of sausage-like limbs of all sizes laid out in the caricature of a human, topped with a mass of dark hair streaked with dark blood and a grey, glutinous gloop. The eyes of a dead fish stared up at her.

Now she stood at the sidelines, watching her husband fondling those same familiar instruments, and wondered, not for the first time, what he would do if things did not go smoothly with her.

Twelve

ND SO THE SNOW FELL AND London shivered.
The menagerie did not open till the sun was well and truly
in the sky and closed as soon as the sky turned the fire orange of
twilight. New show pieces, which had once arrived weekly, were
now sporadic, as were the crowds, and the birds no longer sang so
brightly without the sun streaming through the window to warm
their wings.

The first task of the day for the boys, some with boots but most
barefooted or with feet wrapped in rags tied with string, was to
break the ice on the water bowls and then drag in the extra layers
of straw Grady had begrudgingly agreed to buy. As soon as their
jobs were done, the youngsters would huddle together and scarf
down the extra soup Mrs. Ogden had prepared. Then they disappeared. Lillian was still unsure where they went.

The rhino, which had inconveniently doubled in size over the
summer months with no buyer found, was now too big to enjoy his
rolls in the water bath Lillian had worked so hard to create for him
and stood silent, the cold having robbed him of song. Occasionally
the hyena would let out the most plaintive of wails, which would
make anyone visiting the building stop and give an involuntary

shudder. The wolf puppies curled up between their parents, and the lion, as far he was able, paced up and down his small cell, his warm breath creating little clouds of frozen air, the fresh goat meal lying freezing in the corner. Any drops of spilt water quickly turned to ice, which formed a lethal sheet over the cobblestones; everyone was especially careful where they put their feet or placed a bucket. The snow was bright and white for the first hour of the day, but quickly turned grey and brown when mixed with horse waste and the extra coal being dragged through the streets. The rain would then turn the rest to slush. Sedan chair carriers and link boys complained that their feet were permanently wet and stuffed their shoes with old newspapers, which they hung over the foreside to dry.

Lillian walked slowly, the seven-month pregnancy taking its toll on her back.

But not everything had come to a standstill. Christmas was coming, and back up at Neal Street Mrs. Tomkins filled her days preparing foods for the yuletide feast, making mince pies, plum puddings, and topping up the Twelfth Cake she had made a few months before with extra brandy.

And before Christmas could come there would be a Hanging Day. Everyone was humming with the anticipation of well-known highwayman, Bob Boothroyd, going to meet his maker. He was better known as "Babyface" on account of his florid cheeks, red and round as conkers, and the single curl in the middle of his forehead.

Mrs. Ogden dithered and tittered and gossiped as she sat in the admission booth, quite happy to keep warm sitting on her bedpan, counting the shillings and not having to talk to any visitors. "Oh, but the highwaymen are so gallant," she said, emphasising the first syllable of "gallant" with a nod of her head. "And they say Babyface never laid a finger on a woman, nor hurt a soul, and was the most polite of all of them. Oh, for such a man to be sent to meet his maker . . ."

"I'm sure if you were faced with such a man on a dark country night you would not think he was so gallant," Lillian shouted back from across from the porcupine pen where she was replenishing the water bowl.

"Sitting up there on a bright bay gelding, they say, in his black mask! Oh my!" Mrs. Ogden mused, fluttering both eyelids and hands.

"And neither would he be so gallant if he was on foot and had to run rather than gallop away with his takings," Lillian replied.

"Mr. Grady was telling me that having relieved one squire of his purse he then asked his wife to get down from her carriage and dance with him!"

Lillian laughed and gave a few desultory sweeps with the broom before wandering over to Mrs. Ogden's booth to continue the conversation.

Mrs. Ogden paused for dramatic effect and, looking Lillian straight in the eye, said, "And she did!" clapping her hands together, clearly scandalised but equally delighted.

"Good luck to her," said Lillian. "Why shouldn't she have some fun on such a terrifying occasion?" She wondered what it might be like to enjoy such liberty, to be a man in a mask and able to rove the countryside at will, beholden to no one except the horse. How free she might be astride such a magnificent creature, inviting beautiful young ladies to get down and dance, the disguise hiding both her identity and her gender. She sighed and smiled to herself.

"They give all their money to the poor, you know."

"I very much doubt that, Mrs. O."

"Well, so I heard. Anyway, they are going to hang the poor bugger next Hanging Day. That's only a week or so away. He's quite the fellow of renown, you know, popular with both the quality and the hoi polloi. And only twenty-two years old. Imagine that."

Mrs. Ogden gave a "come closer" nod of her head and, looking around to make sure no one was watching, reached inside her apron and produced a small square of paper about two inches in size, which she passed to Lillian through the ticket booth window. Lillian unfolded it twice to reveal a line drawing of a highwayman in his tricorn hat and mask, a brace of pistols stuck in his belt. The figure was sitting down on a stool, his ankles manacled. Above his head and to the right was a barred window and, in the distance, the hangman's gibbet. The drawing was cleverly done to catch the eye of the beholder, and the artist had made the highwayman look even younger than his twenty-two years, a small tear in his right eye.

"First night in Newgate he got over a thousand visitors," said Mrs. Ogden. "They had to turn people away—one young lady fainted and was almost crushed." She paused to see Lillian's reaction. "It's sure to be a popular event, you know, him being from a good family and all that. I've told Grady, he may as well shut up shop that day. We'll have no visitors, that's for sure."

Lillian looked at the picture for a few seconds, sad at the loss of one so young, then gave it back to Mrs. Ogden without a word. Disappointed that Lillian was not in the mood to talk highwaymen or hangings, Mrs. Ogden shrugged her shoulders, carefully folded her paper, put it back in her pocket, and continued counting the pennies and the shillings.

A FEW NIGHTS later, as Lillian was settling Keebar down for the night, she was disturbed by a lone figure running into the menagerie and towards her. She held out her palm to halt his advance. "I'm sorry, we're closed."

The man, who had evidently been running and was out of breath, stopped and bent to put his hands on his knees, still panting hard. "I heard . . . you have a . . . a . . . lion. I was so . . . excited . . . I've run all the way here just to catch you before you closed."

"Well, we *are* closed," Lillian said firmly but with a little suspicion. The lion wasn't *that* popular. She drew herself up to her full height and, with legs apart and hands on hips, looked down at the man and said, "Can't you come back tomorrow?"

The visitor sported a hat and a blue surtout coat that reached to the floor. He kept looking over his shoulder. Now having fully recovered his breath, he directed a beaming grin up at her, revealing one of his dimples. "Ah, my dear," he said, "Just one tiny peek. I have heard it is the most extraordinary thing and tomorrow, well, who knows? Who knows where we might be?" He flashed the most brilliant smile Lillian had ever seen, his cheeks rosy and red. To her surprise—and annoyance—she blushed. She would later tell Mrs. Ogden that she was sure his eye had actually twinkled.

The man pulled off his hat and gave an exaggerated bow. "Bobby Boothroyd at your service, ma'am. Will not take more than a few moments of your time."

He moved confidently towards her and, despite being at least a foot shorter, took her gently by the waist, leading her further away from the front entrance and towards the back of the menagerie, all the while looking over his shoulder. As they passed the aviary, the birds sprang into life and the sound of urgent flapping wings and screeches from all the different flying creatures filled the air. Lillian let herself be led.

There was something about the man's name that seemed familiar. "Oh!" she said. "You're—"

"Indeed," he replied, the smile falling from his face. "And they are looking for me, so come on. Now."

She allowed herself to be swept along by his urgency and he guided her deeper into the Hall. "Turn right," she said.

The lion roared his welcome.

"Leonidas," said Lillian, walking towards the cage.

The lion padded the few steps towards her. She pushed her face between the bars of the cage and the lion lowered his head to welcome her in the now familiar greeting. Woman and beast rubbed noses. Boothroyd stood back and watched.

"Madame, I have travelled the length and breadth of this country and rarely have I seen such a sight. Is it bravery or foolhardiness?"

"He is my best friend," said Lillian, smiling at the creature.

"And from a woman, too. But such a small place for a living being to call its cot, would you not agree?"

In truth, the cage was hardly more than the length and width of two men lying down head to toe.

"Madame, forgive me, I am quite forgetting my manners," said Boothroyd. "And you in your current state." Spying a small chair by the lion's cage, he pulled it out for Lillian to sit down on. As he did so, his coat fell open and she caught sight of the pistol stuck in his belt. He saw the look and tapped the grip. "You've nothing to fear from me, ma'am. Highwayman I may be but never would I lay a finger on a woman—with child or otherwise—unless invited, of course."

He winked and Lillian felt herself flush. She could not help but notice how fleshy and pink his demeanour—how he differed from the tall, sharp-angled man she had married.

"May I ask your name, ma'am?"

"Lillian."

"Ah, Lillian—the pure flower."

"It is . . . the cage I mean . . . it does seem small," said Lillian, looking at Leonidas once more.

"I am no stranger to a cage, ma'am," said Boothroyd, tapping his nose. The grin was now firmly back on his face. "You must be a very special person to have tamed such a beast."

Ignoring the compliment, Lillian asked, "What brings you here? Surely you could be miles away by now."

"One last escape!" he declared with swish of his hat and laughed. "There were enough who saw me that they will find me here quick enough, but I'm not going to the Drop without giving them a run for their money."

"How did you manage to get out?"

"So many visitors in and out of my cell, lovely ladies with their hair all pinned and powdered. Who notices if a pin falls on the floor? Not the gardy-loos, too busy staring at those apple dumplings. Don't take much for a fellow like me to dig my way out of a lock. One last time, I told myself. And in truth . . . I *did* want to see your famous lion. He is out of Africa, is he not? Like our black brethren?"

Lillian nodded, intrigued by the vibrancy of the man.

"I rode with a negro once," he said. "Always complaining of the cold, but the best of distractions when you are liberating a traveller from their purse!" He laughed. "He was brought to England on a slave ship but managed his escape."

Lillian frowned as she wondered for the first time whether Leonidas minded the temperature.

"He described his homeland to me, a vast dusty open space of red and brown and orange. I wonder if our friend here"—he indicated the lion with his thumb—"would recognise such a landscape?"

Lillian looked from the strange young baby-faced creature to her lion.

"No man nor beast should be kept in chains, wouldn't you agree?"

Lillian slowly nodded her agreement.

Boothroyd licked the thumb and forefinger of his left hand and then twirled the curl on his forehead. "And your better half, ma'am? May I enquire as to his whereabouts?"

"My husband is the veterinary surgeon for this establishment," said Lillian, indicating the menagerie with a wave of her hand. "But he attends many other London folk who keep animals, those with money to pay for his services. Each day he returns with some new bauble or other given as a reward." She added a little sadly, "I presume that is where he is now."

"And he does not mind for his wife to be working in such a place?" asked the fugitive.

"I fear he cares little for me anymore," said Lillian, avoiding

Boothroyd's gaze and surprised that she was confessing such a secret to a stranger.

"Why so?" exclaimed the young man.

She shrugged. "He seems to prefer to attend the lords and ladies with their constipated parrots and little toy dogs, and since he put me with child it seems that all he cares about is his work."

"Ah, now I have heard of this before. It is not so unusual. He will return to you, I am sure, a beautiful woman such as yourself. So tall. Such a prize! Why, if your belly were not so big I'd ask you to dance myself." His blue eyes sparkled.

Lillian laughed. "You're a honeyjack of a man, that's for sure," she said with the faintest of flutter of eyelids. Boothroyd gave a grin and a bow.

"But seriously," he said, furrowing his brow in faux concentration as he stroked his chin with his left forefinger. "I have heard of this and I would take a guess at the problem."

"Please, sir, I'd like to know," said Lillian, looking up at the young man and thinking how handsome he was.

"To put it quite simply, ma'am—" He paused. "He is frightened."

"Frightened?"

"That he may harm you."

"Harm me? How so?"

Boothroyd grinned, pointed at her belly, then made a circular motion with his finger.

Lillian felt her face grow hot. "Well, there's certainly been none of that for some time," she said, again wondering what it was that made her reveal such a personal detail.

"Fear not, ma'am. You may have your way with the lions, but I have mine own ways with the ladies. Let me tell you what to do."

As he leaned down to whisper in her ear, Lillian caught the faintest whiff of a familiar perfume. She sat and listened to what he had to say. Despite the cold creeping up through her feet, her eyes grew wider by the second and her armpits flushed hot and damp.

When he had finished, she could not quite look at the highway-man. Smiling, she stammered instead, "Thank you. Ill pray for the strength to try."

"Please do," said the young man, giving her a wink.

Silence descended between the two.

"Pretty cold in here," he said with a shudder, hugging himself. "Oh, someone must have just walked on my grave. Sorry, that was in poor taste."

Lillian waved away his apology, feeling that it was she who should be apologizing.

"They will be very soon," the doomed man replied.

"But surely you must try and hide, Mr. Boothroyd? Now . . . before they get here."

Bob shook his head and his eyes dulled. He reached through the lion's cage to take a piece of straw and proceeded to pick his teeth with it.

"They will catch up with me, that's for sure, and—may I be honest with you?"

"Of course."

"I am scared."

"You? Why, we imagined you fearless!"

"Ha . . . riding on the back of my horse across the countryside, chasing a four horse and ten, yes, I have no fear, but . . ." He hung his head and sighed. "But faced with going up that wooden ladder to my final resting place . . ."

Lillian put her hand on his arm. "Sir . . ." she said with as much consideration as she could muster.

He lightly shrugged her hand away, becoming increasingly animated as the words tumbled from his mouth. "No, no . . . don't get me wrong. I am not frightened to *die*. We all have to *die*. It's the hanging itself. Everyone watching me, cheering, shouting. I've seen men dangle many a time and it can take up to half an hour to expire, you know, and the piss, running down your legs. So—so—" He searched for the right word. "Undignified."

The blood drained from Lillian's face as she imagined the scene. She had watched a hanging once before and thought little of it, but to stand next to someone whose days could be counted on one hand was another matter.

Babyface continued gloomily, "I've even seen the rope break and the man saved, and standing there waiting for them to fix it, only for his heart to give out before they can put the rope round his neck again!"

Lillian took a sharp breath and turned away.

"I am sorry, ma'am. I didn't mean to—"

"But you will have your hangers-on?"

"I am sure there is enough cutter to pay for them and friends to be had, but . . ." Boothroyd paced in front of the cage. The lion settled on its haunches, watching his every move, occasionally tossing his mane and letting out a low growl.

"But still . . ." His voice drifted off.

"Listen!" Lillian thought she could hear the birds in the aviary call out, but the young highwayman continued as another thought seemed to strike him. "And the surgeons . . . They like a fresh corpse and mine will belong to the hangman to do with what he will . . . and everyone knows that the surgeons like their corpses so fresh that sometimes they—"

Babyface used the cuff of his shirt to wipe a tear that had appeared in the corner of his eye.

"Hush. Hush. You cannot dream of such things. Calm yourself, Mr. Boothroyd."

"And if they cut me to pieces when I am dead, then my body will never see the resurrection."

He laughed suddenly. "I'd like to see the surprise on their faces when they get my body on the slab!"

Dropping down beside Lillian, he took both her hands in his and said, "Promise me you will be in the crowd."

"I—" Lillian hesitated, shocked at the suggestion. "It will be so busy—the pushing, the shoving—my baby . . ."

"Promise me you will be there. I will search the crowd for you. If I can look into your eyes when they put the hood on, it will calm me, I feel sure."

"But don't you have a sweetheart who can take on this task for you?"

Boothroyd stood abruptly. "Ha!" He spat out the single syllable as if he had something unpleasant stuck in his throat. "My so-called sweetheart, that draggle-tail, is sitting right now in the Dog and Duck on Fleet Street supping ale that she's bought with the profit of my betrayal and drunk as Davy's sow by now, I've no doubt. Blast her lights." He looked away and dropped to his knees once more. "Do it for me, Lillian. You are so brave. Braver than any woman I have ever seen."

"I . . . I'm just not sure I can, Mr. Boothroyd."

Then an idea struck her. Reaching around her neck, she removed the lion's tooth that always hung there. She leaned towards the man kneeling before her and placed it over his head.

"This will give you strength," she said. The two looked into each other's eyes for a moment. She noticed his extraordinarily long eyelashes. He leaned forwards and gave her a kiss on the cheek.

"Thank you," he said. "Thank you for the strength to free myself of the tyranny of the scaffold."

Silence fell once more as each contemplated the conversation of the last hour. In the cage behind them the lion rose to his feet.

"What is it, Leonidas?" she asked and was answered by a roar, followed by a voice saying, "Come now, Babyface. Time to get your oatmeal."

From around the corner three men appeared, each dressed the same in long black overcoats and brown wool britches. Thick leather belts held two pistols apiece, along with manacles and chains that hung in loops reaching down to their dirty white stockings and buckled shoes.

The highwayman stood quickly and looked around, to the left, to the right. No exit.

Lillian pulled herself to her feet. "You should have taken your chances while you could. We are at the back, I'm afraid," she said. "There's no way out except through the front door."

"Then I am gutted and busted like a cod on a hook," said Boothroyd, the fire draining from him before it was even lit.

"I'm sorry," said Lillian.

Babyface held out both his hands to his grinning captors, one of whom, ignoring Lillian, quickly slipped on the cuffs while another attached the neck manacle. A third gave him a punch in the side of the head. Bright red blood immediately poured from his ear.

"That's for making us look like idiots," he said, then followed it up with a blow to his stomach. "And that's for making me miss my dinner."

"Come on, then. We are keeping your dispatcher waiting," said the other, pulling the boy by the neck.

"Excuse us, ma'am, but Babyface has got an appointment." They all laughed.

Lillian watched helplessly as the men dragged him away, one on each side. The highwayman turned, and she saw a trickle of blood slowly dribbling from the corner of his mouth.

He shouted over his shoulder, "Remember your promise, Lillian!" The third guard following behind gave the convict a kick in the rear. "Shut it, pig brain."

EXHAUSTED, LILLIAN DRIFTED in and out of sleep as she considered the events of the past few hours and wondered where the young highwayman would rest that night, if at all. She was facing the window when her husband entered the room. He sat down beside her on the bed and whispered her name quietly. She turned and he reached out his hand to stroke her hair.

"I cannot believe you have been through such an ordeal," he said with unfamiliar solicitation. Lillian gave a slight shake of her head, dismissing his concern but pleased nonetheless.

"Don't leave me alone tonight?" she asked and he nodded. She rolled back on her side to avoid watching his undressing, and as he changed into his nightshirt, he chattered on about what had happened and what might have happened and his relief that she was safe. Then he got into bed, gave his wife a kiss, and said goodnight.

Both lay still, back to back, no part of their nightclothed bodies touching, yet Lillian could feel his heat, and her passions, aroused by the day, longed for more. Her heart beat so loudly that surely he must hear. Listening to the steady sounds of the man lying beside her, she tried to recall the highwayman's advice.

She counted her breaths. In "*one . . . two . . . three*," then out "*one . . . two . . . three*," making her own move to his rhythm until both were breathing at the same tempo. Then, as if conducting an experiment, she arched her back—just a touch—and pressed her cold buttocks towards his. His breathing juddered and increased in pace as she inched closer, gaining confidence at the lack of rebuff and becoming aroused by the motion.

She squeezed her eyes closed and a parade of faces appeared— Millie from Mrs. Unsworth's, Babyface, Leonidas, her husband. Seconds passed, she pushed her rear again, and this time he turned silently. Putting his arm around her belly, he whispered into her neck, "I won't hurt you, will I?" Her gesture of reply was met with equal pressure in return.

They now moved together as one. Lillian counted faster. "*One. Two. Three. Four. Five.*" She could feel his excitement as she raised herself towards him and he slithered easily into her. His hand moved slowly from her belly to between her legs. She gasped. "*One. Two. Three. Four. Five . . . Six!*" and both reached their climax at the same time. A few minutes later John said, "I love you, Lillian."

TWO DAYS LATER Button and Lillian stood together, watching a manacled young man with a curl in the middle of his forehead standing on the scaffold's platform.

The occupants of the menagerie had earlier been fed and watered, locked up, and forgotten by the time the sun was up. Last to leave, Grady had roared at Lillian, "Will you ever be getting out of here so we can shut up shop?" while he rolled down his sleeves, buttoned his waistcoat, and checked the silver tiger claw pin was firmly attached to his best cravat.

Satisfied that all was as well as it could be, Lillian hurried out to meet her husband, who was waiting at the entrance. Today would be a heaven for pickpockets and Button had been careful to empty his pockets of all valuables. Devoid of the little adornments and accoutrements of success that he had been acquiring over the last few months, the ambitious young vet now looked just like any other of the twenty thousand souls all waiting to watch Babyface Boothroyd lose his.

The two-mile journey from Newgate to Tyburn would take nearly three hours due to the huge crowd. Seven were due to meet their maker, six men and a young girl, no more than fifteen years old, accused of murdering her own baby. The miserable group, huddled together, sat on their coffins as the wagon made its bumpy way through the narrow streets, surrounded by armed cavalry and accompanied by the girl's continuous weeping. Only Boothroyd refused to sit and stood holding onto the side, smiling at the crowd and giving the occasional wave. The procession was headed up by those who had a job to do, the City Marshal, the prison chaplain, the hangman and his assistants.

All along the route, people hung from windows shouting and cheering, throwing food and worse, whilst the girls blew kisses and hugged each other, grinning if they caught the prisoner's eye. The smell of cooking meat and sizzling fat filled the air, along with the church bells that rang out across the city for Hanging Day. Hawkers of every type were selling their wares—hot pies and muffins, oysters and crabs, oranges, strawberries, roasted apples, and walnuts too. Gingerbread men in the shape of the soon to be deceased were particularly popular with the children, who snapped off the heads with their teeth and then screamed with laughter as they sprayed crumbs and spittle all over their clothes. Musicians escorted the parade as it made its way along the Tyburn Road, playing their instruments all the while and singing songs created especially for the occasion. With much money and merriment to be made, nothing offered greater opportunity for the population of London to enjoy itself quite so much as a Hanging Day. Despite the cold of the last few weeks, the sun had come out to add another layer of warmth to the proceedings.

Button and Lillian picked up the procession at the top of Holborn and reached St. Sepulchre's church in time to hear the minister proclaim: "You that are condemned to die, repent with lamentable tears; ask mercy of the Lord for the salvation of your souls." They watched as friends presented the wagon's occupiers with nosegays and flowers.

By the time it came to the final stop at the Mason's Arms, they had been on their feet for almost two hours.

"Are you all right, my dear?" Button asked for the hundredth time, putting a protective arm around his wife. Lillian smiled at him but, slightly irritated, said nothing.

"You really don't have to do this, you know."

"Yes I do," she replied firmly.

Tradition decreed that condemned prisoners might take a final drink at the Mason's before they got back on the wagon. Lillian and John stayed back in the crowd, having no desire to get involved with the drinking or the laughter. Having taken his final glass of porter, Boothroyd was pushed and shoved back onto the cart and shouted out to the spectators, "I'll buy you all a pint on the way home!" which was greeted with much amusement and celebration of what a fine fellow was Babyface. Stories of his gallantry to women were repeated once more.

And so the crowd, drunk with ale and meat and music and anticipation, wended its way to the end of the Tyburn Road. Was there a moment's pause in the excitement when the crowd finally caught sight of that famous tree, the three bars on the three posts making up the three-cornered gallows? Those who were already there, having paid to take their seats in the gallery, craned their necks as the wagon came into view, cheered when they saw Babyface standing tall in the wagon, and rose to greet him. Lillian and Button searched for a good place to see and be seen—somehow Button, whose elbows could be sharp when he wanted, manoeuvred himself and his wife to the top of a small mound that raised them up above the other spectators, all the time keeping his arm around her waist.

The chaplain was already on the platform reading from the Bible in a monotone voice, not even trying to pretend he cared as he prayed for the souls of those who were going to meet their maker. The marshal's men surrounded the base of the scaffold, checking nervously all the while in case the mob might change its mind as to the destiny of those who were due to die.

The young girl accused of infanticide was first to be dragged off the cart. Her friends had ensured she had drunk more than her fill at the Mason's Arms; she had to be hauled up the ladder to the platform. A voice rose above the crowd crying, "My baby! My baby!" and the condemned girl seemed to rouse herself for a moment, scanning the crowd to find the owner, and stood long enough for the hood to be placed over her head before she fainted.

All grew silent.

The trapdoor fell open. For a few moments the only sound to be heard was the creaking on the gibbet. Then the crowd cheered as she jumped around on the rope and the urine began to run down her leg. Lillian's hand went to her mouth and she turned her head into Button's shoulder.

When she looked back, the girl's body had been cut down and was being taken away, rope still tight around her neck, by the anatomists, Lillian presumed. Parts of the crowd were reaching out to touch the body and clothes for the good luck it was said to bring.

Now the guards were beginning to push Babyface up the wooden ladder to the gibbet. Lillian could see he was still wearing the same clothes from two days before.

A young woman at the foot of the ladder wailed and made to grab the prisoner, only to be dealt a hefty kick from one of the guards. She fell on all fours, mud splashing up on her face and breasts. Boothroyd stood in front of the cheering crowd on the platform, hands tied in front of him. He gave a twirl and a mock bow, which Lillian knew to be bravado. She could see him scanning the crowd, his eyes darting here and there. She did not dare wave lest she draw attention to herself. Instead, she willed as hard as she could for his eyes to meet hers.

And then they did.

Across the twenty thousand souls who had gathered to watch the departure of his own, Boothroyd did not take his eyes from Lillian. He held up the lion's tooth that hung around his neck and kissed it, and Lillian raised the hand that was holding Button's in a salute, hoping he would understand what she meant. Boothroyd glanced briefly at Button then flashed a familiar grin at Lillian.

The hangman placed the noose over his head. At the offer of a few last words, Boothroyd shook his head, much to the disappointment of the crowd, and the hood was quickly slipped on. There seemed to be a collective intake of breath from the gathered revellers. Seconds seemed to go by, then the wooden lever was pulled and the rope quickly unravelled as Babyface Boothroyd fell through the floor.

But instead of the sudden jerk on the neck and the familiar dance of shit and piss that the crowd was expecting, he disappeared straight through the platform. Confusion followed as—just for a moment—the hordes looked away from the scaffold and quizzically at their neighbours and then back again. Angrily, they surged forwards as one into the arms of the City Marshal and his men, who stood resolute with their backs to the proceedings, unaware that anything unusual had happened behind them and that they might be abetting the escape of one destined to live another day.

"Back! Back!" shouted the marshal, as the crowd trampled over each other to get to the scaffold. Unsure of what had happened, and in fear of the crowd's intent, he bellowed, "Reset the trap! Get the next one up," and a scrawny young fellow found himself hoisted from cart to platform by his collar as he screamed, "It wasn't me! I didn't do it!" and the hangman hastily applied the rope without taking time for the hood and let the trapdoor go.

The crowd stopped to enjoy the hood-free entertainment as the man clutched at the rope with his fingers. His eyes bulged, his face grew blacker, and his tongue reached on its stalk to his chin.

Lillian scoured the crowd for the highwayman but Boothroyd had disappeared.

Thirteen

THE NEXT MORNING LONDON ROSE SLUGGISH and hungover, the day having lasted long into the night with many wants and desires raised and satisfied—to the accompaniment of much ale and porter, of course.

Unaware of the events of the previous day, the animals still had their own needs that required attention. The boys who managed to turn up went about their business with red bleary eyes and brains filled with straw, shoes untied and shirts buttoned askew. Everyone moved at half the normal pace, including Lillian, the baby sitting heavy in her belly. Even Giuseppe the hurdy-gurdy man, and his monkey, seemed to be playing at a slower tempo.

Having made her way around the menagerie checking that all the animals had been fed and watered, straw changed and muck disposed of, Lillian went to the entrance to see if Mrs. Ogden had arrived. The last she had seen of her was yesterday evening as Lillian and Button had walked slowly back from Tyburn, a seemingly lawless revelry all around them as they picked their way through the drunken whooping and hollering. Through the propped-open door of the Bell on the corner of Exeter Street they had seen Mrs. Ogden crying with laughter, her mobcap gone, a glass in her hand, and her skirts up above her knees, spread just a little too wide.

Lillian called out for her and then opened the entrance of the admission booth, but it was empty.

"Yoo hoo," said a voice, and a waving and puffing Mrs. Ogden wobbled into view, the ties of her bonnet blowing behind her. "I'm coming, I'm coming," she said.

"Look at the time, Mrs. Ogden," said Lillian, slightly annoyed.

"Can't see no one waiting on me," she replied with a grunt as she settled herself into the booth, her large bottom spilling over the chair cushion.

From the other direction the two beefeaters wended their way towards the place of work, red tunics undone, white stockings around ankles, and hats clutched in hands.

Hands on hips, Lillian scolded them. "Hurry up, you two! Grady would not be happy to see you looking like this."

"Since when did she give the orders?" one muttered to the other in a low voice.

Lillian rounded on them. "Since I became the only one who seems to care if this establishment opens on time or is making any money. Now, hats on and jackets buttoned. Mrs. Ogden, are you ready?"

"I'm here," said Mrs. Ogden. "The big I-Am ain't risen yet, 'as 'e?"

"We'll all know about it when Grady arrives, I'm sure," Lillian replied.

"Ooh, me knees," Mrs. Ogden said before pointing at one of the beefeaters. "Be a love and go fill my bed pan, will yer? Going to be sitting here all day. Need to keep the best bits warm, don't I?" She cackled and started to count out the tokens and the money. Turning to Lillian, she said, "Oh, but did you go, Lill? Did you see it?"

Lillian picked up a broom and started sweeping around the entrance, trying to ignore the sound of the hurdy-gurdy man's tuneless instrument.

"Oh, it were so exciting," said Mrs. Ogden, clapping her hands. "Would you believe he could be so bold?"

Remembering the crowd's reaction to Boothroyd's daring escape, Lillian smiled to herself. "He's certainly a very special kind of man," she said.

Mrs. Ogden's reverie was interrupted by a small boy who appeared at the admission booth. She gave him an expert glance, taking in his raggedy clothing and dirty face in less than a second, then flicked him away with her hand. "No work round 'ere."

"Not 'ere to work," the boy replied.

"Well, you can't come in either unless you got a shilling."

"Don't want to come in. I'm looking for Mrs. Button," said the boy, trying to peer around the booth and into the Exchange. "Got something for her."

Overhearing the conversation, Lillian walked over to the booth. "I am Mrs. Button."

The boy pulled off his cap. "I—I have something for you, missus." From behind his back he produced a piece of folded cloth, no bigger than a small handkerchief, once white but now stained a variety of browns, having been clearly wrapped and unwrapped a number of times. He handed it to Lillian, who placed the package on the counter of the booth.

The two women grinned at each other, raised their eyebrows, then looked back down at the package.

"A present!" said Mrs. Ogden, wriggling her shoulders in excitement and leaning over to better see. "I wonder who from?"

Before they could investigate further, the beefeater returned from his errand. "'ere's your bedpan, Mrs. O." She took it, placed it under the cushion on her stool, and adjusted her buttocks till she was comfortable, letting out a little *mmmmm* of satisfaction.

"Thought you'd had all your bits warmed up last night by Fred the potman," the beefeater said, laughing.

Mrs. Ogden rolled her eyes to heaven and pursed her lips, revealing two dimples in her fat face.

He nudged the other beefeater who'd been leaning against the booth and winked. "Knows how to fill a pot, does 'e?"

"Oh you," Mrs. Ogden replied, doing her best to blush.

Turning to Lillian, the beefeater asked, "What you got there then?" He nodded at the small bundle on the counter.

"Never you mind," said Lillian, snatching it up and walking away towards a quiet corner. The boy followed her. She lay the handkerchief on the ledge of one of the viewing railings and held her breath as she gingerly began to peel back the folds one by one with the tips of her fingers and thumbs until she reached the final layer.

Looking up abruptly, she asked the boy sharply, "Where did you get this?"

"He talked to me, Miss, the night before the drop. Told me he would hide it under the font in St. Paul's church and that I must go there to collect it after he was . . . gone . . . and to make sure not to put it in anyone else's hands but yours, Miss."

It was her lion's tooth on its familiar leather cord.

"I had to search high and low for it, Miss!"

She put her hand to his cheek and smiled at him. "Thank you," she said, then shouted over to Mrs. Ogden, "Give the boy a shilling, and one of those tokens, the one with the lion on."

"Thanks, Miss," the boy said and walked back to the admission booth, where he held out his hand.

Mrs. Ogden made a doubtful noise with her lips. "Puh. I don't know about that, Lillian. What would 'imself say?"

"I'll worry about that," Lillian replied.

"'Ere y'are, then." Mrs. Ogden handed two coins to the boy, who put his hand in his pocket and pulled out what Lillian thought could only be a small sock, into which he carefully placed the coins.

Mrs. Ogden harrumphed. "Nothing to do with me. Giving away the profits."

"Miss. There's something else." The boy reached into his other pocket and produced a single piece of paper, folded twice.

Lillian took the note and turned her back on the others.

If all goes according to plan [the note said] *then I shall be
returning this to its rightful owner, its job having been done.
May the courage you gave to me return to you a thousand fold.
Thank you. PS Maybe one day you will join me for a dance?*

"Oh my," said Lillian, squinting away the tears that appeared
in her eyes, recalling the vibrancy of the man who had been so
scared to die, the twinkle in his eye and its promise of—what? She
did not know. She sat down on the chair by the booth and put the
lion's tooth on its leather lace back around her neck once more,
kissing it as she did so. She wondered where he could be now.

"What you got there then?" boomed Grady as he appeared in
the entrance, swaying slightly, shirt undone and waistcoat hanging
open, his belly sticking out and a pipe in his hand.

"Nothing for you to worry about," Lillian replied, quickly folding the paper and putting it away.

"'Ere she is," said Grady. "How many times do I have to tell you, you
don't need to be here. We can take care of this place without you."

"I've seen what your idea of 'taking care' is like, Grady," she
replied, resuming her sweeping.

"Enjoy the hanging, Lill?" he asked, winking at Mrs. Ogden,
who gave a little smirk, pleased to have the opportunity to share a
joke with the boss.

Lillian briefly raised her eyebrows in reply but said nothing.

"I shook his hand in the Mason's Arms," said Grady, puffing
himself up. Seeing he had the ears of the beefeaters along with
Mrs. Ogden and a couple of the Exchange boys who had been
chasing each other with animal muck in their hands, he ploughed
on. There was nothing he liked more than an audience. "Did you
hear what he said on the way to the Tree? Offered to buy us all a
drink on the way home. Well, I reckon he owes us all a drink now.
Eh? Eh?"

"Ehs's what 'orses eat, Mr. Grady," said Mrs. Ogden.

"Ha! Very good, Mrs. Ogden. Very good."

"Think they'll catch him, Mr. Grady?"

"Babyface will live to fight another day, to be sure." Then, recalling the excesses of the night before, he said, "Drunk as an emperor I was. Feeling it this morning though, dear god." Squeezing his eyes shut, he took another puff on his pipe. He stuck his thumb in his waistcoat pocket. Noticing the mournful tune of the hurdy-gurdy for the first time, he shouted, "Shut that bloody racket!" Giuseppe stopped turning the handle on his machine in the middle of a tune. The monkey ran up to Lillian and rested his head on her knees, staring up at her.

"Not now, Alfred," she said, thinking about the events of the day before, and pushed him away, still holding onto the tooth around her neck. Trying to get her attention, the monkey pulled off his little red velvet hat and, with a screech, waved it above his head. Laughing, Grady bent down and grabbed the hat from the monkey's hand by its gold tassel and threw it out the door. The monkey shrieked and ran after it just as the sound of wheels on cobbles reached Lillian's ears, making her look behind only to see a horse and cart barrelling round the corner right into the path of the monkey.

"Alfred!" she screamed, leaping to her feet, surprisingly agile despite the baby in her belly. She reached out to catch the monkey, stepped on a frozen puddle, slipped, and—just for a tantalising second—touched the fur at the very tip of its tail. The horse reared to avoid the monkey and landed its hooves on the pregnant woman, followed by the sickening noise of the cart running over the prostrate figure.

"Lillian!" shouted Grady at the tableau frozen in front of him: the pregnant woman sprawled facedown in the street, hand outstretched towards the monkey. Motionless. Alfred crumpled and broken on the floor like a puppet—strings cut—a pool of red the same colour as its velvet waistcoat growing ever bigger.

Giuseppe ran towards the accident. "Alfred!" he wailed. Turning to the driver who had got down from the cart, he grabbed him by the necktie. "Could you not look where you were going?"

he shouted in his heavy Italian accent, spitting crumbs into the man's face.

"I didn't see either of 'em," said the driver, in shock at the disaster that had happened so quickly. The beefeaters ran forwards and tried to pull Giuseppe off the driver. The horse rose on its hind legs and one of the Exchange boys grabbed the reins, preventing the hooves from landing on the fighting men.

Grady knelt beside Lillian, checking to see if she was breathing.

"Oh Mr. Grady! Mr. Grady!" said Mrs. Ogden, standing behind him, one hand at her throat and the other flapping in the air like a little bird.

"Lillian. Lillian," said Grady urgently. "Can you hear me?" But there was no sound from the woman lying facedown in the street.

"She can't be dead, she's pregnant!" shrieked Mrs. Ogden nonsensically. For a moment there was silence, then the most plaintive of whimpers came from the monkey, which seemed to be struggling to raise his head from the slick of red, and the scene came to life once more. Dropping his hands from the driver's throat, Giuseppe fell to his knees by his erstwhile partner.

"'eez alive . . . 'eez alive!" he said to the gathering crowd.

Glancing over at the monkey, Grady mumbled, "Not for long." As if in reply, Alfred released a final gurgle from the back of his throat and his head dropped to one side. Giuseppe began to howl.

Lillian stirred. In a voice so low that Grady had to bend his head to hear it, she murmured, "The baby." Quickly he took off his jacket and, folding it up, placed it underneath her head and took her hand.

He whispered, "All is fine, my dear. I've got you." Then, lifting his head, he began to bark orders, hangover forgotten and the leader of old finding his voice once more.

"Charlie, find that mopus of a husband of hers and get him here now."

"Aye," said Charlie, his face ashen.

Pointing to the beefeaters: "Dick. I know they've hired a surgeon. Find out who it is and get him here quick. Mrs. Ogden. Run upstairs to her old room, open the window, light as many candles as you can, make sure the bed is clean, and get a bloody fire going." She nodded and waddled away quickly on her mission.

Grady pointed at the driver. "You! Make yourself useful. Help me. Get her feet."

Lillian lay on the street, her cheek resting on the damp cobbles, but strangely comfortable and insensible to the chaos that was exploding around her. Between Grady and the driver, they made to lift the injured woman. And then the pain began. It felt like the sharpest of knives being thrust between her legs with the most vicious of force. Wave after wave it came, right up inside her womb as if the knife were trying to work its way out through her navel.

Lillian screamed, or thought she did, but little sound came out.

"We can't move her like this," said Grady. Searching around for a solution, his eyes fell on the large wooden board they used to cover the admission booth at closing time.

Still holding Lillian's hand, he shouted at the remaining beef-eater, "Get that," indicating the board. Standing up, he pulled out his handkerchief, gave the wide flat piece of wood a quick wipe, and lay it on the ground. Indicating to the driver to take her feet, between them they carefully lifted Lillian up and placed her on the makeshift stretcher.

"Got to get her upstairs. After three. One-two-three," and the men rose. The board creaked slightly.

The driver moaned. "She ain't 'alf a weight."

"And you wouldn't be carrying it if you'd been watching yourself while you was driving," Grady replied, checking behind him to see where he was going.

The two men carried the injured woman through the Great Hall, past the animals, strangely silent as if they understood some sort of tragedy was afoot, past the aviary, which gave a desultory flutter of wings and calls, and past the lion who let out a questioning roar, moving all the time with kitten steps due to the size of their load and the nature of the makeshift stretcher.

Lillian rolled and groaned and held onto to her belly, muttering all the while, "My baby, my baby." Eventually they reached the narrow stairs of the passage that led upstairs to Lillian's old room. Both men stopped and looked at each other. They lay the woman down as gently as possible and took deep breaths, their hearts beating hard.

"There's no way we can carry her on this thing up those stairs," said Grady to the driver. "Sorry, Lill, there's nothing for it, but I'm going to have to carry you."

He hitched his trousers and rolled up his sleeves. Lillian's eyes were closed, oblivious to the drama. She continued to moan in deep pain. Catching the eye of the driver, who looked like he wanted to be anywhere else but dealing with a six-foot Amazon in premature labour, Grady directed, "I'll grab her under the arms and you take the feet."

But before they could lift her, they heard the sound of footsteps running behind them and an urgent voice shouting "Lillian? Lillian?"

Grady recognised the sound but did not stop his preparations.

John Button appeared. "Good god, man! What happened?" He took in the sight of his wife lying on the board, rolled in a foetal shape and holding her belly.

"Did no one tell you?" Grady snapped, irritated at the interruption to an endeavour he felt he had well under control.

"I heard there had been an accident, but—"

Grady's scorn cut him off. "Then shut your clatter and give me a hand. No time to talk. We got to get her to lying down nice and comfy."

"But why here? We have the room all ready for the lying-in back at Neal Street."

Impatient at the lack of understanding of the scene that was right in front of him, Grady was sharper than he had intended.

"Look at her, you mopus. There was no time. Besides"—he paused before continuing slyly—"she is in familiar surroundings."

"Then let me take care of my wife," Button said and bent down to scoop Lillian up in his arms, but despite his height he had no strength and could not lift her. He stood back.

"I'll do it," said Grady, avoiding Button's eye and picking up the woman in his arms.

All three men immediately saw the pool of blood that had gathered on the stretcher, glanced at each other, then looked away as if ashamed.

Grady shook his head. "The passage is too narrow. Needs two of us. You take her feet while I hold her under the arms."

Between them they managed to manoeuvre Lillian's almost lifeless body up the stairs and into the small room with the large bed that Mrs. Ogden had prepared. The curtains were closed and the shadows from the candles made strange animal shapes on the wall. Mrs. Ogden pulled back the linen and Grady gently placed his apprentice on the bed. Lillian groaned and rolled over on her side, exposing her blood-covered back. Mrs. Ogden noticed the heavy stain and looked at Button but pulled her eyes away first. Footsteps were heard on the wooden stairs and all turned to see a tall stranger filling the doorway.

"Ah, Bernard, you're here. Thank god," said Button with some relief. Bernard was as tall as Button but much thinner and, unlike others of his profession, did not wear a wig, preferring to wear his white hair tied back in a black velvet ribbon, which emphasised his high forehead. But it was his huge hook nose that people noticed first, apt to make an observer just a little cross-eyed.

The visitor smiled and gave a small wave of his hand. "It's Ber-*nard* actually, if you don't mind, but not to worry. How is the young lady?"

Lillian groaned.

Not recognising the stranger on his patch, Grady puffed up his chest and squared up to Bernard, who was at least a head and a bit taller. "And who the hell is asking?"

"For god's sake, Grady," said Button. "This is the surgeon we hired to take care of my wife." He gave a slight emphasis to the word *my*. "He's the best in London."

"I see," said Grady. Sensing he was losing further control of the unfolding drama, he moved away from the door to admit the stranger.

"Thank you," said Bernard, nodding at Grady with a polite smile and removing his jacket. His eyes did not leave Lillian as he untied his neckerchief and rolled up his sleeves. A bowl of water had been set on one side.

Bernard dipped his hands in the water and rubbed them together. "We are going to need plenty of good clean water. Hot. Hot water. Mrs. Ogden, is it? Would you be a good lady and get the kettles boiling on the hob?"

"Yes, sir. Of course, sir," said Mrs. Ogden, giving a little bob and hurrying out of the room.

Bernard knelt down beside Lillian, who still lay on her side.

"Mrs. Button, can you hear me?" There was no answer. Grady and Button stood watching him and exchanged glances.

"Pass me my bag of tricks," said the surgeon, and Button darted forwards to hand over the large bone-handled leather holdall that the surgeon had set down on the dresser when he arrived. Bernard stood and undid the brass clasp. He pulled out an apron, which he slipped over his head and tied around his waist. Dipping into his bag once more, he produced a round circular tube made of leather, a small blue bottle, and a spoon. He placed the bottle and spoon on the table by the bed and then knelt beside her once more as he positioned the tube on Lillian's belly, the other end to his ear.

Long silent seconds passed before he made his announcement. "The baby's heartbeat is very weak and the lady has lost a lot of blood."

He reached for the blue bottle. Holding it aloft, he proclaimed, "First things first. Laudanum. She is in a great deal of pain and we need her to sleep. Let's lift her, Button."

Button positioned himself behind his wife's shoulders and tried to sit her upright. Each movement produced another cry of pain. Bernard poured a measure of the potion onto the spoon.

"She's in so much pain. You must be able to do something. Give her something. Please."

"Make her drink this, Button. It will ease the discomfort. Three should do it."

Turning his back on the couple, Bernard set about laying out his tools on the steel tray. Lillian swallowed the liquid on the spoon, but then, hearing the sound of the metal instruments rattling together, let out a weak "No . . ." before slipping back into a stupor, her limbs growing heavier all the time.

Bernard picked up a long, thin strip of steel with a serrated edge. Then, turning to Grady, he said, "It might be best if you leave now."

Grady blinked in surprise. "I've seen many a birth before. I'm not afraid of a little blood."

Through gritted teeth, Button said, "My wife is not an animal," emphasising each word.

"Human blood has a way of affecting even the most hardened of senses," said Bernard, leaving no doubt as to who was in charge in the room.

Grady pushed between the men towards Lillian and squeezed her shoulder. "May god walk with you, my queen," he said and went to leave.

"Can someone please send for Mrs. Tomkins?" said Button. Grady nodded and left the room.

Bernard stretched out his arms and smiled. "Ah! Room to move at last. Now, let's get on with the job in hand. We need to get those breeches off her." He picked up the scissors from the tray and began to cut the legs of the breeches.

"I've never seen so much blood," said Button.

"By-product of the situation," the surgeon replied cheerfully. "Never fear! Modern science is on our side."

"My poor darling," Button whispered to Lillian. "If we can get through this, then I promise I will not set anything above you again."

THE WARMTH OF the sun flowed through her body. Eyes closed, she could feel it permeating through the pores of her skin and the deepest tissue of her muscles to the very core of her being. She smiled. When she dared to open her eyes, the sun was so bright that she had to squint for a few moments lest it blind her. Slowly they became used to the light and she began to make out shapes. A large mountain of grey rock loomed far away in the distance and, looking left and right, she could see hills of brown as they sat parched in the sun. The whole horizon seemed to shimmer with a golden glow. Above was the biggest sky she had ever seen, white clouds making their journey so slowly you could not tell they were moving. Birds made black scratches on the blue.

She looked down at her feet and was surprised to see they were bare and that she was standing on dark red-ochre sand. It was warm. She wriggled her toes and felt the grains of sand that had lodged between them and then the heat rising up through the arches, then her heels and calves reaching the thighs. She hugged herself, luxuriating in the warmth. But something was wrong. Something was missing.

She held out her hands, turning them palm up, palm down. Who did these belong to? She put her hands to her head, ran them through her hair, the pressure still there when she took her hand away. A small gust of wind touched her face. Licking her lips, she caught the slightly gritty dust, but her mouth was too dry to swallow. She tried to make saliva but nothing happened. The warmth suffused her body like a wave once more and she forgot the feeling of disquiet. Closing her eyes, she breathed in deeply. A familiar smell filled her nostrils. Looking down, was surprised to see the lion standing so close that he was leaning against her. She ran her fingers over his head and through his dirty yellow mane and could feel the purring reverberate through his body and up into her own.

Leonidas looked at Lillian and smiled.

"I know where we are. This is your home, isn't it? We are in Africa!"

Then she shivered. "Why am I so cold all of a sudden?"

And then heard her mother say, "Someone just walked on your grave."

She spun round. "Mum?" she said. "Is that you? Where are you?" But no one was there.

"I'm getting so cold," she said. "Leonidas?" But the lion was gone too. The sky that had been so blue a few moments before was turning dark and grey, the open plain closing in on her like the dark London alleyways that shut out all the light. Something was not right but she could not quite grasp what that might be. She tasted something unfamiliar and bitter on her lips and closed her eyes as she gave in to the easy warmth infusing her whole body once more.

THE SECOND TIME she opened her eyes, she knew where she was straight away.

"I'm home," she thought, but everything was blurred and out of focus as if she'd accidentally rubbed her eyes with goose grease while preparing the bird for the oven. As the mist gradually disappeared, she realised she was floating. Below her there was a woman lying on the bed. Her bed! And what was that smell? Something metallic like iron, something dark. Two men were leaning over the woman. She recognised her husband, but who was the other man? The one who held something glinting in his hand.

"John!" she shouted and Button turned around.

"What?" he said.

"I didn't say anything," said the stranger.

"I thought I heard—"

"You heard nothing. Focus, Button. Think, man. What do you want me to do?"

Now Lillian could hear someone calling her in the distance, a sense of urgency in its tone.

"Lillian!"

She could feel the pull in the voice, but she wanted to hear what the men were saying even more, and they were talking in such low voices that she could not quite hear them. She needed to get closer.

"Who's it to be, Button? Mother or child?"

She floated above the creature now writhing on the bed below her. *What did he mean? Mother or child?* she wondered as she continued to watch the scene. There was her husband, trying to hold up the woman's head with one hand and a spoon in the other. There was another woman in the room, wearing a cap and apron and fussing around, pouring water into a jug, having set a steel pan to one side. It was covered with a red-streaked cloth and looked familiar somehow.

"Pass me more linen. I need to stop this blood somehow. And give her some more laudanum. We can't have her waking up just yet."

That's Mrs. Tomkins, thought Lillian. *What's she doing in my bedroom? And what is in that dish?*

"Mrs. Tomkins!" she shouted, then the urgent voice came again.

"Lillian!"

She was sure she recognised the voice but didn't want to leave the bedroom. The scene then began to recede and the room grew ever smaller as its clarity faded to that of a dream.

"Wait!" she said and shouted her husband's name once more. He again seemed to look around him for the source of the voice.

Then Lillian had a sudden a flash of realisation.

"Oh my god! That's me!"

THE NOW FAMILIAR warmth began to flood through her body once more and she was back in Africa. She could see the lion but he was over in the distance and walking slowly away from her towards a bright white light that seemed to be growing by the minute.

"Leonidas! Wait!" She ran to catch up with him. The lion paused and lay down, its tail *swish, swish, swishing* in the heat.

"Oh Leonidas," she said, burying her head in his mane. "I had such a terrible dream—"

"Lillian," said a voice, and she stood up and spun round to find a young baby-faced man standing and grinning in front of her. He swept off his tricorn hat, giving her the deepest of bows and the biggest of smiles.

Lillian recognised him immediately.

"Babyface," she said, to which the highwayman replied, "Are you ready to dance with me now?" He pirouetted on his heel.

"But you're—"

He laughed. "In a far better place," he said, playing with his hat.

"I thought you escaped."

"Indeed I did, but I couldn't have faced that ordeal without you. I thank you." He gave her another bow.

"Am I dead now?"

"No, my dear, you are not. But . . ." His manner grew grave. "But you are going to need much courage to face the days ahead, as much courage and strength as our good friend Leonidas here can give you."

"Why? What's happening? What's going on? Who are those people in my bedroom? I know my husband and Mrs. Tomkins, of course, but who is that man with the white hair?"

Out of the corner of her ear came a new sound, the sound of someone crying. "Who's that? Who's crying?"

Boothroyd remained silent.

"Can't I stay here with you?" asked Lillian.

Boothroyd looked over his shoulder towards the light and took both her hands in his. "It is not your time, Lillian. I have to go. Be strong. Be brave. I'm watching and so is Leonidas."

THE THIRD TIME Lillian opened her eyes, she screamed in pain as if hit by one of the shovels the boys used to kill the rats.

"More laudanum," instructed the white-haired man she had seen in her dream but knew now was so real she could smell the sweat on him. On one side, Mrs. Tomkins leaned over with a cold cloth in her hand and wiped her brow while her husband held her hand on the other. Barely able to turn her head, she looked from one to the other.

"I don't understand," she said.

Over the body in the bed, Mrs. Tomkins and Button looked at each other.

She heard the sound of a metal instrument being thrown into a pan and joining its brothers.

There was something wrong. If only she could stay awake long enough. "What's wrong? Where's my baby? Where is he?"

But this time when the laudanum made its presence felt she fell into the deepest of dreamless sleeps.

Fourteen

GRADY LEFT THE ROOM, UNFAMILIAR TEARS PRICKING his eyes, and immediately slumped and slid down the wall outside. It could not have been more than half an hour or so since they had all been laughing and messing about outside the entrance to the menagerie. Since then the world had turned on that fabled sixpence.

He was exhausted and he stank. The sweat from his earlier efforts had made rings under his armpits and he could smell himself. Through the thin walls he could hear Lillian's moans and the low rumblings of urgent exchanges between the two men, although he could not make out what was being said.

If anything should happen to her, he thought.

He stood up and brushed himself down. There was only one place he would go when he needed to get away from everything, and that was the Crow's Nest. Located at the very top of the menagerie building, following another staircase beyond Lillian's, there was a heavy oak door to which only Grady held the key. Wearily Grady mounted the stairs. Yesterday's excitement and last night's alcohol combined with the exertions and drama of the day had drained him and he walked slowly, feeling every one of his fifty years. He removed the iron key from around his neck and unlocked the door. The cold immediately rushed at him from the top of the staircase exposed to the elements. He made sure to lock the door behind him, then made his way up the seventeen steps, which were even tighter to negotiate than those to Lillian's room. At the top there was a round turret through which he could peer over the rooftops of London. The black slates looked shiny from the earlier rain and everywhere thin black wisps of smoke were making their way to heaven. In the distance he could make out the Dome of St. Paul's, the Houses of Parliament with their twin towers, and Westminster bridge, where the barges with their flags bobbed about as they made their way up and down the river. Black scavenger kites sat on the sharp angular rooftops.

He remembered the night he had drunkenly confronted her when she had been trying to make her mind up about Button and the shame rolled over him. Jesus. That mopus! He gripped the crenulation with his hands, noticing the black dirt that had settled under his torn fingernails. Knowing he was alone, he howled. The tension released, he stood with his thoughts, occasionally shaking his head, staring across the uneven roofs of London until it started to rain.

Minutes, perhaps hours, passed. He did not know. He wanted to go downstairs to find out what was happening but, at the same time, he dared not.

GIUSEPPE TOOK TO drinking and crying at the Bell. No one wanted to listen to the sound of a hurdy-gurdy without the antics of a monkey falling over or dancing to distract from its discordant tones. A hurdy-gurdy man without a monkey was simply an irritating noise.

"Fifteen years we worked together," Giuseppe cried to anyone who would listen. "Fifteen! There was no one like Alfred. Had him from a baby. Too old to start again. Where would I find another one?"

The Bell regulars sighed and shook their heads and filled up his mug once more. Everyone conveniently forgot that no one had ever really liked the spiteful, screeching little creature. Still, Grady felt guilty. He knew what it meant to rely on an animal for one's living and popped a sixpence in the dead monkey's hat, which Giuseppe set in front of him while he was drinking.

A MELANCHOLIC AIR descended on the Great Hall. The news of the baby generated a sense of loss, which was felt by everybody. The boys tiptoed around in their duties lest their steps disturb the patient. Despite her lack of visibility, Lillian's pain was a tangible thing that permeated the fabric of the animal empire. Everyone wanted to help, but what to do? They all felt helpless.

Grady was leaning on the admission booth discussing the dreadful events of the last two days with Mrs. Ogden just as Mrs. Tomkins the housekeeper was leaving. The only one allowed to see Lillian, she came and went as she pleased.

"Ah! Mrs. T, a word, if you will," Grady said, clearing his throat of phlegm and spitting on the floor.

She stopped and looked at the man, taking in the stubbled face and unbuttoned waistcoat, the disgust plain on her face as she pursed her lips. "Mr. Grady?" As he came nearer, she caught the whiff of last night's ale on his breath and waved it away with her hand.

"What's the plan to send her home?" he asked.

"She refuses to move," said Mrs. Tomkins, pulling a handkerchief out of her apron and dabbing at her eyes.

"I don't understand. It's been two days."

"It's not good, sir. Not good at all."

"How so? Surely she must be on the mend now?"

Mrs. Tomkins shook her head and looked down at the floor. "Sir, she won't speak. She refuses all food."

"That's not good," Grady replied.

"I've been trying to feed her my arrowroot potion mixed with a little sherry and brandy to give her some strength, but she just pushes the spoon away. She won't take no meat nor soup and her milk is coming in—"

"Is she in much pain?"

Mrs. Tomkins nodded and dabbed again.

"And that Barnard fellow came back and he's been giving her some of that sleepy stuff but I don't think it's doing her any good. Ain't natural, it ain't. Ain't natural."

Grady listened with his hands in his pockets, staring at his feet, his usual shoulders-back stance abandoned as one deep sigh followed another. He was the master of his environment, the thoroughly modern Noah in control of his universe. Now he was helpless and at a loss for what he might do to restore Lillian to herself.

"And what about the husband? What does he say?"

Mrs. Tomkins let out a sigh. "Mr. Button wants her back, of course, just as soon as possible, but says she should stay a while, till she feels better, like."

She threw him a quick glance and Grady rolled his eyes to heaven once more.

The tears were now flowing freely. "We all want her home but she's just gone and turned her face to the wall."

"There, there, Mrs. Tomkins," he said, taking the hanky from her hand and dabbing her eyes himself. "What do you mean?"

"She's given up. She just doesn't want to be here—or anywhere—anymore."

"But you're a woman, surely you know how to deal with these things?"

But Mrs. Tomkins just shook her head. "Never seen grief for a lost child like this before."

Mrs. Ogden had been sitting in her admission booth listening to the conversation and smiling to herself while she made small towers of shillings and sixpenny pieces.

"Maybe it's for the best," she said, balancing another sixpence on the top of her pile. "She would only have given birth to a monkey."

And that's when Grady had his idea.

IT WAS ELEVEN o'clock that evening and Giuseppe was crying in the corner of the Bell. At the next table the Exchange boys were drinking and laughing and nicking food off each other's plates, events having quickly passed into ancient history. Grady sat alone with his beer, nursing his idea, while Teddy Diamond lay under the table, head in his paws, ever hopeful of a tasty morsel accidentally falling his way.

Slumped, Grady stared with half-closed eyes at the single candle that flickered in front of him. Occasionally he would lean forwards, make a small dent near the burning wick, and release the hot lava, letting it flow over his finger without flinching. He'd wait for it to cool, then peel it off, adding it to the ball of wax he was rolling between the fingers of the other hand.

"Cor, give it a rest, Giuseppe. It's nearly Christmas," shouted one of boys, flicking a piece of stale bread roll at the bereft Italian.

Chink, went the noise of a coin joining the others in Alfred's hat.

"Only one Alfred," Giuseppe replied, touching his hat in the direction of the hand making the donation.

"Shut the feck up about the feckin' monkey," Grady yelled suddenly, disturbing the dog, who stood up and gave a single bark before returning to his position.

Grady took another swig of his ale. "I'll find you another feckin' monkey," he muttered under his breath, then shouted across the room, "Charlie!"

Charlie rolled his eyes to his mates, ignoring his master, and took another bite of the pie in front of him.

"When's she coming back then, Charlie?" asked one of the boys. "There seems so much more work to do without Miss Lill."

Charlie shook his head and wiped his mouth with the back of his hand, then gave it a lick, smacking his lips. "The animals miss her," he said. "Leonidas just paces his cage then slumps in the corner. He left behind half a goat yesterday."

"I don't dare go near that kangaroo," said another. "It starts jumping around as soon as it looks at me."

"And the fur on the warthog has gone all matted and mangy. Old Grady'll never sell that. It's got bald patches all over it."

The boys crumpled with laughter.

"Charlie!" came the urgent command once more. "Get over 'ere."

Charlie sighed, stood up, and stuffed the last of the pie in his mouth before downing the dregs of his jug. Putting his hands on his hips, he managed to force out a massive burp, which was greeted by much appreciative laughter by his mates.

"Better see what the old fella wants," he said, patting his belly before sloping over to Grady.

"Get yourself down the dock and see which boats are due in," Grady ordered.

"What? Now? Oh no, Mr. Grady."

"Yes, now. No time to waste. Find out where they're coming from and what they're carrying."

"What you after, Mr. Grady?"

"Never you mind. Just do as yer told."

A DAY LATER man, boy, and Teddy Diamond, too, stood on the docks looking out at the hundreds of ships that bobbed on the dirty black waters of the Thames as the rain lashed down. The sound of the ships' tall masts creaking mingled with the noise of the flapping canvas sails and the dull *thunk* of the cowbells and their lonely clanking. Dark warehouses six storeys high loomed behind them and rats lurked in the shadows, oblivious to the night being the Eve of Christmas. They scuttered about, the flick of their tails catching the corner of your eye. Pleasure boats were all tied up for the evening but the never-ending journey from one side of the Thames to another did not cease. Carollers singing "God rest you merry, gentlemen" could just about be heard from St. Mary's church across the river, its windows lit up with candles.

Grady turned up the collar of his greatcoat and tightened his belt while Charlie made do with wrapping his arms around himself and stamping his feet.

"Pass me the looking glass," Grady said to Charlie, who duly obliged. "The *Santa Monica*, you say?" Charlie nodded. Grady scanned the ships in the distance: frigates, sloops, galleys and barques, brigantines, galleons, barges and launches, all making their careful way towards the dock.

"Yes, sir," said Charlie. "That's what I was told."

"Sailing back from the Gambia?"

Charlie nodded. "Dropping cargo here and then on to Bristol."

"Ah. And there she is!" Grady exclaimed, spotting the words Santa Monica on the prow of a rigged schooner with a mainmast.

"I think I've met that captain before," said Grady, squinting with one eye, the glass jammed into the socket of the other. "A man who deals mainly in the black gold, I believe. And that's not someone who we'd call a man, eh, Charlie?"

Charlie said nothing but continued to look out to sea, trying to locate the *Santa Monica* with his naked eye.

"Let's hope he's got some animal gold, tho. Eh? Eh?" Grady continued.

Charlie nudged Grady, who put down the looking glass to see another figure had appeared on the docks. He was dressed the same as Grady, in a long greatcoat, and stood staring out to sea, hands deep in pockets. Grady rolled his eyes and muttered an expletive under his breath.

"Ahoy there, Polito," he shouted to make his voice heard above the rain.

The figure looked over and nodded. "Grady," he acknowledged.

Grady flashed a false smile, then, kicking Charlie with his foot, ordered from the corner of his mouth, "Get a rower and get out there. Get on board. See what they got. Don't let him see you."

Charlie slipped away. Grady patted the pockets of his coat, searching for his pipe. Using one side of the coat to make a shelter from the wind and rain, he packed the bowl with the forefinger of the other hand. He attempted to light the pipe with his tinderbox but gave up.

Polito sidled over to Grady. "You need two hands in this weather, Grady," he said and produced a tinderbox from his coat and proceeded to light the pipe.

"Greetings of the season, Polito," said Grady, taking a satisfying pull.

Polito nodded back and asked, "What you here for, then?"

Grady shrugged. "Same as you, I guess. See what they got." He nodded in the direction of the ships on the horizon and took a few satisfying puffs on his pipe.

His companion sighed. "Two old men standing on a rainy dock with bones as cold as the grave on Christmas Eve. Wasn't meant to be like this, was it?"

Grady took another pull on his pipe, gave a half smile and a shrug.

"Should be shut up in the Bell with a whore on my knee, a jar in my hand, and a belly full of Christmas cheer," Polito said.

The two men stood looking down the river.

Polito was first to break the silence. "You never did like that eye-tie's monkey, did you?"

"You heard what happened?" said Grady, glancing over and quickly deciding that Polito was taking the piss.

"Ha! All of London's heard. You can hear that bloody Italian weeping into his cups all the way from the Bell," he replied with a sneer more than a laugh. "No way to do business, Grady. Killing off the merchandise."

"You know full well it weren't one of mine," Grady gruffly replied.

Polito laughed again.

"Was sorry to hear what happened to that big woman . . . the one you were quite sweet on."

"Sweet? Weren't sweet on no one," said Grady, sticking his chin out.

"Well, you know who I mean."

Grady sighed and looked up at Polito, then down and shook his head sadly. "Lost the bairn along with the will to live, it would seem."

Polito wrinkled his nose. "Shame," he replied, but with little sincerity, "One thing the world's not short of and that's babies."

The two men stood in silence as the wet from the sky tried to make its way into their unprotected crevices. All around them the labourers on the dock went about their work, lifting and hauling, rolling barrels and pushing trolleys, oblivious to the elements and only occasionally stopping to rest a hand on a weary back, wiping palms down their aprons or sweat from a brow. Someone disturbed a pile of wheat sacks and at least twenty fat rats scurried away and disappeared into the dark corners of the warehouses. Polito passed Grady a flask and he took two big swigs.

"Reminds me of when we were just starting out, eh, Jacko?" Grady said, handing it back.

"Aye, we had some fun in those days, that's for sure," Polito replied, pulling a handkerchief from his pocket and wiping his face. "Remember the time that captain made us draw cards against each other for that cargo of birds of paradise?"

"Ha! Indeed! And when I won and got them back and up the Strand they were all dead."

"Always take your time to check the shipment first, Grady."

"Just like you always do, eh, Jacko?"

"Cut from the same piece of cloth, you and me, Grady." The two men stood quietly, reflecting on the past.

This time it was Grady who broke the silence. "You stole my Rose from me."

"I didn't steal her, Grady. She wanted nothing to do with either of us. As soon as that fancy pants, Captain Whatever-it-was, turned up at the Bell, flashing his gold tooth and heavy wallet, we were both history."

Grady shook his head, closed his eyes, and took in a deep breath.

"I can still remember the smell of her," he said, smiling.

Polito laughed. "You're going soft in your old age, Grady. Be careful. That's when a man trips up."

"Everything has its price, Jacko," Grady said sombrely. "Everything has a price. Now, where's that young mopus of a boy?" Grady lifted the looking glass to his eye once more, searching for signs of the *Santa Monica*, and was gratified to see Charlie at the prow of a small boat accompanied by a boy about the same age rowing furiously for shore.

Looks like we will have news soon, he thought, then said aloud to his companion, "Too wet to be standing around, Polito," and abruptly walked off in the direction Charlie's rowing boat was heading for.

THE BOAT WAS about six feet away and Grady shouted out to him.

"What news, Charlie?"

Charlie put his hands to either side of his mouth and shouted back. "I'm not built for water, sir. Need to get me on dry land."

Grady walked down the three stone steps that led to the river, holding his hand out to catch the line and then tying it to the iron ring set in the wall, tethering the small vessel. Charlie got out first, followed by the rower who held out his hand for a coin, which Grady pressed into his palm, dismissing him with a wave. The rower ran off. Charlie's face was white as a sheet.

"You look green, Charlie. Seasick off the rowing boat?" Grady asked.

"Never seen nothing like it," he replied, wiping a lock of wet black hair from his forehead with a shaking hand.

"What you talking about, boy? You been on the animal ships before."

"Nothing like this, though," said Charlie. "The boat was a broad as you've ever seen and now I know why. All along the deck there were these grated hatchways guarded by one of the mates who stood there, holding the meanest of whips."

"A whip?" said Grady.

"Wicked beast it were. I swear it had more knotted strands than the 'airs on me 'ead. Hands were reaching up through the grates, black hands, trying to catch the rain as it fell and this mate kept cracking the whip over the hatches at these fingers—all bloody like—and laughing his head off."

"Black gold," Grady interrupted and spat.

". . . but still these fingers kept reaching up through the grate," Charlie continued, clearly in shock, "and he kept on cracking this whip."

Charlie stopped and wiped away the rain and river water, mixed with a few tears, from his face with his sleeve.

"All I could hear were cries and moans coming from below. You should 'ave 'eard them, Grady. I ain't 'eard nothing like it. Piteous it was. Piteous."

"Wouldn't treat the animals like that," said Grady.

"And all the mates were laughing and just going about their business. I mean . . . I peered into the hold through one of the hatches and there was man after man just crammed in together. They couldn't even stand up as the space seemed no higher than my shoulder. Black as soot they were and all you could only see were the whites of their eyes rolled up looking at me."

"Go on."

"And the heat! You'd swear they had a furnace going down there. The stench was worse than that summer's day last year when the water boys were late in coming and no one turned up to clean out the cages. Remember?"

Grady nodded and wrinkled his nose in agreement.

"Then men appeared with buckets of water and they started emptying them over the hatches and the screams just got louder."

Charlie looked down shaking his head. "I'll never forget what I've seen today."

"But the animals, Charlie! What of the animals?"

"Everything's in crates, sir, but I'm sure I saw monkeys like you asked. They weren't small and stringy like Alfred, though. They were different. Bigger. Chunkier. Black and hairy. Don't know if Giuseppe will be happy with one, to be honest. Fair miserable they all looked as well. They didn't look no happier than them down below but at least they were above deck. All huddled together they were, in a pile, sticking their hands out in the rain and licking them.

"A family, you say?"

"One of them monkeys was suckling a babby, that's for sure."

"Good work, Charlie. Now, let's see about securing this infant."

"Securing? What do you mean? Giuseppe won't like it, sir. It's nothing like his Alfred," said Charlie, surreptitiously inspecting Grady.

A strange smile appeared on Grady's face. "Who said it was for Giuseppe?" he said.

TWO HOURS LATER, Grady and Charlie were on their way back to the Strand, a small bundle in their arms, the deal having been concluded on the ship's arrival in dock with little fuss save from when they went to remove the infant from its mother's arms. The mother had refused to give up her baby and the mate with the whip gave her a vicious whack around the head with the handle, dazing her long enough to drop her bundle. Another chimp jumped onto the mate's back, digging his teeth into the arm that held the whip. In one seamless action the mate spun around, gripping the scruff of the chimp's neck, kicking it in the stomach and sending it flying overboard. Charlie had rushed in to grab the infant while the mother was still dazed.

"That must have been the male," said the man with the whip, holding onto his arm, his shirt growing darker with the blood from his wound. "Can't separate 'em. That's good cutter down the 'ole, that is.

"I'll make good your losses," said Grady, opening his pocket-book and thrusting more coins into the overseer's hands. "Now, if our business is concluded, we will take your leave. Come, Charlie. We must hurry."

THE MENAGERIE WAS closed for the evening and the low December sun had turned the sky a deep blood-red, tinged with yellow and orange and black, as it shimmered above the rooftops. Charlie had gone to join his mates at the Bell. Grady stood at the top of the stairs up to Lillian's garret with the bundle in his hands. He tapped lightly on the door he'd closed behind him in such despair just a few days before. Expecting no answer and, indeed, receiving none, he gently twisted the door handle and entered. The smell hit him first. The window had not been opened for many days and the air hung thick with the smell of dried blood and bad memories. The only sound was the relentless ticking of the clock. Lillian lay with her back to him.

"Lillian," he whispered.

"Go 'way," came the numb and weak reply.

"Lill," he said gently.

"Let me sleep."

"Got something for you."

"I want nothing from no one and certainly not from you."

Grady crept closer until he was no more than a few feet away.

"See 'ere. See what I bought yer," he pleaded, offering the bundle to her stern back.

As if on cue, a mewling sound emerged. Slowly Lillian turned her head to look over her shoulder.

"What's that?"

Grady made his offering once more. "Bairn's lost its mammy," he said, nodding down at the bundle and up at her, forcing a smile all the while.

The baby gave another weak cry.

Lillian turned the rest of her body to look at what Grady was holding.

"I think it might be hungry," said Grady, looking at Lillian. "Do you think it might be hungry? Need feeding?"

The heavy, painful breasts Lillian had been supporting with the palms of her hands suddenly grew wet as her milk started to pulsate and flow between her fingers. Smelling the milk, the baby mewled even louder. Lillian gave a low animal cry as her milk started to pump in shafts as thin as a pin but strong as her heart, wetting the front of her nightdress, making it translucent.

She held out her hands. "My baby . . ." she moaned, showing an interest in something for the first time in days.

Grady held on the baby, keeping his eyes away from Lillian's chest. "No. No it's not. Not really . . . well, it could be . . . it might be," he said, stumbling over his words. He was unsure how he had come to find himself here in this hot and stuffy room with this grieving woman, nor what he had intended, apart from his desperation to alleviate her pain.

The clock ticked loudly.

"My baby," she said, stronger now, eyes fixed on the bundle and holding out her hands towards him. A slowly dawning realisation of the unorthodoxy of his actions, and what they might mean, started to grow in Grady's mind. For a moment he hesitated, faced with the reality and possible consequences of his good intentions. But it seemed he could no more turn back from this course of action than he could stop the tide flowing up the Thames. He was committed and Lillian would have her baby after all.

He handed over the mewling infant and took a step back to look at the mother and child.

Slowly, Lillian pulled back the blanket covering its face to reveal the infant chimp procured two short hours earlier. She looked into the baby's brown eyes and watched its mouth open and close, running its tongue over the lips of its wide muzzle.

"It's a—well, it's a *special* type of monkey. It's a chimp," Grady said, but Lillian was not listening.

Grady gave a nervous laugh and now the words fell quickly from his moth. "Comes from the Gambia in Africa."

"My baby," she said, smiling at the infant in her arms.

Grady tried not to focus on the intimate moment he had created but was mesmerised by the tableau in front of him and watched as Lillian put her hand to the infant's mouth. It greedily licked the milk from her fingers, making a tiny mewling sound more like a mouse.

He turned and left the room.

Fifteen

ANYONE PASSING BY THE EXCHANGE THAT Christmas Eve might have looked up and seen a yellow glow at the very top of the building. Few would have guessed at the unusual bonding that was taking place inside.

Lillian lay in the huge bed in the flickering candlelight, staring at the wiggling, mewling infant in her arms. She ventured a finger into the baby's mouth and tentatively felt the hardness along the gum line. Immediately the baby pulled vigorously on the digit and—it seemed the most natural thing in the world—she untied the strings on her soaking nightdress, released her hard and heavy breasts, and allowed her nipple, slippery with milk, to be snatched into its anxious mouth.

She gave an involuntary "Ow" as the baby bit too hard in its enthusiasm, but then it settled and there it suckled. Lillian closed her eyes and smiled while the baby chimp took its fill, feeling relief at last for breasts that had grown solid and painful with milk not yet needed. Sensing the baby's urgency dissipating, she gently pulled it from her breast by the scruff of its neck and it latched onto the other as if it had never known anything else.

She stared down at the small dark creature as her eyes swelled with tears once more. She luxuriated in sweeping waves of love. Her uterus contracted, the milk pumped stronger, and the baby sucked even harder. Its features were set in a pinky-beige face the shape of a heart, surrounded by light brown fur. Every now and then it would slowly open its eyes and she could see they were round and brown, set close together over a protruding muzzle with large flaring nostrils and grey whiskers. She touched the top of its ears, which were huge and disproportionate to the rest of the face and set well back. *Like handles on a milk jug*, she mused. A small pink tongue poked out from between two lips that seemed to smile. It searched with its tongue for any drops of milk that might have escaped.

The body felt hard in her arms, not soft and fleshy like other babies she had held. While the baby satisfied its hunger, she took one of its hands in hers, turning it over every which way and marvelling at the similarity between her own fingers and the four long, dark brown fingers, which she kissed, each one in turn. Gently she examined the feet and was surprised to find them not dissimilar to the hands and not at all like her own. As she checked over every inch of her new charge, she found a little white tuft of fur on his rear and gave a small laugh out loud.

Lillian did not know how much time had passed when the baby eventually relented its hold on the nipple and its mouth fell away, a white dribble trailing from the corner. Its eyes tight shut, she gently shifted the baby's weight, tied up the strings of her nightdress, closed her eyes, and fell into a deep sleep. Mother and child dozed in and out of sleep as the clock by her bed steadily marked time. *Tick. Tock.*

There was a knock on the door.

"Come in," said Lillian, raising her head from her pillow and unconsciously checking her modesty.

Grady appeared.

"Oh, it's you," she said, letting her head drop back on the pillow.

"I've brought thee vittles," he whispered, as he shuffled into the small, stuffy room, hunched over a tray, which he placed on a small table by the side of the bed, all the time trying—and failing—to avoid looking at the pair in the bed.

"No one else been in yet, have they?"

"Sssh!" Lillian commanded. The baby was fast asleep on her chest, making a gentle whistling sound as it breathed out. A small dribble of milk made its way down the muzzle.

He walked around the bed to the window.

"Hot in 'ere, Lill. You don't mind, do you? Let a little fresh air in?"

Lillian shook her head without looking up. He opened the window a crack and it began to rattle.

"Mrs. T's arrowroot medicine, a little porridge, and some beer for you," he said, indicating the tray. "Give you strength."

He bent down in front of the small fireplace and placed another faggot on the fire. "Mother and—er—doing well?"

"Boy," said Lillian, stroking his head and taking a quick glance up at Grady. "It's a little boy, Grady."

"A-ha," he said, standing up and looking down at the pair for the first time.

The two gazed quietly at the creature lying in her arms, the peace punctuated by the ticking of the clock.

"May I?" Grady looked at Lillian, who nodded. He reached out to stroke the top of the new arrival's head.

"Isn't he beautiful?" said Lillian, continuing to stare at the infant.

Grady raised his eyebrows. "Indeed he is, but Lillian . . ."

"But what?" She smiled, never taking her eyes from the small beast that clung to her chest.

"Your husband. Button. What will *he* say?"

Her face darkened as she pushed away the reality of the situation to which she appeared to have committed herself. She knew she could blame it on the laudanum, a moment's madness that might be squarely laid at Grady's feet, he having taken advantage in her loss and grief—although for what reward she knew not. She could, maybe should perhaps, say goodbye to the strange little chimp that had already suckled at her breast, the once motherless infant that had found its way to her. In the same way her life had changed when she reached out her hand to save Alfred, she knew things had now altered once again. She could no more give up this baby than she could bring back their own child from the dead. She squeezed the sleeping infant a little tighter.

"I'm not sure I should have done it," he said.

"What's done is done. Won't my husband be glad to have me alive and well and caring for something? Now let me have a taste of that porridge. I find myself so very hungry."

"But Lillian. It's not a child, it's a—"

Lillian took a few draughts of beer and another spoonful of food. Speaking with a full mouth, she said. "I know what it is and I don't care. It's an infant that needs a mother."

"I'm just saying. It's not a usual thing, Lill. Not something *everyday*, like. You know that."

Lillian put down the beer and pulled herself up on the bed, checking that her night dress stayed in place, and gave a small shrug. "Sometimes God sends what we need."

The baby began to stir. Grady sucked in his breath and gave a sideways nod of the head.

"Pass me that linen," she said, "on the dresser."

Grady did as he was directed and picked up a pile of white linen, which had been laid out in anticipation of another event and passed it to Lillian. She gently lay the baby to one side and sorted through the various shapes and thicknesses of cloth until she found what she was looking for. She folded the selected item into a triangle, lay the baby chimp inside, and deftly wrapped the clout around the body. Searching again, she found a thicker piece of cloth to secure the dressing.

"A pin or two, please," she said, indicating the hedgehog of metal quills that sat on the dresser. She neatly secured the ensemble.

Now she picked up a larger piece of white linen decorated with curving stems bearing flowers, leaves, and berries and worked with white linen thread in a variety of drawn threadwork stitches. Having wrapped her charge in the shawl, she selected a small cap, which she placed on its head and fastened under the chin. She settled a series of small whimpers with a long, gentle *sshhhhhhhh* and, satisfied all was well, gently lay the baby in the small wooden box Grady had brought and placed by the bed.

Grady stood back, watching the display of new motherhood. When she was done, he went to plump up her pillows. "You've always had a way with the babies, Lillian," he said with a wink.

Lillian tried to smile but, exhausted with the effort, sank back with a huge sigh against the pillow. It seemed she had barely closed her eyes when there was another knock on the door. Without waiting for an answer, her husband's head appeared.

"Hello?" said a forced but cheery voice.

"John," said Lillian, hefting herself up in the bed and pushing fingers through her hair to bring it under control. The unspoken decision she and Grady had made was to be tested sooner than expected.

"It's good to see you," she ventured with a weak smile, recognising the lie as soon it left her mouth, that his presence was an intrusion on the bubble she had created with her baby. Her heart beat faster.

He stood at the end of the bed, both hands clasped behind his back, looking down at his wife. The box was to the right of the bed and out of sight.

"And how's the patient today?" he said, looking around the room, sensing something had changed but not yet sure what. His eyes fell on Grady, who stood on the other side of the bed. "Grady," he said, nodding at the man. "I'll be alone with my wife now, thank you."

Grady had been holding his breath since the knock on the door, his eyes darting between man and woman. Now he let it out with a jumble of words, "Right, right, yes. I must be off." He hastily rearranged the scabby wig on his head. "Leave you two alone."

Lillian reached a hand out to Grady, holding him for a second by the wrist. "Thank you, Grady. For everything," she said, looking him directly in the eyes.

Grady nodded at Lillian and briefly at her husband. "Glad to see you eating, Lill." He left.

Button said nothing as Grady made his departure but had noted the look between them. When the door closed, he picked up the small stool from the corner of the room and sat down beside his wife on the left side of the bed. He began to caress her head.

"You've had something to eat today, then? Mrs. Tomkins's special potion?"

Lillian nodded.

"That's good. You'll soon be back on your feet again."

Lillian smiled weakly, aware that her breasts were starting to leak again, and pulled the shawl that covered her nightdress tighter around her shoulders. Button picked up a blue bottle and spoon that lay on the small bedside cabinet.

"Ready for your medicine?" he said, pulling out the cork and about to pour the liquid onto the spoon.

Lillian turned her head away. "I don't really want to take that anymore. It makes me feel all cloth-eared and I can't think properly."

He soothed, "And what is there to think about, eh? It's to help you feel better."

She shook head and held up her hand. "No, really. John, listen, there is something I need to—"

"Just one spoon for me," he coaxed, holding the spoon so close to her mouth she could smell the liquid.

She gulped at it, then continued, "Now will you listen to me? I—"

He sat back with the bottle in one hand and the spoon in the other.

"What you got to thank him for, eh?" he asked suddenly.

Lillian's pulse was racing hard, the closeness of the small room making a steady beat against her eardrums which reverberated in her head. She did not reply, not trusting herself to speak.

The silence was interrupted by the most plaintive of mews from the box on the floor by the side of the bed.

Button turned sharply. "What was that?" he asked.

"John. I've been trying to explain—"

The noise came again.

Her husband stood up and pointed. "It's coming from over there."

Lillian struggled to pull herself up and reached out to stop him. "John, wait," she said as he moved around the bed. As he swept past, the candle flickered on the mantelpiece, causing shadows to dance on the walls. He looked down at the box. The coverings writhed. It was clear there was something living under the blanket. She couldn't help herself. "Ssssh," she urged.

"There's something in that box."

"Please . . ."

"What is it? What have you got in there?" he whispered, wide-eyed.

"John . . . I . . ." She put a hand out to stop him but he threw it off.

"Let me see, Lillian." He knelt down beside the box, pulling back the blanket to reveal the source of the mournful noise.

"Good god!" he exclaimed before clamping a hand over his mouth, standing up, and stepping away from the bed, his eyes mesmerised by the newborn bundle of fur wrapped in fine linen and lying in the box. Lillian picked up the infant and held him tightly to her chest.

"What is this grotesque impersonation, Lillian?"

She whispered, "A baby that needs a mother."

"But where has this . . . this . . . *thing* come from?" he hissed.

Lillian did not look at her husband but silently played with the baby's linen wrappings with her fingers.

"When? When did it appear? I was here but a few hours ago."

"And I am a mother in need of a child," she said, mustering as much strength as she was able and looking him full in the face.

"I've no need to guess, have I? Grady. Grady, I suppose," he said, clenching his fists and then spitting out the words. "You two are thick as bacon fat, always have been." He wiped spittle from the corner of his mouth with the back of his hand.

Lillian did not reply. Button paced the small garret room, shaking his head and occasionally knocking it against the rafter in the low ceiling, muttering all the while to himself.

"Sssh," said Lillian as the chimp began to stir and she slowly filled her lungs to summon her strength. "Grady was doing his best for me in the ways he knows how."

The room grew silent and hotter. The clock continued its relentless ticking.

"I can't breathe in here, Lillian. I need some air, for god's sake." He pushed the window open beyond the crack Grady had made, then ran his finger around his neck collar, shaking his head all the while.

Neither said a word.

He knelt down beside her. He licked his lips. "You must see this is madness. This . . . this is simply not possible." He reached out to stroke her face with the back of his fingers, but the gesture was shrugged away.

Holding the baby even closer, she said, "I won't give him up."

He reached again for her hand. "Lillian. There will be other children, you know. In time."

"This one needs me now."

"This is a—a—"

"A motherless child."

"An abomination."

"In whose eyes? I was set to die from my grief."

"An abomination against nature."

"I don't care what it is. Folks have called *me* the same," she said and started to cry quietly. "I *won't* give him up."

"Hush. Hush thyself."

Silence descended once more. John resumed his place on the stool, legs apart and an elbow on each knee, head hanging between. Looking up, he said, "What on earth do you think people will say?"

Lillian shook her head. "I . . . I . . . ."

The baby started to squirm in her arms and began to arch his back while making a *mupp* sound with his lips.

"He needs his feed, John."

Incredulously: "His feed? You mean you—"

"Of course," said Lillian defiantly as she began to undo to the ties on her nightgown.

John watched as his wife began to suckle the young chimp at her breast. The smell of the milk was sweet in the air.

"This is not right," he said. "It is against God."

"There is nothing more natural in the world than a mother using her milk to suckle an infant."

"But what will people say?" he repeated.

Lillian did not reply.

"I . . . I must take your leave. I beg you, Lillian . . . consider your actions. Give up this . . . animal."

"John. Don't!" She reached out to catch his sleeve.

"I—I must think about this . . . I must go," he said quietly and left without kissing her goodbye, closing the door firmly behind him.

Lillian turned her attention back to the baby, a smile now spreading on her face. "Who's hungry then?" she asked the infant who reached out his hand, opening and closing his mouth all the time. Lillian undid her nightgown and exposed her nipple for her baby.

JOHN LEFT THE building and turned right, walking down Fleet Street towards the Thames, where he wandered alone and along, thinking about the stifling room from which he had just come. He could not shake the image of his wife and the chimp lying on that sunshine-yellow bed cover. He thought of those small curled hands as it lay on his wife's chest and was surprised at its similarity to a human baby. He stood and watched as the lights were lit one by one along the Blackfriars Bridge, the early twilight greeted by the birds and their evensong. Then he remembered the milk running from its mouth and a wave of nausea overtook him and he stopped and spat on the ground. He felt around for a handkerchief and wiped his brow and his mouth. He needed to get home and discuss this with Featherstone.

"TWO CUPS OF chocolate, please, Mrs. Tomkins," he demanded as soon as he walked through the door in Neil Street.

"Right away, sir, I'm sure," said Mrs. Tomkins. "Nothing better to do," she muttered.

Button knocked on the door of Featherstone's study and entered without waiting for permission. Immediately he felt relief at being back in the familiar surroundings, books piled everywhere and Silver the parrot sitting on his perch. The giant boar's head with its gross underbite and two upturned fangs stared down at him from above the fireplace. Featherstone was also in his usual position, bent over his desk, one hand on his microscope and the other making notes.

"Too much rum! Too much rum!" shrieked the bird as soon as it saw Button.

"Oh, shut up, Silver," said Button, flopping down on one of the two stuffed red velvet chairs placed in front of the fire, barely alive in the hearth.

Featherstone turned from his work, removed his glasses, and placed them on his desk. He rubbed his eyes. "What is it, boy? Has something happened?"

Agitated, Button stood up and began to pace. "Sir, you will not believe—"

Featherstone indicated the chair. "Sit! Calm yourself down and tell me. How is our patient? Ready to come home?"

The apprentice took a deep breath and sat. He gave a shiver and wrapped his arms around himself.

Featherstone took a newspaper from the pile by the fireplace, got down on one knee, opened it out, and held it against the mouth of the hearth. Within a few minutes it was throwing out heat once more. Satisfied, he selected another log and placed it on the blaze, then took his seat in the other armchair. He leaned back, crossed his legs, and began to fill his pipe as Button told him what had happened.

"As men of learning and knowledge, it will be most interesting to see how this—er—experiment develops," Featherstone said, taking the scientific approach.

Button did not look so sure. "Sir. With respect. This is not an experiment. This is my life. Our lives."

The room fell silent apart from the crackling of the fire. Button loosened his collar. Featherstone selected a wooden spill from the bronze holder by the fireplace, leaned towards the fire, and lit his pipe. He let out a long thoughtful plume of smoke.

"We should be grateful, Button. Nature has provided us with an elegant solution and we shall also have our Lillian back in time for the Christmas meal. Would you not agree?"

Button sighed and shook his head. "I am so grateful to you for the way you have taken me in this last year—me and my wife— allowed us to be your apprentices and taught us all you know about the animals. I think of you as a father, you know that, but I cannot ask you to do this. Your reputation? What will people say?"

Featherstone picked up his spectacles once more, cleaned them with the tail of his shirt, and popped them on his nose.

"Whose reputation are we talking about, precisely?" he asked slowly, looking over the top of his glasses.

"We are building a great practise here. People of quality trust us with their animals. Business is good. We can hardly keep up with our appointments between us. I would hate for Lillian and her—" He searched around for the words to define his wife's relationship with the new arrival. "Lillian and her . . . her *ape* to threaten that."

"Leave me to worry about reputation and you worry about your wife," said Featherstone coldly. "We survived well enough before the so-called quality, as you call them, found their way to my door."

Button glanced at Featherstone, surprised at the unfamiliar admonishment in his voice.

Featherstone clapped his hands. "Besides! Look around you," he said, indicating the inhabitants of the study, which were mainly stuffed, pinned, or spread open under the microscope. "Everything is dead. Everything, except Silver, of course, and—"

Silver interrupted, "What's an old man to do? To do? To do?"

Featherstone stood and leaned towards his apprentice to give him a hefty whack on the back.

"And I look forward to a live specimen! It's not so unusual to have a live chimp as a member of the household. Sir Thomas More himself had one, I understand."

Button attempted a smile. "I am not sure if I can be a father to this creature."

"Father? Who is asking you to be its father? You are thinking too much, man. Lillian is keeper to the menagerie. She is merely taking care of a motherless infant."

"But Featherstone, she . . . she suckles that infant."

Featherstone raised his eyebrows and stroked his chin, looking away before pronouncing. "Of course, that's perfectly possible," he said. "I've heard of lost children in the African jungle being suckled by monkeys, so why not the other way round? Eh?"

At this moment Mrs. Tomkins bustled in and placed the chocolate on the table between the two men. "Suckled by monkeys?" she asked. "That's disgusting." She turned and left the room.

Featherstone ignored her and the chocolate and stood up at

the mantelpiece, picking up small objects—bits of bone, feathers, teeth of unknown origin—and rearranging them in new positions. It helped him think, he said.

"Seriously, though, Button. What is the alternative? You leave her there at the Exchange with Grady? Or see her return here to us with a small creature that is taking away the pain of her—and your—most terrible loss."

Button hung his head in thought.

"Lillian is alive and well and returning to us, yes, and her charges at the menagerie. This can only be a good thing, surely?"

Featherstone stood and placed a hand on Button's shoulder. "She is your wife. Sometimes it's about doing the right thing, regardless. Eh?"

Button nodded.

"Drink your chocolate. It's getting cold."

Button took a mouthful but hardly tasted the sweet brown drink as his thoughts continued to fight with each other.

"Go. We will get a separate room made up for her and her charge—until you two get used to each other again. Mark my words. Don't leave her with Grady. You will lose her."

Button put down his cup and stood up, giving a small, resolute nod of his head.

"Go now," Featherstone said, pushing him towards the door of the study, which he held open for Button to pass through before shouting across the hall to Mrs. Tomkins.

"Good news, Mrs. T! Our Lillian's coming home. Can you make up a room for her, please?"

The front door of the Neal Street house closed behind Button as he set off back to the Strand.

LILLIAN LAY PEACEFULLY with the small infant in her arms, drifting in and out of sleep. The force of the laudanum was weakening but could still exert itself when she closed her eyes. In the distance, she thought she could hear the roar of the lion, which made her think she was back at her old mistress's house on Tottenham Court Road. A small breeze through the window, and its intermittent rattle, would occasionally nudge her awake, carrying the mixed aroma of lavender and oranges that drifted up from the theatre courtyard next door, taking her back to being a young girl sitting at the kitchen table with her sisters, tying posies.

Every now and then the breeze also brought a whiff of roasting meat that she could taste on her tongue. Along with the realisation she was hungry came the thought of what on earth was she going to do now. Her husband had made his feelings perfectly clear. Grady would let her stay, she was sure, but what compromise would she have to make? She felt like she could just stay here in this room forever.

A small tear made its way down her face and gently fell on the sleeping infant, who opened his eyes, looked at Lillian, and raised a paw to wipe away the moisture. He then licked the salt from his fingers before snuggling down further in Lillian's arms and closing his eyes once more.

There was a gentle knock on the door. Lillian kept her eyes closed and held her breath. She seemed to recite a thousand prayers in her head before she said, "Come in."

The door of her bedroom pushed open and her husband appeared. Nothing had changed since he had made his rapid departure a few hours earlier, but Lillian sensed something was different.

"You came back," she ventured.

He knelt down beside her. "Evidently," he said with a reluctant smile. "I couldn't leave you here alone."

"I . . . I'm so glad, John. Thank you."

"Come, Lillian. It's time to go."

"Where? Where are we going?"

"I'm taking you home. Both of you."

"Really? Back to Neal Street?"

John nodded.

"Mr. Featherstone? What does he say? And Mrs. Tomkins?"

"He can't wait to see you and meet . . ."

"Samson," she replied, looking down at the sleeping infant. "His name is Samson."

"So be it." He paused. "We will tell people that you are simply taking care of this . . . this infant . . . as you would as manager of the menagerie. There cannot be any public displays of—"

She did not let him finish. "Yes, of course," she replied, already pushing back the covers and keen to get home.

"Let's gather your things. There's a carriage outside."

It only took a few minutes for Lillian to dress and gather her belongings in a small holdall. So much had happened since she had found herself unexpectedly back in her old bedroom four long days ago. She had little to collect. She blew out the candle on the mantelpiece.

Having carefully wrapped the only thing she really wanted to take in his shawl, the couple slowly made their way downstairs. Still weak from the events of the last few days, she held onto the rail as she made her way down, step by step. When they reached the bottom, she suddenly heard the lion roar.

"I must go to him," she said, flashing a smile at her husband. Energised by the thought of the lion, she headed towards its enclosure.

"Lillian, I just want to get you home," Button sighed.

"Ten minutes, John, please. He's not seen me for days."

John followed his wife as she made her way to the lion's enclosure. Leonidas stood as soon as he saw her and put his muzzle through the bars of the cage. Lillian said nothing as she felt the familiar hot breath on her face. She presented the baby to the lion.

She turned to her husband, who put his arm around her and guided her out of the menagerie and towards the waiting carriage.

Sixteen

"HERE HE COMES NOW!" GRADY DECLARED to those watching the wild boar lying on its side chewing a mouthful of straw with disinterest, impatiently looking over their shoulders, waiting for the real stars of the show to appear.

"Why there you are, Teddy Diamond, m'lad," he said, "and with your very own young charge."

He held up his hands to welcome the new arrivals. The crowd let out a collective "ooh" as a young chimpanzee appeared, riding on the dog's back as if he were a small horse, one hand holding on to his fur and the other waving in the air. They were followed by half a dozen boys running after him, pointing and laughing. Excited visitors nudged each other and patted pockets that contained the treats they had bought for both dog and chimp.

Grady let his hand drop to his side as the dog, with chimp on back, pushed his muzzle into Grady's open hand, inviting his head to be stroked. "See that, ladies and gentlemen? *Never* a more loyal dog, a true *family* of animal lovers."

Samson would then beat his chest from atop Teddy Diamond while the braver visitors held out a tasty morsel between their fingers. The chimp would jump down, run over to the proffered treat, and snatch it up.

Six months had passed since the arrival of the new addition to the menagerie, and everybody loved him. Grady strolled his empire with a smile on his face as he planned a new imprint of tokens to feature a chimp on one side. Hands on the lapels of his new yellow and black striped satin waistcoat, he looked like a man enjoying an increase in good fortune, as indeed he was. Trade was brisk and Mrs. Ogden complained that she barely had time to use the chamber pot, so frequent were the callers.

He nodded at the visitors and graciously stopped to answer questions, never revealing any irritation with even the most banal query handled many times before. Where did this one come from and what did it eat? And is it true that his cassowary bird once laid a golden egg?

There was a sense of relief about the place, as if disaster had been averted, and all were thankful to return to normal. The boys at the Exchange began to whistle again and the yips and barks, snarls and roars of the animals returned to their usual enthusiastic levels.

"The *real* proprietors of this establishment—Teddy Diamond and Samson, his chimp!"

LILLIAN WAS LESS inclined to allow Samson to be used as a side-show. As she went about her day supervising the boys and checking the animals, Samson would hold on around her neck, occasionally swinging down to snatch something intended for one of the other creatures. The rhino, no longer a baby, would give an incensed wailing *"Num a num?"* at the disappearance of his favourite treat, whilst the boys soon found the fun in dangling a pear in the chimp's direction, pretending they were unaware the fruit had caught his eye, then snatching it away as he reached out a paw to make a grab.

"Don't tease him, boys," Lillian admonished them. "How many times do I have to tell you?"

"Can I hold him, Miss?" said another.

"No, you can't. He's far too young to be passed from pillar to post." But she said nothing, just smiled, when Teddy Diamond padded by and Samson swung down onto his back. She had always loved the dog and he drew attention away from her real relationship with the chimp, with whom she was learning to communicate by using a series of signs made with her hands. Her baby knew how to make the sign for milk, but any feeding of the more intimate kind would only take place in strict privacy.

One of the younger boys leaned against Lillian's leg, looked up, and said in the smallest voice, "It's so good to have you back, Miss."

Lillian hugged him to her and replied, "It's so good to *be* back."

Summer was just around the corner, and there was a suggestion of perfume in the air and a lightness in step and smile as all rejoiced in the return of Lillian—accompanied by Samson, of course. The evenings were growing longer and the menagerie stayed open until the sun began to fall behind the roof of the theatre at Drury Lane.

But whilst the days quickly returned to the easy comings and goings of animals, workers, and visitors, the night held its own challenges as Lillian and her husband kept separate bedrooms with Samson occupying his own cot.

GRADY TOOK HIS time as he sauntered past the cages and pens. The afternoon sun was fast disappearing and the cold was starting to seep up through the flagstone floor. The evenings were still cool and damp—exactly how the animals liked it. Feeding time had been an hour before and there was that sense of peace that came when bellies were full and appetites satisfied.

He stopped by the stuffed cassowary bird and paused to reflect on earlier travels and triumphs. He rolled his eyes when he remembered how those so-called "intellectuals" in Cambridge had forcibly taken his egg from him and cracked it open in order to prove it was real and the stupid look on their faces when they got yolk and albumen all over their hands and their subsequent pitiful exclamations of "Sorry, Grady . . ."

"Ha! Those mopusses," he said out loud.

He cast his eyes around for a chair and, eyeing a small stool, sat down and began to tap the pockets of his waistcoat for his pipe and contents. He was in the process of tamping down the tobacco in the bowl when he heard the sound of running footsteps. Charlie appeared from around the corner.

"Grady!" he shouted. "Grady!" He was out of breath and panting.

"Jaysus, boy, I nearly dropped me baccy. What's got you all worked up?"

Charlie stopped and bent over, his hands on his knees, panting to catch his breath.

"There's a man here . . . says . . . says he's from the Prince of Wales!"

"Good god, boy. From the Prince you say?"

"Yes, a small feller he is."

"Why didn't you tell me? Where is he?"

"He's at the ticket booth . . . talking to Mrs. Ogden. Wants to meet you, Grady!"

"What d'you leave him alone with her for?" he said, horrified, starting to make his way towards the front entrance while buttoning his waistcoat, pulling up his stockings, and straightening his wig. Charlie trotted behind him.

"Wait, sir, wait," said Charlie.

"What? What is it?"

"You've done the buttons on your waistcoat all wrong," said Charlie.

"You cheeky little mopus," said Grady and gave him a cuff round the ear.

Charlie indignantly put his hand to his cheek.

Grady marched ahead but stopped just around the corner before the main hall to catch his breath and adjust his buttons. "Right. Now. Will I do?" he said, presenting himself to the youngster.

Charlie nodded with a sulk. Grady gave him a conspiratorial smile and a wink and a gentle punch on the shoulder, took a deep breath, and turned the corner. Immediately he spied his prey standing with his back to the hall, chatting with Mrs. Ogden in her admission booth. From the very end of the hall he advanced towards him with wide-open arms and at the top of his voice declared, "My good man, my good man."

The visitor turned. A short, hatless man, no more than five feet tall, his high snow-white wig adding the inches he doubt-less felt he lacked, Grady surmised. He stood with one arm fully extended, leaning slightly on an ivory bone-topped cane which Grady immediately recognised as a highest-quality pizzle walking stick. He sported a white satin waistcoat decorated in a delicate and intricate gold thread, not Indian spice-stained imitation, but real gold, Grady was sure. Clean white stockings and shiny black patent shoes meant that this gentleman had not arrived at the emporium dodging the shit and piss of the gutters of London. A duck's-egg-blue top coat (carefully chosen to enhance his eyes?), edged again with the same gold thread, completed the effect.

In the time it had taken him to complete his short walk, Grady had quickly sized up the specimen that stood at the entrance to his empire with a knowing and experienced eye. Here was a man who had money and who liked to spend it.

"Thank you for visiting this, my most humble of animal empo-riums. Whether it is fleet of foot or sharp of claw or bearing teeth the size of a crocodile, I am proud to say we have it here for your delectation for an afternoon with a lady or—ahem—simply a friend," Grady purred, tapping the side of his nose. "Or indeed to take home and keep and care for your good self and show all your friends just what a wonderfully successfully man you have become"—he paused—"to afford such exotic creatures." He com-pleted his entrance with the deepest of bows.

The creature turned and looked at Grady.

"Ah, so you are Mr. Grady," he said, jutting his chin and looking him up and down, making his own assessment of the proprietor. His voice was deeper than Grady had expected from one of such diminutive size.

"Indeed sir, I am, sir," Grady replied, sticking his thumbs in his waistcoat and drawing himself up to his full height. "You may have read about me, the Aerial Fascinator and the truly modern Noah." With a flourish, he produced the weathered piece of newspaper from his waistcoat. The visitor took the paper unfolded, read it, and handed it back wordlessly with a nod of approval.

"Grady . . . of Grady's Emporium," he clarified, carefully putting the paper back in his waistcoat and giving a sweep of his hand as he bowed. He indicated to Charlie with his thumb, never taking his eye off the visitor, "Charlie, get the gentleman a chair."

Charlie duly obliged. Mrs. Ogden flapped her hands in the background.

"At your service, sir," said Grady. "Pray tell. What is your desire?"

"Indeed, your servant, sir, Sir Thomas Kraven-Cleavens," The visitor matched the bow, crinkling his nose and ignoring the chair Charlie offered.

"Perhaps a little snifter of refreshment following your long journey?"

"Who would decline such a kind offer?" the visitor replied, cocking his head to one side and smiling.

"Mrs. Ogden. Two glasses and a drop of the old author for Sir Thomas here."

"Yes sir, right away, sir," said Mrs. O, bobbing up and down and dashing away.

Grady indicated the chair once more and pulled up one for himself. Both men sat. Grady knew the power of silence and now let the sound of the yips and barks from the menagerie take over as he patted his waistcoat for baccy and pipe and filled the bowl, all the while giving the visitor time to take in the surroundings and atmosphere of the establishment in which he now found himself. Charlie darted forwards with a tinderbox for the pipe, which Grady lit and then sat back as a cloud of sweet smoke appeared above his head. Mrs. Ogden arrived with two glasses and a bottle of brandy, which she placed on a small table between them.

Sir Thomas crossed his legs, sat back in his chair, and graciously allowed Grady to pour him a drink. He lifted the glass to Grady's and with a "Good Health" their glasses met. He then set his down and made a temple with his fingers. The business was begun.

"Mr. Grady. I have come from His Majesty the Prince of Wales, who has quite an interest in the exotic." He paused to let Grady take this in. "You may have heard how the good Queen Charlotte herself kept some interesting beasts at Buckingham Palace?"

Grady nodded, trying to affect a sage air. "A pioneer in the science of animal care, sir."

"And how sadly her elephant died a few years ago?"

"Indeed so. A loss to the nation, may I be allowed to say, sir?"

Sir Thomas waved his hand with indifference. "So it is said. Well now, my master has a desire to create his very own menagerie at the new summer residence in Brighton."

"Ah, Brighton by the sea," said Grady. "I have heard much of this place."

"Indeed, it is very modern, Grady. During summer season the place doubles in size with all the gay and fashionable folk from London heading to the sea to enjoy its many delights. The assemblies! The balls! The theatres! And the gambling! A man who enjoys a wager can always find something to place a bet on—if the Prince hasn't thought of it first, of course!"

Grady took another puff on his pipe and nodded as he imagined such a fabulous gathering of the great and good.

Sir Thomas continued. "His Highness's new residence has been designed by none other than the great Henry Holland himself. It is in the most *chicest* of French style. The corridors in blue and ceilings of grey and white. My my," he said, patting his heart with his hand. "But I digress. I am here today to find—and to make purchase—of the strangest, the most exotic animals from around the world."

Grady rubbed his hands. "Then, my lord, you have come to the very place. We have all you might desire. Come!" He made to stand. "Allow me show you around."

Sir Thomas raised his hand towards Grady.

"Indeed, I can barely wait a minute longer before we tour this . . . this . . . *marvellous* emporium of yours, but first, let me ask you. Word has reached the Prince of a *particularly* special creature who, we understand, resides within this good establishment." He placed great emphasis on the word *particularly*.

"To what do you refer, sir? To our magnificent polar bear? The only creature on God's good earth that is not hunted by another? To our wonderful singing baby rhinoceros, which seems to grow inches by the very day?"

"No, no . . . not the four-legged variety." Sir Thomas laughed and took another sip of his drink. "If I may be so bold . . ."

He glanced up to determine Grady's reaction. "We hear tales of a rather tall, very large creature?"

Grady frowned. "Oh yes?"

"Dresses like a man but is, in fact, a young woman?"

Lifting his chin and narrowing his eyes, Grady looked down his nose. "My head keeper is certainly such a woman."

Sir Thomas carried on. "And is it true that she can actually talk to the animals?"

Grady stroked his chin and thought fast. The businessman, the showman, and the man himself were all conducting their own arguments inside his head. But there was never any doubt as to who would be the winner.

He gave a slow nod and chose his words carefully as he replied, "It has been commented upon that indeed she has a particular . . . affinity, shall we say? . . . with many of the animals in her charge."

Sir Thomas seemed to forget the superior composure he had

affected since they began their conversation and now said hurriedly, "And can it be true that no creature will dare place a finger—ha! or a claw even!—to hurt her?"

Here Grady looked at Sir Thomas squarely in the eyes and firmly nodded his assent. "Well, that is most certainly true, sir. I have been with her in the very lion's cage itself and she can lie down with that magnificent beast like a veritable lamb in the Garden of Eden."

Sir Thomas pondered Grady's replies, then gave a little clap of the hands.

"The Prince *will* be pleased. Now. To today's mission! We are going to need our new menagerie populated with the most exotic and, needless to say . . . may I say, Grady? May I be frank?"

"By all means, sir."

"With no doubt the most *expensive* of God's great creatures. I have a full purse here, sir." He tapped his thigh. "So maybe today we could take a look at some of your more *exclusive* items?"

"Certainly! Certainly! Charlie, run ahead and check all is as it should be—"

"One moment, Grady. Maybe the good lady of whom we speak might be able to show us round herself?"

Grady opened his arms wide with his shoulders raised and his palms turned upwards. "Ah, Sir Thomas. As much as it grieves me to disappoint a gentleman such as yourself, I am afraid that our young Miss Lillian is, today, ah . . . indisposed." He wasn't sure what prompted him to keep Lillian away from Sir Thomas but hoped she might take a little longer than usual with the horses at the theatre.

"Oh, now that *is* a shame . . . I had so hoped to be able to report back to the Prince that I had met her and that such stories were true and that my budget for this little enterprise might be increased . . . ."

"I am sorry, Sir Thomas. If I could I would, but you see, we had a little accident here just a month or so ago . . ."

"Nothing too serious, I hope?"

"Maybe you heard of it? Such is this great lady's love of the animal kingdom that she hurt herself trying to save the wretched worthless life of some no-good organ grinder's monkey. Run down by a stupid mopus who should not have been in charge of a bottle of ale, let alone a horse and carriage."

"Really?"

"Poor Lillian ended up sustaining a slight injury. Come, let me show you round and I'll tell you all about it."

And with that the two men set off on their tour of the menagerie.

SIR THOMAS'S EYE was caught by the wolves' enclosure.

"Romulus and Remus, you say? And what a most apposite setting!" He clapped his hands. "You've bred a wolf with a dog, I heard?"

"And produced a litter of most disagreeable whelps!"

"Marvellous, marvellous, Grady. Simply marvellous. The Prince is always pleased with the unusual and I think we have made an excellent selection."

Grady gave a desultory bow and murmured, "My lord," and watched as Sir Thomas appeared to toy with his pocketbook.

"And the elephant?"

Grady puffed himself up, stuck his fingers in his waistcoat, and proclaimed, "The word is out amongst my *many* associates and I am confident we can secure a most *prestigious* example of that most *respectable* of *all* the world's animals. Indeed, a creature that has *surpassed* all other terrestrial creatures in size *and* intelligence. An animal that—"

"Yes, yes, Grady," Sir Thomas interrupted. "We know all this, which is *why* we need the damn thing."

He directed a hard smile at Grady, who gave a small indifferent shrug at having his patter interrupted. He knew when to stick a cake in the hole.

"I might add, Grady, that Sheridan plans to stage his magnificent show *Bucephalus* at the Brighton theatre. I understand you provided the horse before?"

"Indeed we did. A most magnificent beast and trained in ways that most horses—"

"Yes, yes, I'm sure . . . A deposit now and the rest on delivery?"

Grady nodded. "For sure." He greedily watched as Sir Thomas began to count out the notes of promise.

"Which we can expect . . . ?"

"As soon as you give the word that the new place is ready, I can have the animals down there in three days."

"Thank you. And I am *most* keen of course to meet this lady who has given birth to a monkey. The Prince will be very interested."

Grady squirmed. In his enthusiasm to show off his empire he had let the lie escape, almost bounding, from his lips.

"What a marvel that is, a creature that can commune with the animals, lie down with lions, and now mother a baby monkey. You'll make a fortune with this creature, Grady," Sir Thomas said. "When the Prince hears of this, everyone will want to come and visit this place."

Grady gave a weak smile.

"I shall return in a few weeks and maybe you will have news for me then."

Sir Thomas completed his visit with a handshake and the most elaborate of twirls and bows and was gone. Grady rubbed the back of his neck as he watched him depart.

Seventeen

LILLIAN WAS MAKING A FINAL INSPECTION of the animals before leaving for the night and briskly strode up and down both sides of the hall, peering into the stalls to check that the supplies of water and straw were adequate for the night ahead, putting off the inevitable return to Neal Street and another awkward evening. She paused by the heifer, who had just given birth to a calf, and thought back to the previous night and how Button had taken too much wine at dinner.

Her husband had started to talk loudly with his eyes closed, and she noticed Mrs. Tomkins trying to catch Featherstone's attention as she served the pudding with a pursed mouth. The old vet would not meet her gaze and had quickly cleared his plate, mumbling something about "not leaving the preservative on the butterfly too long" and disappearing into the refuge of his study.

As Mrs. Tomkins made herself ready to depart, Button had demanded, "Leave the bottle, my good woman," in the pompous tone he had adopted since Lady Charlotte Beauchamp and her peacock had become a client.

The fire crackled, and as the room got hotter Button grew even more flushed. He slumped in front of the fireplace, all clothing askew, and began to mumble to himself.

"I can't quite hear what you are saying, husband," said Lillian.

Suddenly he leaned over towards her, grabbing her by the wrist. "I love you and you're mine," he said urgently. "Mine. My wife."

"I—I love you too, John. You know I do." She felt aware of her lack of insistence.

"Then why won't you let me—" The sentence hung incomplete in the air.

"I—I have not denied you," she said, pulling her arm away.

"I cannot attend your bedroom with that . . . that . . . ape watching me."

"He's just a baby—"

"What? No! That is exactly what he is not!" Button slumped back in his chair. "Bah."

John, Lillian, and Samson had then gone upstairs to bed, but as Lillian went to close the door of her room, Button had stopped it with his foot.

"I want you," he said, breathing fumes from the wine he had taken earlier that evening directly into her face.

"You've drunk too much," said Lillian, push the door back on him.

"I want you," he repeated. Lillian dropped her eyes and opened the door wider to allow her husband access.

"Just let me lay Samson down."

Button grunted assent and flopped onto the bed whilst Lillian quietly and gently lay the baby chimp down in his cot. Undressing as slowly as possible, she glanced over at her husband as she did so, listening as his breathing became deeper and more steady until it eventually turned to a snore.

She climbed in beside him stared down at him for a few moments, wondering what had happened to the enthusiastic young bird man just up from the country, so keen to read books and learn about this modern world full of new ideas in which they were so privileged to live. What did she need to do to get him back? A short time later, Samson crawled into the bed and Lillian's arms, where he pulled at the strings of her nightdress till he found what he was looking for.

When she woke in the morning, she was alone. Button had left for his duties before breakfast and she had not seen him since.

HER THOUGHTS WERE interrupted by a strong smell of perfume that rose above the straw and the animals, making her nose twitch and causing her to look around and come face to face with a short little man sporting a huge white wig and a duck's-egg-blue coat, trimmed with golden thread. He was accompanied by a female companion in matching white wig, at least a head taller than he but still not reaching Lillian's shoulders, most fashionably dressed in blue and navy satin stripes with two layers of lacy cuffs on the arms and a matching headdress. The woman clung to his arm, her large popping eyes darting around the room but the rest of her face hidden by a fan decorated with a rural scene, which she waved with great vigour. Lillian found herself wondering what her mouth might look like.

The man gave a deep bow. "Madam, it is an honour to make your acquaintance."

Lillian gave a suspicious nod at the couple in reply, unconsciously putting her hand up to Samson, who held on to her neck, and pulling him down to settle on her hip.

"Hello," she said and, sensing they were her betters, followed with a quick bob. "Are you looking for Mr. Grady?"

Samson gave a screech, startling the man's companion who pulled away, fluttering her fan even harder and tugging at the top of her gown, which had fallen slightly to reveal the white skin of her shoulders.

"How charming!" said the man in the duck's-egg-blue coat, smiling at Samson. He produced a sweetmeat from a pocket and held it out to the chimp, who quickly took it and put it in his mouth. His companion picked at his sleeve to pull him back from the monkey.

"Don't fret so, my dear," he said.

"Sssh, Samson," said Lillian, making the sign for "stop" with her hand and then smiling at the woman. "Don't worry. He won't hurt you."

The man moved his gaze to Lillian, the smile fixed in place. "No, it's you I wish to see."

"Me?" she replied, looking around for Grady and wiping her free hand on her leather trousers.

"Allow me to introduce myself. I am Sir Thomas Kraven-Cleavens—emissary to the Prince of Wales—and this is my, er, companion, Miss Letitia Nimbletongue."

Finally, the woman appeared from behind her fan, revealing a tightly closed mouth and a dimpled smile. Her eyes grew even larger, as if she were laughing, and she gave a small bob. Lillian felt she was being mocked in some way but was unsure how and could not pull her gaze away from the woman.

Instead she mumbled, "Miss Letitia."

The woman grinned and seemed to slightly shimmy her shoulders, as if she were familiar with people responding to her presence in this manner.

"Let me speak directly," said Sir Thomas, closing his eyes and making a steeple with his fingers. "It is said you have a"—he paused—"a way with the animals, ma'am. Indeed, that you have developed a special system of *signs* to enable you to talk to them in their own language."

"I—I—" Lillian hesitated, trying to work out how to respond, when she was relieved to see Grady appear from the other end of the hall.

"Why, Sir Thomas," he boomed in greeting. "Ma'am," he added, quickly acknowledging the companion. "How good you have returned. I did not hear you arrive."

"Ah, Grady," said Sir Thomas, waving a hand in the air, evidently irritated to be interrupted in the middle of his speech. "I could wait no longer to meet this wonder of yours and hear what she thinks of our plans." He tapped the side of his nose. "I presume you have told her now, Grady?"

"Told me what, Grady?" said Lillian, shifting Samson to her other hip but watching the back of Sir Thomas's companion as she wandered away from the group.

"All in good time, my dear," Grady mumbled nervously.

"I thought so. Let me enlighten her myself," said Sir Thomas. "My dear Miss Lillian, the Prince himself is planning a new menagerie in Brighton—by the sea, don't you know—and has requested that we develop the most *modern* of places to house the very *best* examples of the animal kingdom.

"To borrow a phrase—a veritable modern Noah's ark. Now, a deal has been struck—a very *generous* deal I might add—with your good employer here, Mr. Grady"—he affected a small smile and a mock bow—"to supply this new menagerie with a selection—a collection—of the most exotic that our kingdom has to offer."

"And what relevance do I have to this enterprise?" asked Lillian.

"If I may be so bold, ma'am, your fame has spread before you. Your, ah, *endorsement* of our project will mean so much to the Prince."

He stood back and smiled as his companion, who, still waving the fan, took his arm once more, her eyes fixed on Lillian and revealing two rows of small white teeth set in a smile.

Lillian looked at the menagerie owner. "Grady? What does this mean?" She watched as a vein began to throb in Grady's neck.

"He wants you to go there, Lill. To Brighton. Cast your eye over this new place. See what you think. Give them a report, like. Tell them what you think."

Sir Thomas nodded. "Indeed, our new venture will offer the very *best* to be seen in England, and who better to oversee than a woman who can talk to the animals, who can lie down with the lion and the sheep and one who has actually given b—"

Letitia suddenly interrupted, putting a finger to her brother's lips. "Oh, *do* say you can come, Miss Lillian."

"I don't know what to say, I'm sure," said Lillian, running her free hand through her short hair. "I am not sure I am worthy of such tributes."

"Your modesty commends you, young lady. Come. Meet with our Mr. Barclay, who is the head of the menagerie," said Sir Thomas.

"Barclay, you say," said Grady. "Tall thin fella, always scratching?"

"That'll be the one," said Sir Thomas.

"Was on the circuit with me a few years back. Used to specialise in oddities, two-headed sheep, five-legged goats, all that. Our little Irish fella was with him awhile. Didn't think he'd ever get as far as a Prince's palace though," said Grady, shaking his head.

Letitia leaned forwards and grabbed Lillian's hand, fixing her large unblinking eyes on hers. "Please say you will come. I will make you my very special mission and show you all the nicest places to visit."

She beamed at her and Lillian was mesmerised by the attention of this pink powdered perfumed creature. She had never left London before, let alone seen an expanse of water bigger than the Thames.

"I—" she faltered, noticing for the first time how Letitia's jacket matched the blue of her eyes.

"We shall have the most tremendous fun in Brighton," Letitia insisted.

"But my husband?" said Lillian.

"That mopus," muttered Grady under his breath.

"I am sure he can spare you for a short time in the service of your future King," said Sir Thomas.

And Lillian, excited by the prospect of a new adventure and leaving London even for a short while, thought that of course Button could spare her. It might even do them both some good to get away for a while. Still she hesitated, trying to ignore a small feeling of disquiet that had lodged at the back of her mind.

"Oh, I knew you would say yes," said Letitia. Lillian nodded and smiled.

"If my husband agrees, of course," Lillian said, but already making up her mind that she would go anyway.

PART THREE

Part Three

Eighteen

1 July 1790
Dear John,

I am writing this letter in haste, balanced on my lap, as there is a mail coach leaving for London almost as soon as I arrive in Brighton and I am anxious to let you know that both myself and Samson are well.

It is so kind of Sir Thomas to ensure I had passage on the faster coach. We should reach Brighton by midnight so twelve hours travelling at the very most. We have only had to get out of the coach and walk up a hill twice so far but, to be honest, I was so keen to stretch my legs by then that the order to disembark came somewhat as a blessing.

The journey has been most bearable and Samson, I am glad to say, has made no inconvenient noises which might have encouraged my fellow travellers to enquire as to his well-being. Please be assured that I have been most discreet in feeding and have always sought a private place.

Now I must rush as they are calling for the mail. I hope you will excuse the imperfect letters. I will write properly as soon as I am in my lodgings.

Your wife
Lillian

4 July 1790
Dear John

So, I am arrived in Brighton.

True to Sir Thomas's word, a man was there to meet me and take the trunk to my lodgings.

And what lodgings they are! I am in a small house called the Evening Star which is located in Bartholomew Street. There are four floors in all and two glass-paned bay windows on either side of a heavy wooden door which I swear could keep out the French. The outside is decorated in cobbles which have been painted black while all the sills are contrasted in white. I am quite at the very top of the house and if I open the window and stand on my tiptoes and lean forwards enough I can just about see the sea. I can most certainly smell it—and how invigorating it is too. They say the sea air is a tonic for the spirits and I swear I can take in the deepest of breaths and hold it till my head goes dizzy then let it out and the smile remains on my face.

Did I say window? I meant windows. For I have two. A bedroom and a sitting room. Both quite small but perfectly adequate. I have arranged my toilet on the piece of lace Mrs. Tomkins gave me and your books are beside my bed. Grady was very generous (would you believe) and plucked a feather from his precious cassowary bird and said I might use it as a book mark. And of course, I have your handkerchief with me always.

Thank you, husband. Thank you for giving your leave for me to visit here with Miss Letitia and Sir Thomas. I know things have been difficult for some time now but hopefully the distance between London and Brighton will be large enough to enable our hearts to repair over time.

There is a small fire in my room which is tended by a young girl called Molly, quite a sullen little thing and not the cleanest either. I understand her father is a fisherman so that might account for the pungent smell. Ha. But look at me. What must they say of me coming from the habitué of animals and birds? I think it might take more than lavender water to hide my own particular aroma.

There is a wonderful picture above the mantelpiece, who it is by I cannot credit, but it shows Noah (to whom Grady does bear a passing resemblance) and his wife outside the ark with the skies darkening above them and all the animals from around the world slowly making their way towards the boat and safety. I look at the picture at least two or three times in the hour and remember all our magnificent charges back at the Exchange and think of ways that we might take better care of them.

I have only one complaint and I am sure, my dear husband, you have already guessed what it might be. The bed is so short that it barely covers my ankles so it is either my head that is cold or my feet. At least the bed is not positioned in the alcove so there is space for them—albeit in the air.

My landlady is called Mrs. Fortescue and she is most genteel and nicely spoken. The man who brought my things said her husband had been quite a wealthy captain but had died at sea and now she makes her living by renting rooms to visitors. Brighton is growing so fast, they say, that it can be hard to find a decent place to stay and providing lodgings is a lucrative and growing trade. Of course the quality always take rooms at the more prestigious establishments—The Old Ship or the Castle Hotel where they have balls and assemblies—but I am more than happy with the Evening Star. I believe there are six other lodgers residing under this roof but I have yet to make their acquaintance. I shall be sure to write and tell you all when I do.

But now I am quite overcome with fatigue and must lay me down for an hour or so. I shall give this letter to Molly and it will be in your hands in a few hours.

Please write as soon as you can and tell me all the news of home.

I remain,

Lillian

9 July 1790

Dearest John

What joy to receive your letter today and how reassuring to hear that all is well at Neal Street and at the Strand. And yes, I miss you too, even though I find myself quite stimulated by all the new sights and sounds there are to be seen in this seaside town. Thank you for your apology. While it is not needed it is appreciated.

Brighton! Oh Brighton! More come to visit every day and I understand why. This little place was a poor fishing village just a few years ago and now it is so gay and full of colour. London might be the greatest city in the world but there seems to be an energy here, inspired by the sea air they say, that lends itself to smiles and a lightness of being.

I woke this morning and found Molly had already been in and laid a fire and to my surprise had laundered my cambric shirt and placed it alongside my leather britches. Maybe I have underestimated that girl?

There is a cot beside my bed for Sam but when I awake he seems to have found his way into my bed. So far, and despite entreaties to see the babby, I have managed to keep him wrapped in his muslin. But it can only be a matter of time. As the guest of Sir Thomas I am counting on his protection from those of ignoble and ignorant thought, as he solemnly promised.

I wrapped myself up in my large greatcoat—not to keep me warm mind, as it is July and the sun is doing its best, but I am not yet used to the winds which sweep up from the sea and it is also good to shield Samson from the elements.

Miss Letitia came to call for us today and we went for a walk down to the Foreshaw to see what we could see and I couldn't believe how many boats there were. Not like in London, where they are always dodging back and forth across the Thames or down on the docks where the ships are so huge and built for travelling the seven seas. No. These are the smallest of vessels, built for nothing other than the man and the net. The fishermen seem most industrious as they pull in their nets and shout to each other about their catches above the noise of the waves and the clanging of the cowbells on the boats. Mackerel is the thing and it is the freshest in the country, so they say. Mrs. Fortescue presented me with a fish for my breakfast this morning and it was if she had plucked it from the sea and thrown it on my plate so fresh it was. When I exclaimed upon this she told me: "It's good for the visitors Dearie but believe me you can get sick to the back teeth of the mackerel." I cannot imagine ever getting sick of so fresh a repast.

We continued walking towards the East where there are the most glorious cliffs of the finest white chalk and that's where we saw the visitors who are taking the water cure. I watched as these wooden huts on wheels, decorated in all sorts of colours, were led down into the sea by both horses and humans. The men are attended by so-called "bathers" and the women have their own assistants (of course) who go under the extraordinary name of "dippers." I spotted a crowd of young misses, obviously from London due to their high fashion wigs and hats, all giggling and holding hands and making their way inside these wheeled contraptions still fully dressed. The huts were then pulled out into the sea and, once in position, the assistants pulled down the canvas to form a small tented arrangement and the bathers slipped into the sea. I couldn't see them from where I was standing but you could certainly hear their screams of delight. Oh how I longed to join them but it would be well beyond my means. I asked Letitia if she had ever tried it and she looked at me with horror and said she did not believe all this nonsense about taking the waters and that to immerse your entire body in water could not possibly do you any good. Still, I would like to try it for myself.

My eye was caught by a reflection of the light and looking up I could see two young fellows—again from the City I am sure—nudging each other and pointing a telescope at the huts. I wonder if the young misses knew what entertainment they were providing for all around them.

I am pleased to tell you, and I am sure you will be delighted to hear, that Samson is becoming more and more independent by the day and is enjoying a more adult diet. We usually dine alone in my rooms, as this is easier for the other guests, and he will often steal a tit bit or two from my plate. He is very smart and is starting to express himself in his own unique way, forming different noises and signs with his hands to express his needs. I don't know how this has happened, it just seems to have evolved somehow, that we each know what the other is thinking. He knows how to ask me for the things he wants, simple things such as "yes" and "no" and "wait." He points at himself and thumps his chest twice and I say "Samson" and he gives a noise like a yelp in reply. We have worked out signs for all the different foods that he likes—mainly fruit, just like Keebar. Mr. Featherstone would be fascinated, that's for sure. I know you feel uncomfortable about his taking of milk and I am pleased to say he is no longer so demanding of this refreshment, it being mainly reserved as a treat for late at night.

One thing I must confess to you that made me slightly uneasy were the few strange looks Letitia and I received on our walk. It took me back to my days in service when I had to trail behind my mistress. Maybe they are looking at Letitia, so pretty and petite she is. Her frame seems so small and well-formed, yet so well-proportioned, and she has the longest and most noble of necks, which only seeks to emphasise the bones of her shoulders, the whitest of skin and the yellowest of sunlit curls. If only I could look in the mirror and claim that sight to be my own.

Samson's heritage is blessedly still hidden and I am certain I heard a voice say "Oh it's a woman," so I know it was myself attracting the adverse glances. I must admit I allowed myself the slightest of smiles when I thought of what was under my coat.

Only a few more days until my appointment with the head keeper of the new menagerie. I am very excited to see what we might learn and put to good use in our own rather humble establishment on the Strand.

The light fades and I must save my stub of candle. I am blowing kisses to you in the dark my darling.

Your wife, Lillian

13 July 1790
Dear John

I have the most wonderful news to report.

I promised that I would tell you about my fellow lodgers and this morning I finally made the acquaintance of a young woman about my own age who I hope will become the most delightful friend.

I was in the entrance hall of the Evening Star looking through the letters on the hall stand when I turned and bumped into this most solid of characters, almost as tall as myself (but not quite) and wearing a dark green worsted jacket and carrying a pile of books under her arm which she said she had obtained from the library.

Her name is Emily Lovetrue and she is in the room underneath mine. And would you believe, she too is from London and has performed at our very own Drury Lane around the corner? She told me she remembers the Bucephalus spectacular and the wonderful performance of Caesar and has confided that Mr. Sheridan himself has been in town and is in talks to have the very same play performed at the theatre in Brighton's Duke Street. She says she is sure to have a place in the show herself and will ask about Caesar having a role. Can you imagine?

Emily is a steady character and when she speaks one cannot help but be struck by her demeanour, her confidence of voice and strident manner. Worldly considerations aside, Emily has a good and wise head about her and tells me she writes frequently to the magazines. She talks of the position of women in society and how our oratory might be just as valid as those of our fellows. She is passionate about the importance of women receiving an education and has been quite flattering to me about my recent learning and training as a doctor to the animals. There are no less than three libraries here in Brighton and Miss Lovetrue says she prefers Widget's Library because it is run by a woman. The proprietor is also a milliner, I understand. Nothing in this town surprises me. She has promised to take me to the next gathering of the Brighton Literary Society where they discuss all sorts of ideas and I cannot wait.

Now, a small confession. I know I promised you and Sir Thomas and Miss Letitia that I would keep Samson to myself for a while but Miss Lovetrue was so complimentary and curious about my stories of the Exchange that I revealed Samson to her and she seems quite delighted with him—and he with her—but when I told Letitia she did not seem happy at all and told me it was "too soon." Too soon for what, I do not know.

When Letitia called for me this morning she was quite insistent that I should abandon my greatcoat and simply carry Samson in my arms *when we go for our walk—from which I have just returned! Letitia was completely correct and, whilst we drew a few glances as we walked across the town towards the cliffs, Letitia was with me and I didn't feel awkward at all.*

But now I am quite exhausted by the walking and the sea air and I swear my face hurts from smiling so much. I must run and post this.

  Yours
  Lillian

---

15 July 1790,
Dear Husband

  Thank you for your letter which I received but an hour ago. I must declare I am most concerned to learn of the proposed acquisition of an elephant at the menagerie. This is something that Grady and I have discussed on many an occasion. You know this. You have been party to my thoughts and considerations on the matter. He has made me a promise that he would not make purchase of such an animal, there simply being not enough space to hold a creature of such size.

  I beg thee, beseech Grady on my behalf that he will do no such thing?

  Your wife (and colleague), Lillian
  (written in haste)

---

23 July 1790
Dear John

  I must confess to holding my breath until I received a reply from you regarding Grady's intentions. It is a relief to learn that the elephant is not due for settling in London but here in Brighton. The day after tomorrow I visit the site of the proposed menagerie and will be delighted to report the lodgings they have set aside for the elephant. Be assured you will have my most scrupulous of professional opinions.

  I am slowly starting to develop a routine. We rise, break our fast with a little fish, bread, and beer, then dress and wait for Letitia. Sometimes I see Miss Lovetrue in the hallway and we stop and pass the time and she might make a recommendation for a book she has been reading.

Today, she showed me the response she had received to a letter printed in The Lady magazine where she had suggested that girls learn to read and write quicker than boys and how girls might actually exceed the boys if they were given the same access to education. Letitia was there and gave a most unbecoming snort at the idea.

Later that evening I saw Miss Lovetrue once more as I returned from my day and she asked how well I knew Letitia. She said she looked familiar but she could not quite place her. I explained how she was the companion of Sir Thomas and how he held high position in court and she seemed satisfied with that.

Together, Letitia and I make our way across the cliffs towards the bathers. Many other Brighton visitors have the same idea to take an early morning walk and, as the days have grown hotter, I have abandoned my greatcoat and started to let Samson swing on my neck. People have stopped to point but Letitia says I should ignore them. I am sad that Samson doesn't seem to care for her and his own sign for her is most rude.

Emily has told me that the sea water is reputed to cure the most purulent swellings and abscesses and that taking a draught of the sea water when emerging from the sea will purge the body and prevent the blood flying to the head. We discussed what else this marvellous drink might cure. Could it apply to animals as well as humans? Indeed, what sort of animal ailments might it cure? It is said that "the sea washes away all the ills of mankind." I wonder, would it wash away the ills of animals as well? I am keen to seek out the works of the good Dr. Russell—dead these twenty years—who, it is said, is responsible for this interest in the cures of the sea. There is talk at the library in a week or so and I plan to attend if I am still here. Dr Russell was a Fellow of the Royal Society and I would be curious to know if he is an acquaintance of our good Mr. Featherstone?

Could you see a day when Grady takes all the animals to the seaside?

Well, he likes to term himself the "modern-day Noah." When I told Letitia about using the waters in this way she and I quite laughed at what a sight that might be, all the animals from the Exchange making their way down to the sea!

With this letter I am sending you a bottle of sea water and I pray you try it on that annoying swelling the kangaroo is prone to get on his foot in the hot weather. Do not let him drink it but do try bathing the foot in the seawater and let me know if it is a success.

Your loving wife, Lillian

24 July 1790
My dearest husband

Of course, I understand your concerns about the company I am keeping, but please be assured they are completely unfounded. Emily is a most wonderful young woman. Just because she is on the stage it does not mean she is not well-read or educated. It was she who told me all about Dr. Russell and we have the most passionate conversations about the situation of women.

And Letitia is Sir Thomas's companion.

I have never had a real friend of my own before and they are both the most wonderful company.

Please do not be alarmed!

Today it was hotter than the previous days and there seemed to be even more people than usual gathered along the path where we walk. I am sure it is not my imagination but it seemed that people were turning and looking at us as we made our way along the top. A woman and her small child came up to us and asked if they might say hello to Samson. I said "yes, of course" and, before I knew where we were, a small crowd of about ten or so people had gathered around us, asking his name and trying to offer him little delicacies. I must confess to feeling slightly overwhelmed and Samson made the sign for "scared." Letitia was wonderful of course and made everyone take a step or two back so that we might continue our walk. I am certain I heard someone use the words "Monkey Lady," but Letitia said she did not hear so I might have been mistaken.

Tomorrow is the day I am to visit the new menagerie so I will take your leave and bid you good night!

Much Love

Lillian

25 July 1790

Dear John

I am pleased to relay news of a most marvellous day!

I have visited the proposed menagerie and I am relieved to tell you that it is everything we had hoped it might be.

First thing this morning Letitia, Samson, and I made our usual walk along the top to take in the fresh air and watch the bathers. Today it was so strange but there were at least double the number of fellow walkers from yesterday and yet the weather was not half as warm. And I am sure I heard the words "Monkey Lady" spoken quite distinctly and one even pointed at me, but I did not mention this to Letitia as she had seemed quite angry when I remarked on it yesterday.

Following our walk, Samson and I went to meet with Mr. Barclay who is the head of the new menagerie. Mr. Barclay is quite a long tall man, so thin that his fingers appear like dark dry sticks or twigs and he is constantly scratching his face, his side, the back of his neck. I tried to ignore it but it really is quite irritating, so much so that it gets me scratching. I noticed Samson doing it too! He has quite a haughty manner and even though I am easily the same size as him he talks with his eyes closed like he is looking down his nose and never seems to look at me directly. He says he is very well acquainted with Mr. Grady and that my own reputation had preceded me but says it in such a way that I'm not sure if it is a good thing or a bad thing! I enquired "how so?" and he replied "your way with the animals."

He took me on a tour of the new quarters which are recently built and using all the most modern of materials and designs. It certainly bears little or no resemblance to our exhibition on the Strand. The place is so different and yet familiar—without the smell, for there are no animals as yet. Everything is on one floor and the cages are far bigger than the meagre space allowed at the Exchange. There are even water pools for the animals that like such a thing and room for many a creature to be both displayed and enjoy life—not that many will see them, apart from the Prince and his friends, as there are no plans as yet to open to the public.

I know Samson enjoyed the visit as he would jump down off my back and run around and then jump back on again screeching all the while with that smile on his face. I am fairly sure he thought he was at home once more but he missed Teddy Diamond. Mr. Barclay held his hand out and Samson went towards him without a moment's hesitation. I did my best to show a little knowledge of animal care as we made our way around the premises and I think Mr. Barclay may have started to warm to me by the end of our visit.

He told me some stories about the old days when he and Grady were on the road together. It's hard to believe that Grady wandered the roads of England with a caravan of animals before he settled at the Strand. He told me how he was always chirping merry with a good glass of liquor. He also spoke about the scholars at Cambridge breaking his cassowary egg. I always believed they had stolen it from him but, of course, Grady had sold it. Is there nothing that man would not do for a shilling or two?

I have a better understanding now of the animals which will shortly be making their way to populate this wonderful new establishment and Mr. Barclay seems quite knowledgeable and capable of their care. We moved on to a caged area with a door in the rear which opened onto a far wider space at the back and Mr. Barclay said that this would make the most perfect lodging for a lion as it could enjoy both shelter and the open air, as the elements dictate. My first thought was Surely Grady would never sell my lion but then I thought that maybe Leonidas would be better in this place with more space and earth beneath his feet and sky above his head, with the opportunity to roam and feel even a little bit free. Sadly I have to accept that here he might have a better quality of food and care than we can give him at the Strand and I have made up my mind to not stand in the way of his being sold, should Grady decide.

I told Mr. Barclay that I was excited to learn that an elephant was coming from India and he said that yes the elephant would be the centre piece of the new menagerie but he did not have time to show me the proposed location today and that I should return in a few days.

And now I must rest. My senses are quite overwhelmed.

I remain, always, your loving wife

29 July 1790

Dear John

Today has not been good.

Samson and I rose as usual, broke our fast, and headed out to the cliffs for our morning walk with Letitia. And today there was no mistaking the crowds which were quite easily double the size of yesterday. People were jostling and pushing and reaching out their hands and I could hear the words (Forgive me for relaying this) "Monkey Lady, Monkey Lady," now repeated directly rather than the sotto voce of yesterday. Samson started screeching in fear and Letitia stood in front of us saying "Stand back. Stand back" and that they would all "get their turn."

I was shaken by both the crowd and her words. "What turn, Letitia?" I asked but she did not reply as she seemed engaged in an animated conversation with another man on the edge of the crowd. I did not wait any longer for a reply but grabbed hold of Samson firmly by the wrist and walked just as fast as I could back to the Evening Star.

When we arrived back Emily was just leaving, with her books under her arm as usual, and could see that I was in a state of distress.

"My dear, what has vexed you so?" she said. "Is it Letitia?"

I shook my head and her hand off my arm as I had barely a few minutes to freshen myself and make the fifteen-minute walk to the menagerie of the Prince's Marine Palace for our meeting with Mr. Barclay.

When I arrived we immediately walked towards the quarters where

Mr. Barclay said he planned to house the elephant. We walked past the various empty enclosures where I could imagine all sorts of exotic creatures would be housed—a zebra, a bear, a kangaroo?—until we reached a space at the very end of this horseshoe-shaped arena. I could not hide my surprise. It could not have been more than ten foot by ten foot at most. Not that I have ever laid my eyes on one, but elephants are reputedly such gigantic beasts—surely the largest of any animal which walks on the earth, bigger even than the rhinoceros? I firmly believe—as I know you do, my dear husband—that any animal must be able to at least turn around and lie down at night. Mr. Barclay could see my face and asked me what I thought. I could only be honest. I felt that Mr. Barclay and I had reached a level of understanding and that I might be confident enough to express my opinion—that the proposed enclosure was simply too small to house an animal the size of an elephant. He was not happy at all and turned quite cold on me. So much so, that I soon made my excuses and left.

But that was not the worst of my day.

A little later that evening there was a small knock on my door and I was most surprised to see Letitia standing there looking quite contrite. She begged that she might come in to talk to me and she has a way about her that I find impossible to deny her request. She seemed quite shame-faced and the whole story poured out of her. She fluttered and flapped with her hands and shook her hair and her head and ran her fingers though her curls.

But I know her now for the actress she is.

And that is how Miss Lovetrue recognised her.

Letitia has betrayed me.

It would appear that she is not a true friend of Sir Thomas's at all but some crooked rib of Eve. She knows Grady and Mrs. Ogden and over porter at the Star she heard that silly story of how, in my state of enceinte, I tried and failed to rescue poor little Albert and believed that, as a result, I had given birth to a monkey myself. Mrs. Ogden is a stupid ignorant woman but Grady? Grady? He knows the truth but did he dissuade her? I cannot believe he would allow that lie to take root.

That is why Sir Thomas came a-calling.

But there is worse.

Letitia has allowed—nay encouraged—the word to spread that myself and my "child" would go walking on the cliffs each morning and demanded a penny—a penny!—to see me—the Monkey Lady—which accounts for the whisperings. It transpires she had an accomplice who would follow us and take the pennies! She even had a young boy selling bits of fruit behind us to give to Samson.

I cannot believe that this was all going on before my very eyes and I knew nothing. But you knew. You were right all along and I did not listen.

I apologise that this missive is wet and that the words run into each other. These are my tears which blur the words from my pen.

I thought Letitia was my friend but instead she is my exploiter and I, her Freak.

Letitia stood before me and wrung her hands and cried her tears and I saw her for what she was. But I will be no one's exhibit. Suddenly, Samson sprang from nowhere screeching at the top of voice and attached himself to Letitia's pretty face. I screamed "No Sam, no!" but he just screeched all the more and scratched and pulled and she cried and screamed. And the blood. She ran away clutching her face.

My bag is packed. I am on the early coach and will not tarry another moment.

In haste
Lillian

Nineteen

IT WAS A QUIET DAY AT the menagerie and Grady took the opportunity for a little "plotting time," as he liked to call it. He pulled up his chair beside the admission booth, plumped up the horsehair cushion, and took his seat. The sun was beating down and he removed his jacket and hung it on the back of the chair, then rolled up the sleeves of his shirt and rubbed the tattoo of a roaring tiger on his left arm. Teddy Diamond was never far from Grady's side these days and waited till his master had settled before lying down beside him, head in paws, and immediately falling asleep in the warm sunshine. Grady carefully filled his pipe, lit the tobacco, closed his eyes, and took in a deep lungful of smoke. "Elephants!" he said aloud and let the smoke go.

He had been fascinated by elephants since he was a child, when his father had told the story of Hannibal and his magnificent journey across the Alps. Together they had gone to watch the arrival of the Bengal elephant gifted to King George and Queen Charlotte. Eyes still closed, he remembered how his father had clutched his hand tightly as people lined the streets of London to catch a glimpse of the elephant as it wended its way towards Buckingham House Gate. Everyone knew of elephants, just like they knew about unicorns and mermaids, but they hadn't seen those either. Few would miss the opportunity to see an elephant in the flesh. The boy Grady was too small to see anything over the tops of the throng and so had to dip down to watch the men on either side of the eight-foot-high grey walking mountain as they took turns to poke him with long poles to keep him moving in the right direction. Two other men kept a firm hold on the ropes tied around its neck. Grady had freed himself from his father's grip to take up a position on the ground between somebody's legs, lying on his belly, head in hands, propped up on his elbows, where he watched the elephant make its slow and steady progress, head hung low, trunk waving in front like a pendulum. Sitting right on top of the elephant was its keeper, a boy no older than Grady, dressed in a red scarlet turban and keeping his balance by pressing his knees just behind the animal's ears. The mahout, as Grady later learned he was called, carried a large stick with which he would prod the huge beast and shout commands in a language Grady did not recognise. He was sure the mahout looked him right in the eye and grinned. Oh, what he would have given to have been up there on that elephant, higher than anyone else in London, waving and smiling at the crowd. He grinned at the thought and reached his hand down to Teddy Diamond and let his fingers play in his fur for a few moments.

But Queen Charlotte's elephants had not lasted more than a few months. He knew that taking care of an elephant would not be easy. Other owners had not had much luck either. He knew of one travelling menagerie that had walked their fellow up and down the roads of England to an early death from the damp and the cold and fever, and another that had been fed on a diet of wine to keep it warm in the winter and that had barely made it through till spring.

He had always dreamed of owning one.

Acquiring an elephant was not going to be an easy matter, and Grady was quite perplexed as to how he could go about the task without rivals knowing what he was up to and getting in there first.

How could it be so much harder to get his hands on an ele-phant, he wondered, than it was a lion or a tiger? Such beasts could survive the six-month journey from India on oats and straw alone instead of raw flesh. Was it just the sheer size of the beast that made it so difficult to transport? And then, recalling the walking mountain, he thought, *that's an awful lot of food.* That was the clev-erness of the East India Company for you, transporting such large beasts across such vast distances.

He filled his pipe once more and ran through various scenarios in his head. Should he send Charlie off to scour the country and nego-tiate with one of the travelling menageries? Or a circus, maybe? Or should he send him abroad to one of those foreign places, Paris per-haps, or Berlin? He had heard he had counterparts across the water. Ha! Wouldn't that be an adventure for the young mopus. Ooh la feckin' la. He could always sign him up to the East India Company, of course, and go and catch one for themselves. *The British have got the matter all sewn up over there in India,* he thought. If he had been a younger man himself then he would be out there with the rest of the lads, setting elephant traps, training them, and then selling them to the British army. Of course he would.

A WEEK LATER a chance meeting in the Great Hall set Grady on the road to finding his elephant. An elderly gentleman, rather portly and well dressed, but in a fashion that would have been out of date ten years ago, was walking the Hall accompanied by two youngsters who dashed from one side to the other in great excite-ment. He wore a red tailcoat with gold epaulets on the shoulders which had grown a bit scraggy, having seen better days. No wig, quite bald on top, but the largest white sideburns and matching moustache, which met on either side of his face. His cream-white shirt parted below the last button of his tailcoat to reveal a little flesh and some wiry hair, same colour as his whiskers. The man strolled with his nose in the air, a swagger stick under his armpit and hands behind his back, every now and then admonishing the youngsters with, "Now now, boys, keep it down," which the boys ignored.

Grady could always smell money and attached himself to the visitor as he inspected the rhinoceros stall. He sidled up to him. "We call him Keebar," said Grady. "You should have seen him when he was a baby, sir. Would almost sing for his supper, he did. Grown a bit now though and, between you and me, sir, needs to be thinking about moving him on to a new place."

The visitor swung round. "Ah. You must be the eponymous Grady, I presume?" he said, removing the swagger stick from his armpit and giving Grady a gentle poke in the belly, which Grady took with great patience.

"In the flesh, sir. And I have the pleasure of making the acquaintance of . . .?"

"Diggory-Diggins . . . Colonel Diggory-Diggins . . . British Army . . . retired . . . at your service, sir."

"Delighted to meet you, sir."

"Likewise," said the Colonel. Both bowed.

"And where were you stationed, sir, if I may be so bold as to ask?"

"West Indies, the Colonies, India. Not many places I haven't seen."

"Then our collection here must seem quite familiar to you."

"Indeed, it quite takes me back, Grady."

"India you say, sir?" Grady enquired.

"India! Up in the North in Sylhet," the Colonel replied. "Elephant territory."

"That's just what this place needs," said Grady, his mind ticking faster than the hearts of the canaries he kept in his aviary. "An elephant."

"Not much I don't know about elephants," the Colonel continued, twiddling the whiskers under his right ear with his finger and thumb. "Used to catch a hundred and fifty, two hundred elephants a year in my heyday."

"That many!" said Grady quite impressed.

"At least!" the Colonel boomed.

"A great asset in battle, I've heard?"

"The best! A high point to shoot from or simply a force to batter the enemy. Good workers too. Get 'em well trained and they can pick up logs and build their own quarters!"

In his mind's eye Grady imagined his own animals creating their own menagerie.

"You want to hear how we used to catch 'em?" the Colonel asked. Without waiting for an answer, he continued, "We would round up a few thousand of the local wallahs, all making one hell of a noise with drums and trumpets and fireworks, and then we would drive the elephants into a ditch which we filled with fruit and vegetables and let them fill their boots. Took a few days, mind, but that was half the fun of it! However . . ." He paused for dramatic effect. "With the really wild ones we would always use a coonkie."

"A coonkie?" said Grady.

"Female decoy," said the Colonel, smiling. "I don't have to tell a man of your experience, Grady, that the animal kingdom is no different from the human world. And what does a young wild bull elephant need but a willing female? Eh? Eh?"

Grady listened, his eyes growing bigger as he allowed his imagination to transport him to the villages of India and the sounds of the animals running riot. He was interrupted by the sound of Teddy Diamond barking.

"Sshhh, boy," said Grady.

The Colonel went on. "We'd set the female up in a trap and she would encourage the lovesick creature in and as soon as he mounted her the elephant drivers would dash out and wrap ropes around the legs of the beast and bring him down."

Teddy Diamond continued to bark. "That must have been quite a sight," said Grady as the two men turned the corner and the lion's cage appeared at the end of the corridor. The Colonel's two boys were in the process of climbing over the low wall.

"Algernon! Nigel! Get down off there," the Colonel shouted.

But Grady was ahead of him and grabbed the boys by their breeches before they could get any nearer the lion's cage.

He wagged his finger at the boys. "You want to be lion fodder?"

The boys looked up at him sheepishly.

"You know how hungry that lion can get for young boy meat?"

"Grandkids, eh?" said the Colonel, laughing. "Easier to handle a drunken troop of press-ganged soldiers from Hull. You got any, Grady?"

Grady laughed and shook his head.

Algernon began to cry.

"Pull yourself together, boy," said the Colonel, giving the boy a cuff. "Spoiled rotten they are. Youngsters today. Useless. Could learn a thing or two from the way those mahouts handled their elephants."

Grady rolled his eyes and tutted in sympathy.

The Colonel continued, "Oh, I've seen some sights, sir. Been on a hunting party with forty thousand men—forty thousand I tell you—and fifteen hundred elephants and god knows how many camels, horses, and bullocks. Those days are behind me now, though." He went back to playing with his whiskers.

"Colonel, may I ask you? I'm keen to obtain an elephant for my . . . my exhibition . . . this emporium of the exotic animal kingdom. Educational, of course. I wondered if you might . . . er . . . have any connections?"

"Well, I certainly owe you one, Grady. Wouldn't do to get back to my daughter's house and tell her little Algernon had been eaten by lions. What? What?"

Algernon cried louder.

The Colonel turned towards Grady, pulled out his swagger stick, and once more gave him a poke in the belly, a bit harder this time, and fixed him with his eye. "Ah, but you've got to go careful with elephants, Grady. One swipe of his trunk and you'll be out cold. He'll use his trunk to pinch any man that comes near you."

"So I've heard."

"And the story of elephants in our cold northern country is not a happy one—nor an honourable one. An elephant does not fare well in fair Albion. Mark my words, Grady. Remember Queen Charlotte's own elephants? And that one up in Dundee, walking the roads of England and falling into a ditch and drowned?"

"Another for the knife of Mr. John Hunter," said Grady, gravely.

The Colonel nodded in agreement. "Those wretched intellectuals can't wait to get their hands on the dead."

Warming to one of his passions, Grady spat and said, "Intellectuals! Where are they when these fine beasts are walking the Great Hall of our menagerie? Tucked up with their books! But as soon as they're dead they are like vultures with their sharp knives ready to cut and carve and splice and slice and hold up the very bones and organs and skins of the carcass so it becomes no more than a novelty."

The Colonel nodded his agreement.

"That elephant in Dundee?" Grady continued. "Why, they peeled that skin off him like an apple and salted it and before you knew where you were it was stuffed and standing in the hall of the Royal Society less than a mile from here."

Grady conveniently forgot to mention the fifty pounds he had been so pleased to receive from Hunter when the baby polar bear he had purchased had been found dead one morning and had already begun to stink.

"And the bones in Dundee's own Repository of Rarities," he added, again failing to mention the abortive bid he had made for the very same bones.

Both men shook their heads.

Moments passed before Grady said, "Colonel, you mentioned royalty earlier. May I share a secret with you?"

"Why certainly, Grady."

Grady looked left and right to check if anyone might overhear, then leaned forwards and said quietly to the Colonel, "I have been tasked from the very highest authority"—he paused to ensure the Colonel understood just how high the authority was—"to obtain an elephant. An elephant of the very best calibre to be the show piece of a brand-new menagerie in Brighton, owned by the Prince himself."

"Go on," said the Colonel, now twisting the whiskers on the other side of his face.

"But I have had no success with finding such a creature. I am quite at my wit's end, and if I ask any of my so-called animal colleagues then they will simply go ahead and procure the creature for themselves. And of course it cannot be just any creature. It is for the future King himself, and if I provide him with an elephant that dies after such a short time then my name—and the name of Grady's Menagerie—will be mud. And I will be ruined."

"Ah, Grady," said the Colonel, opening his hands wide. "Did I not tell you that I know more about elephants than these so-called sailors and traders who bring them to our shores? I think this calls for a drop of the old author."

A FEW HOURS later Grady was shutting up the Exchange for the evening, wondering what Lillian and that chimp of hers might be up to, and wishing that she were there to help close up shop and check on all the creatures. The place felt empty without her, somehow. Not for the first time he gritted his teeth and shook his head and cursed himself for the vanity of the stupid lie he had let escape about Lillian having given actual birth to a monkey.

As he closed the door and locked it behind him, the words of the Colonel resonated in his head. "The elephant is an intelligent beast, Grady, probably the most intelligent animal you or I will ever set eyes on. Do not underestimate him and remember this: you think they love you, but it only takes one swing of the trunk, one stamp with that huge foot of theirs, and you are a dead man."

IT WAS ONLY a week or so later that Grady watched Big Bertha stroll up the Strand without a care in the world. It was love at first sight.

She swung her hips as she walked, taking the occasional glance from under her eyelids as if to see who was watching, grinning all the while. Each step Bertha took was accompanied by the ringing of a set of bells attached to her front feet and the jangling of the heavy chains attached to the back. She was still a very young elephant and only a head taller than her would-be mahouts, Charlie and Jack, who walked beside her, matching smiles on their faces.

Grady had given Charlie the honour of collecting Bertha from her previous owner, a Duke of something or other on an estate in the west country, and a friend of an ex-East India Company man who, in turn, was a friend of Colonel Diggory-Diggins. The Duke had kept his own private menagerie with a small selection of exotic animals to entertain his friends but when his old brown bear was savaged by the lion, and one of the wealthy spectators was killed in the process, the victim's offspring were now demanding some restitution. The Duke had no choice but to sell the elephant.

"One thousand guineas, Charlie," Grady had declared. "Daylight feckin' robbery. Let the old man drink himself to death on it. And mark my words, he will. See if I care." He rubbed his hands together. "I am going to make my fortune with this animal. Maybe open myself a little drinking establishment. Something for the quality mind." He wagged his finger at Charlie. "Those pox-ridden, second-hand, laced mutton, Drury Lane vestal virgins be damned. Only clean whores round my gaff. Ha."

As Charlie walked up Fleet Street towards the Strand, he proudly held onto the decorated harness, which went over Bertha's trunk, behind her ears, and around her rear. The Duke's animal keeper had been at pains to point out the quality of the elephant's tail. "They don't get much better than this. See how long it is? And how very thick at the insertion? See how it tapers well to the end?"

As they passed a horse and cart loaded with loaves of bread, Bertha gave a little swing of her hip, knocking the cart and causing the horse to rear up on its back legs and the bread to roll off the back and scatter all over the street. Big Bertha raised her trunk in the air, gave a victorious bellow, and proceeded to tuck into the loaves.

"Come on, Bertha. Leave that, it's not yours," said Charlie, realising for the first time that Bertha did not go where she did not want to as he and Jack tried to pull her away from the cart, without success. The driver of the cart jumped up and down, asking who was going to pay for it all. She ate for about ten minutes, sprayed herself with a trunkful of dust, and then began to stroll again.

The commotion with the baker's cart had attracted the attention of those who were going about their business at the end of day and now people were leaving the various shops, grocers, coffee houses, and drinking dens to see the elephant for themselves, pointing and nudging each other as Bertha walked by.

The three commenced their journey once more, Bertha sashaying down the road and Charlie keeping to the same slow pace. Kids no bigger than him skipped along beside him and the elephant, firing questions as they walked.

"What is it?"

"Is it a boy or a girl?"

"Is it dangerous?"

"Where are you going?"

Charlie's self-assurance grew and he took off the three-cornered woollen felt cocked hat that Grady had given him to celebrate his promotion to "Number two assistant" and waved it in the air.

"Grady's!" he shouted. "We're going to Grady's Emporium."

Suddenly Bertha's trunk whipped the hat from Charlie's hand and held it just high enough above his head to make Charlie jump for it. Jack laughed and the crowd roared.

"Give it back. Give it back," demanded Charlie, his confidence now replaced with red cheeks. Bertha duly obliged.

"You're a clever girl you are, and no mistake," said Charlie, brushing the dust from his new hat and placing it back on his head. Bertha made no more sudden movements until they were almost home and she spied the trough for watering horses outside Simpson's fish shop. It was time for a drink, accompanied by a very long emptying of the bladder, which resulted in cries of disgust from the crowd that had been following them both—a horse's evacuation being nowhere near as voluminous as the elephant's. Charlie however, having learned from a master showman, shouted to the crowd, "Elephant piss. It's good for you! Proven to give whoever uses it superior health and intelligence!"

Then, to the surprise of the gathering crowd, Bertha suddenly rose up on her hind legs, placing first her left foot and then her right into the trough. The people responded with a collective "Ooh!" as they craned their necks to better see what the animal was up to. Bertha beat the water with her trunk and pummelled the trough with her feet before taking a trunkful of water and spraying herself and then the gathering crowd whose "oohs" turned to good-natured "Oi!"s.

The boys had run ahead to alert everyone at the menagerie of imminent arrival of the procession, and Grady and Button were standing at the entrance, ready to greet her. By the time Charlie, Jack, and Bertha finally arrived, they were followed by a procession of almost a hundred people, all gabbling and chatting and pointing and discussing the various events that had occurred along the way. As she walked towards Grady, she seemed to fix a purposeful eye on him—until becoming distracted by the display of fruit and vegetables in the grocer's a few doors down. She stopped once more and gave another "harrumph," then tucked into a meal of apples and turnips. The greengrocer, who had retreated to the back of the shop, shouted, "You'll have to pay for this, Grady."

But Grady didn't care. All he could think was, *Polito is going to be pea-green about this.*

BUTTON HAD WORKED his way through the crowd and now joined Charlie and a couple of the Exchange boys as they led the elephant through the open doors to take up the place that had been prepared for her. The crowd surged forwards, unwilling to say goodbye to their entertainment, the smaller children at the back using shoulders to jump up and get a last glimpse of the animal's rear as it disappeared into the menagerie. As she made her way towards her new home, Teddy Diamond ran around her feet, barking all the while, until Bertha pushed him away with a gentle nudge of her trunk.

Sensing a disappointment that might turn ugly, Grady climbed up on his chair and addressed the mob. "Ladies and gentlemen, you are privileged to be amongst the first—the *first* I say—to welcome the new addition to our family of animals. Tonight our young lady will rest and take her evening meal. Some may say she has eaten enough already—" He paused to check the mood. "But we are going to be feeding that growing creature at least one hundred and fifty pounds of hay each day!"

The crowd "Ahhhhed" its approval.

"I urge you to return tomorrow when Bertha is settled and ready to, er, receive her visitors." He gave a knowing smile, scanning the assembled with his eyes, seemingly meeting the gaze of each one, and gave a bow. The crowd chuckled.

"In the meantime, please take one of our tokens, our specially minted tokens, and when you return, on presentation of this 'ere coin, you may gain admission for *half* . . . yes, *half* . . . our normal price at just ninepence a head."

"It's usually a shilling to get in!" cried a voice that Grady ignored.

"Now, please don't rush at once. Mrs. Ogden, get those tokens ready."

As soon as the doors were closed behind them, Grady stood in front of Bertha, inspecting his purchase. Man and beast were roughly the same height and he was able to look her directly in the eye, taking in her thick grey hide, the enormous ears, and the big black eyes framed with lashes. Bertha held his gaze, opening and closing her eyes, and something inside him melted. Meanwhile, Button walked around the elephant with his hands on his hips, affecting an air of knowledge but making sure to get out of the way whenever she swung her trunk.

On impulse, Grady reached in his pocket for one of the sugar lumps he kept for the horses and offered it to Bertha, who took it delicately with her trunk as if she were using a pair of sugar tongs. She popped it in her mouth and then patted Grady's head as if to say "thank you."

"Did you see that?" Grady exclaimed, beaming.

Charlie nodded, eyes open wide. "She's a really clever girl," said Charlie. "She nicked me 'at earlier!"

"And look at the length of her trunk," said Grady, reaching out to stroke between her eyes. "The Colonel said that was one of the signs of a great elephant."

"Let's get her in the pen, Grady," said Button, producing a bag of apples from a satchel that swung round his neck. "We can take a better look at her when she is secured."

Grady snatched the bag from him. "Give that to me, Button," he said. "Come on, my darlin', let's get you settled." He let Bertha take one of the apples from his hand.

"Come on. This way," Grady said as he set off and Bertha followed, chomping on the apple as she sashayed through the Great

Hall towards her new home, tail swishing from side to side, seemingly oblivious and unafraid of the other caged exhibits despite the huge noise with which they greeted the new inmate. Charlie held on to the harness and Button followed them, keeping his distance but taking the opportunity to examine her all the while—the steady gait, the length of her trunk, the thick black toenails.

There had been a reorganisation of the various pens and cages in order to make extra space for Bertha. She would now have her own presentation room, set up with twenty stools for the audience on one side of a low wall about waist high and the star of the show on the other. A new admission booth was placed at the entrance, and a poster tacked above it, which proclaimed Bertha to be THE ONLY LIVING ELEPHANT IN LONDON!

When they reached the newly created pen, she pulled up short, giving a loud harrumph, and began to bang her trunk on the floor.

"Ouch!" cried Charlie. "She almost pulled me arm off!"

Much coaxing and wooing and dangling of the apple bag got her moving again, and the boys ran round and quickly attached her leg chain to the large ring that had been set into the wall. Grady fussed around the pen.

"Do you think she's got enough hay? She'll be warm enough, won't she, Button?"

Charlie piped up. "She likes the water, Grady. You should have seen her earlier with her feet in the trough outside Simpson's."

"Good call, Charlie. You!" he said, pointing at the smallest of the Exchange boys. "Run and get that old tin bath Mrs. Ogden uses for washing out the tea cloths. And get that water barrel set up too."

"Yes sir," the boy said and disappeared.

Half an hour later, the water barrel and tin bath had both been installed to Grady's satisfaction. The impresario stood back and folded his arms to admire the elephant, which was tucking into the feast of hay.

"So what do you think, Button?" Grady asked. "A fine specimen, is she not?"

Bertha proceeded to dip her trunk in the water barrel and spray her back. She then did the same again and sprayed the boys, catching Button in the face in the process.

Everyone laughed. "You've got a winner there, Mr. Grady," shouted Charlie.

BERTHA RECOGNISED GRADY'S footsteps from down the Hall and would stand up as soon as she heard him coming, then pat him on the head with her trunk by way of greeting. Everyone soon learned that if they were looking for Grady, they should go straight to the elephant room where Grady would most likely be found, either on all fours cleaning between Big Bertha's toes and ensuring the chain was not rubbing her legs, or calling for more buckets of water as he supervised the boys scrubbing down her tough hide to keep it as moist as possible. Button would often look in on the new addition but was careful to keep his distance.

Fifty miles away, as Lillian, Letitia, and Samson took their daily stroll along the cliff, the relationship between Grady and Bertha continued to blossom, with Grady taking great delight in the little tricks Bertha would reveal. She basked in his approval. A particular favourite included reaching over from her side of the low wall to shake the pockets and handbags of her audience and see if they jangled. Visitors soon took the hint and would place an old penny on the tip of her trunk, which Bertha then dropped into a box Charlie nailed to the wall of her enclosure. When they broke the box open, the money would be used to keep her plied with sugar lumps. It soon emerged that the elephant was quite adept with her trunk and was able to pick up the smallest of objects, such as a watch or a coin, as well as quickly sifting through the hay to find the sugar no matter how hard they tried to hide it.

"Welcome, ladies and gentlemen, boys and girls, to the greatest and largest animal on the earth and the only elephant in captivity in the whole of the city of London!" went Grady's patter, which he performed at least six times a day in front of the elephant's pen. "I give you Big Bertha, ladies and gentlemen, the latest in a long line of elephants to grace our shores, the first being a gift to the good King Henry from the French king over five hundred years ago . . ."

While Grady was talking, he would pretend to ignore Bertha reaching into his pocket with her trunk in search of her favourite treat. Alerted to the theft, he would turn and express shock and surprise as the audience laughed.

"See how she flaps her ears," Grady would say, and Bertha would give an obliging flutter. He had no idea how she had learned to perform in this manner but was delighted all the same at her ability to both entertain and be a marvel that visitors would pay to see.

"And they wash themselves with dirt, ladies and gentlemen, and it keeps them cool. We prefer to use water, though, don't we, boys and girls?" Bertha would take a trunkful of water and spray it over herself and then the audience, who roared with delight.

Then he would adopt a more serious tone.

"But do not let the docile look of this beautiful creature deceive you. Oh no! With just one swipe of her trunk, she can knock a man down dead. Why, the Emperor Akhbar the Great himself had an entire fleet of elephants that he used as his own grim executioners to destroy anyone who spoke out against him.

"The elephant can taunt its prey or just kill with one stamp of his foot," Grady would continue, at which point Bertha would lift her front foot and bang it against the tin bath, causing the assembled audience to jump.

ONE EVENING, AS the boys were settling the animals down for the night, Grady was lingering in the elephant room, chatting away to Bertha and planning a final smoke of his pipe before he left for the night.

"Join me, Charlie?" he said to his young assistant and pulled up a chair to the small table and set out a bottle and two glasses. Charlie sat down opposite him.

"Miss Lillian should be back soon, shouldn't she, Grady?"

"Who knows?" Grady sighed, shrugged his shoulders, and continued to fill his pipe. "We miss her, don't we, Teddy Diamond?" he said, reaching down to stroke the dog, who was busy scratching away at a flea on its leg that he couldn't quite reach.

"Just tip us a drink, Charlie."

The boy uncorked the bottle and poured two glasses.

"You've told Miss Lillian that you're keeping Bertha, then?" Charlie asked.

Before Grady could reply, Bertha's trunk appeared, snatched the glass just as it reached his lips, and knocked the contents into her mouth.

"Hey!" said Charlie.

"That was your one, Charlie!" said Grady, laughing. "You liked that, didn't you, my lady?" Bertha replied with a harrumph and tapped her trunk on the floor.

"Run and get a jug of ale, Charlie. Let's see what she makes of that. And while we're waiting, let's 'ave another, shall we, Bertha?" He poured two more shots.

"Of course I'm bloody keeping her," said Grady.

Twenty

IT TOOK FAR LONGER TO GET back from Brighton than it had taken to get there. Lillian reserved the first coach with an available seat, but unfortunately it was the slow service, which seemed to stop at every available stagecoach post. The journey had been quite uncomfortable as she attempted to keep Samson wrapped up whilst squashed between an elderly couple who chatted to each other and ate throughout the entire journey. Each time one turned to talk to the other, she would be sprayed with crumbs from some pastry or cake. They had waved away her offer to change seats so they could sit together, as both needed to be near the window "just in case." All she could do was lean her head back or else receive a spiteful dig in the ribs should it fall on one or the other's shoulder.

Samson slept quietly in her arms as the countryside swept by. As the wheels on the coach turned, they made their own music which seemed to say, *The nimbletongue is a false tongue . . . the nimbletongue is a false tongue.* How on earth could she have fallen for such fake platitudes and protestations of friendship? How quickly she had put her trust in Letitia! What sort of complete fool was she to have believed that silly little madam and her pretensions, when all along . . .

And Grady, how on earth could he have told such a terrible lie? That she had given actual birth to a monkey?

Letitia's face! The way Samson had clawed her cheek and produced so much blood!

All Lillian wanted to do was to get home to her husband, but she feared the reception that lay ahead.

She drifted in and out of sleep, the picture of Noah's ark from her lodgings in Brighton vividly in her mind whenever she woke. And suddenly she was home.

LILLIAN WAS QUITE exhausted by the time she found herself at the door of 23 Neal Street. Samson hung around her neck, groggy from travel. She had not even raised her hand to the knocker when the door was thrown open and Mrs. Tomkins was standing there, her arms open wide and looking as if she were about to cry.

"Lillian!" she exclaimed. "Mr. Button, Mr. Featherstone. Look who's home!" Before she could take another step or draw breath, her husband was standing in front of her.

"Lillian, my darling," he said, staring at her, not knowing what to do. "We weren't expecting you for hours."

Featherstone appeared at the door. "What's this? Why are you standing there, man?"

Lillian swung Samson round. "Please take him, Mr. Featherstone." He hoisted the chimp onto his hip.

"John," said Lillian, holding out her hand. Her husband moved forwards, took his wife in his arms, and held her. She felt the rough weave of his woollen jacket against her skin and took in the smell of tobacco and fireside smoke. The warmth from his body enveloped her and she put her cheek to his and whispered, "I never want to go away again," to which Button replied, "And I will never let you."

Featherstone smiled as he watched the two embrace. "My dears, let's get this young lady by the fire and then we can hear all about her seaside adventures."

Silver the parrot greeted her with an almighty screech as soon as she entered the room, and ten minutes later Samson was fast asleep upstairs in his cot and all were seated on chairs around the fireplace with cups of hot chocolate in their hands.

Featherstone said, "I hear they go into the water up to their heads and with all their clothes still on?"

"Well not quite," said Lillian, smiling at the family surrounding her and delighted with the unexpectedly warm homecoming.

"We tried your sea water," Featherstone said. "I drank the whole bottle, but it didn't seem to agree with me at all."

"I told you not to drink it, you silly old fool," said Mrs. Tomkins, and turning to Lillian, she confided, "There's no telling him, you know."

Lillian gave half a smile and nodded.

"Now now!" said Featherstone, wagging his finger and leaning forwards to poke the crackling fire as a companionable silence fell on the room.

Eventually Featherstone said, "We heard about your terrible experience with that young lady you met."

"Letitia," Lillian replied.

"She told everyone you had given actual birth to Samson?"

Lillian nodded and her bottom lip trembled. Mrs. Tomkins handed her a handkerchief.

"And conspired to sell tickets to see them both behind her back," said Button, standing up and pulling the shawl around his wife's shoulders.

"She told everyone I was called the Monkey Lady," said Lillian, dabbing her eyes with the handkerchief.

"Oh my dear!" Mrs. Tomkins said.

"I expected something of the sort, but not to be her freak."

"And this is all Grady's doing, I take it?" Featherstone asked.

Lillian nodded.

"That man," said Featherstone, shaking his head. "Do anything for a guinea."

"I must get me to bed," said Mrs. Tomkins, standing up with a huge sigh. "And you must be very tired."

"I must go to bed too," said Featherstone. "Got Mrs. Pickles and her polly parrot to visit tomorrow. Always a strain."

He leaned forwards and gave Lillian a peck on the cheek.

"It's good to have you home again, my dear."

"Thank you, Mr. Featherstone," said Lillian. "It's very good to be here."

"I'll get you a candle to take up with you," said Mrs. Tomkins and the pair departed, leaving Button and Lillian on their own.

Husband and wife sat in silence for a few moments until Button finally asked, "What about Sir Thomas and the arrangements for the new menagerie? Did he know what Letitia was up to?"

"I am fairly sure he did not. On the one or two occasions I met him, he always asked if Letitia was looking after me and I did not suspect any foul play on his part."

Button nodded as Lillian continued.

"I don't think for a minute that he even considered I had given actual birth to a chimp. He had brought Letitia along with him that day we met at the Exchange as an entertainment and when he saw how . . . enamoured I was of her he used her to encourage me to Brighton. I think it was all her own idea."

"And who is Barclay?"

"Mr. Barclay is the man really in charge of the new establishment for the Prince, and he certainly knows what he is doing. Sir Thomas is simply the procurer of the animals. Oh, John, it really *is* the most wonderful place—so new and clean. The animals will be so happy there. Leonidas will have his very own run, not cooped up like he is now."

Lillian fondled the lion's tooth that hung around her neck.

"And Keebar the rhinoceros. Not such a baby now, of course, but she should go to Brighton as well. She's just too big for the Exchange."

Button agreed. "I think you're right, my dear."

Lillian looked at her husband. "And did you manage to stop Grady from getting that elephant?" she asked.

Button was silent and did not meet her eyes.

"He's gone ahead and got it, hasn't he?" she said with a sigh.

"Don't judge straight away, my dear. I think you might be quite surprised about developments at the Exchange. Grady seems to have changed somewhat."

"I can't wait to see everyone. It feels like I've been gone so long," said Lillian, closing her eyes.

"First thing tomorrow we will go together. But for now, you must rest. Get your strength back. Your room is ready for you and I will be next door."

Button placed a hood over Silver's cage and set the guard in front of the fire. They lit a candle and together they walked upstairs, hand in hand.

When they reached her door, Button said, "Samson is quite asleep, I believe?"

Lillian nodded.

Her husband opened the door and pulled her inside.

That night Lillian luxuriated in stretching out her long legs in bed once more, and when she reached out her arm, her husband was beside her.

As THEY TOOK their breakfast the next morning the postman arrived with a letter.

"It's for you, my dear," said Mrs. Tomkins.

"Who can it be from?" Lillian wondered as she unpicked the red seal, unfolded the letter, and began to read.

My dearest Lillian (she read),

I came to call for you today but was surprised to hear from Mrs. Fortescue that you had already left—and apparently in such a hurry. I had so enjoyed our talks and discussions and was looking forward to many more.

I wanted to write and tell you something that had been niggling at me for some time now, about that young lady, Miss Nimbletongue. I was so sure I knew her from somewhere but I could not quite place her, especially when you said she was the companion of Sir Thomas. I thought she must be a person of breeding and quality. I must confess I did not know how you could spend so much time with her as she never made much of an impression on me, her responses always being so short and sharp.

I saw her a little earlier today in the hallway and she had two long scratches down the side of her cheek. When I asked how she had come about such an injury she just shook her head, turned away from me, and pulled a scarf around her face. Indeed, she seemed a little distressed but walked off before I could say anything.

And then it came to me.

She had briefly been in the same company as I when we performed Midsummer Night's Dream *at a little theatre just outside of Cambridge. That would have been about two years ago now. But she had been dismissed for dipping in the pockets of our fellow troopers. Not the done thing at all darling, as we are not the most flush of professions, as I am sure you know, and to steal from your own? Well . . .*

I thought I should let you know what I had remembered just as soon as I possibly could, which is why I came looking for you today only to find that you are gone. Hence my letter. I am sorry to say I do not believe her to be worthy of the status of "friend" and do not believe Sir Thomas's interest to be of the pure nature one might expect from a man of his standing.

But what do I know? I am merely a woman.

I do hope that dreadful creature has not done you any harm and that she had nothing to do with your abrupt departure.

I shall return to London in a few weeks and look forward to renewing your and Samson's acquaintance once more and, of course, to meeting your husband.

Please look out for my letters in The Lady *magazine and I shall see you in London before the winter.*

Your very dear friend

Emily Lovetrue

LILLIAN FOLDED THE letter and put it in her pocket.

THE FIRST FEW drops of rain were just starting to splash in the gutter as Button and Lillian, with Samson on her hip, opened the front door. A hackney carriage was called for to take them the short distance down to the Strand. The road had already turned to mud and the wheels of the carriage moved slowly as the couple sat and watched the street sellers take cover from the weather.

"Not seen weather like this before," the driver shouted back as they made their way through Covent Garden, past the shops and theatres, down Bryden's Street, Catherine's Street, and at last onto the Strand. They got out of the carriage and ran towards the entrance. The old familiar smell of the place hit Lillian's nostrils straight away. She took a deep lungful of the familiar menagerie aroma and smiled.

Despite her caution about keeping an elephant at the Exchange, Lillian was excited at the prospect of seeing one for the first time. But first she needed to run of the gauntlet of hellos and how-are-yous. As soon as young Charlie spotted her, he grabbed her hand and started pulling her towards the back of the Hall. "This way, Miss!" he said. "You must come see. This way."

She could hear the babble of excitement and a scraping of chairs from the other end of the Great Hall over the sound of the rain, which continued to beat steadily on the roof of the Exchange. As she turned the corner, she saw at least fifty people tightly packed into the space allocated as the elephant's room, although there were only chairs for twenty. They were all jostling for a better position, standing on their toes or laying claim to the chairs laid out in three short rows—all to get a better look into one of the enclosures.

"There's more here than those who visited the baby rhino or the kangaroo," said Lillian to her husband, who had caught up with her.

"A large beast draws a large crowd," Button replied.

As Lillian walked towards the gathering, she could just about see the wrinkled grey skin and the tops of two flapping ears, but not quite over the heads of those already watching. Charlie ran before her, his slender frame threading through the crowd till he reached Grady, who had just finished his elephant speech and taken his seat and was reaching underneath his chair for a sneaky drop of the old author. Teddy Diamond leaned against his thigh. Charlie whispered in Grady's ear and pointed at Lillian. The menagerie owner's eyes widened with pleasure. He jumped to his feet.

"Ladies and gentlemen, boys and girls," he boomed and with a sweeping gesture of his hands made the introduction. "Meet Lillian, the mistress of this fine establishment!" Those who had been listening to Grady's talk turned as one to see Lillian standing there, six feet tall and a bit with cropped blonde hair in leather trousers and white cambric shirt, a chimp on her hip and the vet by her side. Teddy Diamond barked in joyful recognition and ran towards them. Samson immediately jumped on his back and the pair trotted off as the crowd made way for them.

"She is newly returned from consulting with our very own Prince George," Grady proclaimed, only to be interrupted by a large clap of thunder. For a brief second there was silence whilst everyone looked up at the ceiling. Then he continued, "Consulting on the opening of a brand-new menagerie in Brighton, which this very establishment has been called upon to be the supplier of its most exotic and rarest of specimens in order to populate aforesaid enterprise."

The crowd murmured their approval and Lillian gave a small nod of acknowledgement.

"Lillian, may I have the pleasure of introducing you to our newest resident attraction—Big Bertha." The crowd leaned away to let Lillian see Bertha for the first time.

The elephant was sitting on her bottom, big grey ears twitching and sounding like flapping sails as they brushed away the various flying insects that called the menagerie their home. Strange symbols had been painted down her long trunk, which she now dipped in and out of an enormous manger of hay. She appeared to be chewing in the corner of her mouth, staring at Lillian and smiling all the while.

"Pleased to meet you, Bertha," Lillian said and gave a small dip and a curtsey, keeping half an eye on her husband's reaction. To her surprise, and the delight of the watching crowd, the elephant pulled herself up to her fullest height, raised her trunk in the air, and gave a deafening harrumph. The crowd leaned into each other for safety with an uncertain "Ooh?"

She knew it would be big—bigger than the rhino even—but nothing had prepared her for the sheer size of an elephant. Bertha did not disappoint.

The crowd watched spellbound as Bertha knelt down on her forelegs and sneaked her trunk over the low wall towards Lillian. She proceeded to walk it around Lillian's head and face and up and down her body, finally taking her hand and gently pumping it up and down in a gesture of greeting.

"Oh Grady," Lillian exclaimed. "Isn't she the sweetest thing?"

"Ah yes," he replied, as he sucked in his breath with a contented sigh. "That's my beautiful gel."

"And look at those eyelashes!"

Lillian turned to look at the old showman who was patting his pockets, for his pipe and tobacco she presumed. His face seemed changed somehow.

Turning to see if her husband was watching, she said, "Isn't she charming, John?" unaware that Bertha's trunk had now found its way into her pocket and was surreptitiously looking for whatever tasty morsel she might have secreted. Slowly Lillian became aware of the tickle in her trousers and twisted around to see Bertha triumphantly holding up a large piece of sugar that Lillian had saved from the recent journey. Playing to the crowd, Bertha gave a victorious bellow. Sensing the theatre of the occasion, Lillian stood with hands on hips and said in mock surprise, "Why Bertha. You naughty girl." The crowd roared with laughter.

She glanced at Grady, who was also laughing.

Ah that's it, she thought with a grin. Was his face softened somehow?

Grady, who had found his pipe, now commenced to fill it, tamping it down with his forefinger. He gestured to Charlie, who darted forwards to light it, but before he had a chance, Bertha's trunk swept forwards and knocked the clay instrument out of Grady's hands.

"I don't think she likes your pipe, Grady," said Button with secret delight, and the crowd laughed as Grady looked about him in mock confusion.

Lillian stood watching while Bertha entertained her audience, the long trunk finding its way into various visitors' pockets, taking pennies and popping them into the box behind her, helping herself to a watch on a chain and passing it to someone else. Grady's eyes did not leave her and Lillian noticed he did not try to light the pipe again.

As they watched, Lillian whispered to her husband, "Grady certainly seems quite fond of that elephant."

"Indeed," her husband agreed. "He seems to have completely forgotten the rest of the animals around here."

"I've never seen him so . . . so . . . sentimental!" said Lillian.

"We did say you might find matters slightly altered." Button smiled.

"And is she in good health, John?"

"I am not entirely sure. Mr. Featherstone said he had had the opportunity to get close to an elephant many years ago but did not have enough experience to make an assured assessment. We talked to Grady's friend, the Colonel, and he said she seemed about the right size for an eight-year-old. She has had a thorough once-over and we are all agreed she is in fine health for now," he said.

"For now?"

"Elephants need a lot of care and have never fared well in England, I understand. The change of diet, temperature, et cetera. One of the biggest lessons I have learned from Mr. Featherstone is that it is no easy matter to simply transplant a creature from one climate to another and expect it to thrive."

Lillian nodded her assent, thinking of her own experiences in Brighton.

"I expect it is a lonely existence to be only one of a kind. The Colonel says elephants are quite social creatures and need to be with their own, that they do not breed in captivity. And her enclosure seems so small for such a large creature."

Lillian sighed and took in a deep breath. "It is a bigger pen than Mr. Barclay was prepared to offer in Brighton. Still, Bertha is young and will need room to grow."

THAT NIGHT THE rain continued to beat down on London and did not stop for many an hour, the Thames filling up the Fleet ditch that lay beneath the Strand until finally it had nowhere to go but up into the street.

And along with the dirty river water came the rats.

Twenty-One

THE RAIN CONTINUED TO BATTER THE roof of the Exchange throughout the night, but over at the Bell Grady slept right through it, ably assisted by a drop of the old author and, for only a few hours more, blissfully unaware that nightmares could happen in the daytime too.

When he walked in the front door the next morning, the first thing he noticed was silence. The boys were not going about the daily business with their usual slow lack of enthusiasm. Instead they stood talking quietly in small groups of two or three, hands on hips or holding their caps and scratching their heads, taking in the scene in front of them.

Overnight their place of work had been transformed.

The Thames had taken more than its fair share of the night's extraordinary rainfall and had overflowed into the ancient sewer known as the Fleet. In turn, the effluent from the Fleet had nowhere to go and had made its way up into all the establishments along the Strand, including the menagerie, to claim Grady's empire as its own. It rose as high as a man's knees then slipped silently away to leave behind an unwanted gift of black sludge soup made up of the various sweepings, fish heads, mud, bones, and dead things that were usually content to sit undisturbed in the riverbed. The muck lay everywhere like discarded piles of old clothes. It dripped from the bars people leaned on to watch the animals in their cages. And it stank to the point of gagging even Grady.

"What's happened?" he asked quietly, surveying the disaster.

"Been flooded out, Mr. Grady," one of the boys replied, pulling his shirt up over his nose.

"Flooded out?" he repeated, then spat on the floor and surveyed the room. "What about the animals? What have we lost?"

Small black puddles of water remained throughout the Great Hall. Except for a heavy drip of rain, like a fat man taking his seat in an overstuffed chair over and over again, all was silent. *Plop. Plop. Plop.* None of the yips and barks and tweetings that usually greeted the start of a new day.

In just a few short seconds Grady took in the entire scenario before his thoughts were interrupted by the loud urgent harrumphs of the elephant, interspersed with shrieks of fear and panic.

"God's wounds!" he shouted. "What's happening to Bertha?" He was greeted by the boys' wide-eyed stunned silence as they stood gripped by inertia, their familiar environment now transformed into a monster's den.

"Don't just stand there!" he shouted and began to run as fast as he could to the back of the Hall. He slipped and slithered in the black sludge and slime, once, twice, picking himself up and almost slipping again in his anxiety to get to her. Bertha's screams grew louder.

When he reached the elephant, she was thrashing her trunk from side to side, eyes wide and white with fear.

"Bertha! What is it? What is it Bertha, my love?"

When he looked down, he saw the rats. Hundreds upon hundreds of them—a rabble, a swarm, a disgusting pack. Many were already dead, stamped on by the furious and frightened elephant, brown furry bodies split open and innards spilled all over the straw, a pink-red stinking mess of blood and guts. But there were still just as many alive as dead, and they were crawling over each other to get to their prize of the tasty morsels lodged in between poor Bertha's toes.

Grady seized one of the brooms leaning against the side of the enclosure and began to beat at the vermin, shouting all the while, "Tom, Charlie get in 'ere!" interspersed with, "It's all right, Bertha, it's all right" and "Get those fecking rats out of here!"

Now the menagerie seemed to rouse from the shock and burst into life with the inhabitants responding to the screams of the elephant with their own fearful retorts. The wolves howled, the lion roared, and the hyena made its strange strangulated half-bark, half-frenzied cry. The birds screeched and flapped in their aviary and the boys awakened from their stupor.

Grady pointed at the brooms and barked his orders. "Grab something, anything, just beat the little feckers."

The boys looked at each other with open mouths and, turning this way and that, searched around for something with which to tackle the horde of rats. Shirts and waistcoats came off and the air was filled with a whipping sound as the rats were beaten away.

It was all over by the time Lillian, Button, and Samson arrived and Grady was in the process of dispensing sixpences to the boys, who recruited their friends to come and help clear up the black mess.

It had taken nearly twenty minutes to quell the rats' attack and the rest of the morning to clean up the corpses, which were being collected in buckets or on shovels. Teddy Diamond and Samson ran in between everyone's legs; the dog grabbing rats that were still alive and finishing them off with a vigorous shake in his jaw; whilst Samson scampered screeching, picking up dead vermin and making a thorough inspection before surrendering them to the boys' pleas to "'and it over, Samson, will ya?"

The rain continued all day as if God were wringing the last few drops from his dishcloth. The doors to the menagerie stayed shut. Mrs. Ogden arrived for normal opening time and immediately went home. "You don't pay me enough to deal with that, Grady," she said and turned on her heel. The few visitors there were on that black drizzly day were refused entry. The only real casualties had been in the aviary, when the birds had taken fright and flight and crashed into the bars and each other. The boys collected endless buckets of mud and slime and tipped them outside the Exchange in a growing, stinking pile. The dead rats and birds were delivered to the other residents who had never eaten so well.

Leonidas sat in his cage, one paw crossed over the other, running his tongue around his muzzle, for once enjoying an unusually full belly.

By nightfall the dead things had been removed, the sludge soup cleaned away, and the straw replaced. Having satisfied herself that all was well, Lillian joined Grady at the entrance to make her report.

"I'll be bloody bankrupt," he said.

Lillian lay her hand on Grady's sleeve. "Charlie told me he thought Bertha was going to knock that wall down," she said.

Grady gave a small shrug without looking at her.

"It's too small a space, Grady," Lillian insisted. "She won't always be a baby. Look how Keebar has grown."

"Maybe," he mumbled quietly, still not meeting her eye, instead patting his body for his pipe.

"I know how precious she is to you."

"Aye, she is that." He pulled the tobacco from his pocket, his hand shaking.

"What if the Fleet rises again?"

He turned on her, shaking her hand from his sleeve. "Just leave it, will you?"

But Lillian would not. "She can only get bigger."

Then Grady had an idea.

THE VERY NEXT day visitors to the menagerie were surprised to see men and women hurrying through the Exchange carrying piles of dresses over their arms. Backwards and forwards they scurried, leav-

ing the garments on the cart that waited patiently outside, the horse
tucking into a bag of oats hanging round its neck, only to return ten
minutes later with another armful. Grady stood leaning against Mrs.
Ogden's admission booth, smoking his pipe and smiling.

"What is happening, Grady?" asked Lillian when she arrived.

"Getting rid of those seamstresses," he replied.

"Whatever for?"

He turned to face her. "Needs the room, don't we?" he said and
strode off.

Getting Bertha to move into the new display room required a
reinforced ramp laid over the staircase and Grady and Charlie at
the front with a bag of apples, sugar, and a flagon of beer. Four boys
pushed and heaved from the back, encouraging Bertha to walk up
and into her new home. All the time Grady whispered endearments in Bertha's ear: "You'll be alright here, my love," and "No
more rats," and "Never leave you again."

Three hours later, Grady stood back to admire the new arrangement. The room was even bigger than he had expected, now the
seamstresses had taken out all their cottons and silks, feathers
and bows, and other assorted paraphernalia. There was certainly
room for a table and a few chairs for visitors, although it was much
smaller than the spectator space downstairs.

The exhausted team sat down, wiped their brows with the backs
of their hands, and called for refreshments They exchanged puz-
zled glances as Grady cleared a corner of Bertha's enclosure and
unpacked his bedroll. Bertha chomped happily on the fresh hay,
occasionally stopping to dip her trunk in Grady's beer while Teddy
Diamond scrabbled around in the hay trying to make his own nest.

Grady found a chair, leaned back, crossed his legs at the ankles,
and filled his pipe. "This is where I will sleep from now on," he
declared. "Be on the safe side. Just in case."

THAT EVENING BUTTON and Lillian sat together in front of the parlour fire, Featherstone having long abandoned the pair to attend to matters in his study. There was an uneasy quiet, as each sat with their own thoughts.

Button broke the silence. "I've been thinking, Lillian," he said.

Lillian looked up from the book she had been reading.

"Maybe Grady has the right idea, special quarters for the elephant and all that," he said.

Lillian nodded her head. "I *am* a bit worried about him being alone with her so much though, especially as the majority of the animals are going to Brighton."

"It's not just him on his own though, is it?" Button persisted.

"And it means that we cannot charge extra admission to see her," Lillian mused, flipping the pages of her book.

"Teddy Diamond is never far from his side, though, is he?" he continued. "And Samson loves Teddy Diamond."

At last Lillian understood that her husband was trying to make a point, put down her book, and turned her attention to him. "What is it you're trying to say, exactly?" she asked.

Button looked at her. "I am saying that maybe it's time for you to let Samson go, let him live full time at the menagerie, along with the other animals."

Lillian blinked but said nothing.

"I mean, it was Grady that brought him into the house in the first place," Button insisted.

Still she said nothing.

Button raised his voice. "It's time to choose, Lillian," he insisted. "I've been a patient man, but everyone thinks you gave birth to him. I've heard them call you 'monkey lady' behind your back. And what does that make me? The monkey man?"

Tears pricked her eyes as she looked at her husband and said, in as calm a voice as she could muster, "What has become of the man I married? The man who wanted to take me to the Tower to see the lions? The man who delighted in seeing birds that could talk, who wanted to provide a better place for the animals?"

He let out a sharp breath and leaned forwards to take her hand.

She flicked it away and stood, fists clenched, teeth gritted as she tried to control her anger. "I will *not* choose between the man I love and the poor creature which has been placed in my care by whatever higher agency has seen fit to entrust me with this task."

"Lillian, I—"

With as much dignity as she could muster, she picked up her book once more, walked towards the shelves by the fireplace, and calmly put it back in the gap she had made just an hour or so earlier. She dusted a few crumbs from her shirt, drew in a deep breath, and with her back towards him said, "I had hoped we had reached an understanding, you and I, but . . ."

She let the rest of her sentence hang unfinished, as if expecting an answer.

When none came, she turned to look at him. He sat with his head hanging, hands clasped in despair.

"I love you, John. I love you from the bottom of my heart."

He looked up at her and she could see tears starting to form in his eyes.

"But don't ask me to give up Samson."

She walked towards the door, opened it, then turned towards her husband once more. "I'll pack my bag now and leave in the morning."

Button opened his mouth to say something, then closed it. He wiped his eyes with the sleeve of his coat and when he looked again the room was empty.

Twenty-Two

"THIS WILL BE AN EVENT!" DECLARED Grady, clapping his hands. "All of London will know my name."

Lillian had been living back in her old room at the Exchange for two weeks when the day finally arrived for the animals chosen by Sir Thomas to make the long-planned journey to the Prince's menagerie in Brighton. In order to transport the selection Grady had rented a number of wagons, adding metal bars to six of them so they became, in effect, cages on wheels. A fleet of six white Arabian horses had also been acquired, which would pull the rhino's enclosure. Two horses would suffice for Leonidas. Ever the showman, Grady employed two of the seamstresses he had just thrown out of the Exchange to create banners in red and yellow satin, with gold tasselled trim, which displayed the words GRADY'S EMPORIUM—LONDON TO BRIGHTON. BY APPOINTMENT TO HIS MAJESTY. These were draped along the wagons.

Joining the departing caravan would be two llamas, a tiger, a tapir, a black swan, two porcupines, a warthog, a hyena, three wolf cubs, and a dozen or more small cages of birds—including a Brazilian condor, a pair of Indian doves, and an Egyptian ibis.

Work had begun before dawn and the boys hugged themselves

and stamped their feet to keep warm. Grady was already dressed for the occasion in his finest waistcoat, silver tiger claw proudly on display, wig on straight for a change. He stood barking orders and pointing and directing the boys as they rushed in and out of the Exchange carrying buckets, brooms, leather harnesses, bales of straw, and various other animal paraphernalia needed to keep the animals fed and secure on their journey. Teddy Diamond chased amongst the boys' legs, barking, Samson riding his back, clinging onto his fur and screeching.

The wagons and horses stood patiently in the street outside the menagerie, ready and waiting to receive their occupants. A crowd was starting to form as passers-by on their way to work stopped to see what was happening. In anticipation of the event, Grady had commissioned a ballad singer to write a special song in commemoration and he sang the words to himself as walked up and down the caravan checking straps and ties.

It was a glorious sight to see, you see,
When the animals went to sea, you see . . .

LILLIAN STOOD AT the Exchange entrance watching the proceedings. Mrs. Ogden was with her, arms crossed, lips pursed, and disapproval oozing from every pore.

"Is he doing the right thing, though, Lillian?" she asked, shaking her head, mind seemingly made up. "All he seems to care about since the flood is that bloomin' elephant."

As if on cue, a loud *harrumph* could be heard from the back of the hall.

Lillian smiled. "Bertha knows something is going on and doesn't like not being the centre of attention."

"Only be Bertha left at this rate and that's not enough to run an animal business, is it?"

"Plenty of stock left, Mrs. O," said Lillian, as bright as she could muster.

"The good stuff's going to Brighton. All he cares about is that bloody elephant." Mrs. Ogden crossed her arms beneath her chest, which was getting higher the more agitated she became.

"I'm sure that's not the case. You are worrying unnecessarily. Really. The animals are all going to the Prince's own Brighton palace. They will be well taken care of—"

"It's all very well you worrying about the animals, but what about me? Where's the new stuff, eh? Eh? And I'm too old to be getting work anywhere else."

The two women were interrupted by Charlie shouting directions to the boys as they began to move Keebar the rhino towards its wagon.

"Careful now, lads," he ordered.

The commotion was starting to attract an audience, and those who had gathered to watch the proceedings glanced uncertainly between themselves, then back again to the huge creature which had been secured, they hoped, with a complicated contraption of leather straps.

A few days earlier Grady had told Lillian, "What you need to know, my dear, is that the rhino and the elephant are deadly enemies. Bertha does not like the rhino being here at all. No, not at all. I can tell. And the rhino is simply too big. Too big." Then, mumbling to himself, "I think a thousand guineas might be in order. Certainly cover some of the costs we've had since the flood."

She had said nothing. She knew when not to argue with Grady. She also knew he was right. Keebar was now almost twelve feet long and had quite outgrown his enclosure. Along with his size, he had developed a bad nature and a large horn and needed to be handled with care.

Lillian watched as the rhino was led out of his pen by six of the boys. He was no longer the sweet little baby so popular with the children who would sing "*num a num*" whenever Lillian walked by, enjoying milk and fruit and a roll in the mud bath she had made for him. She remembered how she and Button had rubbed

Keebar's stomach to ease the bellyache and wondered whether her husband missed her as much as she did him. Her life as a married woman seemed such a long time ago.

"Nothing to worry about here, ladies and gentlemen," Grady was saying to the worried faces who had gathered to watch the proceedings. "A more docile creature I've yet to give shelter to at this 'ere 'umble establishment!"

The boys exchanged glances and rolled their eyes as, one by one, they darted forwards to check the strong leather harness that had been wound around the rhino's seemingly armour-plated body, all the time keeping an eye out for any unexpected movements. The animal had been given a hefty draft of laudanum and was cobbled by chains around his three-toed feet, which caused him to tread in a slow and swaying motion, his great head swinging from side to side with each step and hanging heavy beneath the weight of his huge horn, which pointed forwards as if ready to charge. As he walked, he made a snuffling noise like a man snoring in the deepest of sleep.

One of the boys ran ahead to open the back of the cage on wheels whilst two others held onto the harness of the lead horse, which kept whinnying and rising up on its back legs.

"'E's caught a whiff of the rhino," one shouted to the other, eyes wide with fear.

"Keep that horse under control," shouted Grady, pointing at the boy who was desperately trying to hold onto the reins of the horse's harness.

"I'm trying, I'm trying," the boy yelled back, no more than four feet tall and being lifted off his feet each time the horse reared.

Panicked by the noise of the horse, the rhino made a lurch forwards. "Don't let go!" Charlie screamed at the boys who were now digging their heels into the ground, the leather straps cutting into the palms of their flesh, in an attempt to guide the rhino in the direction they wanted him to go. One of the younger boys ran to get out of the rhino's path, then slipped on the horse-muck-smeared cobbles and fell to the ground right in front of the rhino, who bent his head, scooped up the unfortunate child with his horn and tossed him over his head. The boy flew through the air and landed with a sickening thump at Grady's feet.

Grady looked down at the young boy lying in front of him and gave him a cursory kick. The boy was grimacing, stretching and rubbing the back of his neck.

"Still alive?"

"I think so, sir," the boy replied slowly, rubbing his belly where the horn had tossed him.

"Any blood?"

The boy looked down and held out his shirt and shook his head.

"Well, get up and give the others a hand, then, you lazy article."

LILLIAN AND MRS. Ogden watched the proceedings, hands over their mouths as agonising step followed agonising step and the boys slowly guided the rhino towards its new prison, up the ramp and into the cage. Once inside, Charlie dashed around the back to ensure the door was firmly closed and locked, then leaned against the wall and let out a large sigh. The crowd burst into applause. Grinning, Charlie whipped off his three-cornered hat and took a mock bow. The watchers gave a small cheer.

But before anyone could have a chance to take a rest, Grady shouted, "And now for the lion!"

Lillian swallowed and nodded. She always found it difficult when the animals in her care left for a new home, and this exodus would be particularly challenging. As she followed Charlie towards the lion's pen, she thought back to how she had lain in her bed in Tottenham Court Road and listened to his roar, how she had found the handbill advertising his existence and set off to find him. How long ago had that been? Only eighteen months? She shuddered when she remembered the terrible accident when she had lost her baby and how the thought of Leonidas had sustained her in the laudanum nightmare.

And now it was time to say a final goodbye.

She walked slowly and with a heavy heart as the boys dashed about carrying out their tasks.

"Excuse me, Miss," said one as he dodged out of the way. "Sorry, Miss," said another, weighed down by a bucket of water in his hand that was slopping over the edges.

Lillian stopped two feet from the cage and watched as Leonidas padded up and down in his cell. The lion turned to look at her, giving that familiar, almost indiscernible nod he always made when he saw her. He opened its mouth slightly to let out a gentle growl. He had been fed an hour before, and the heat from his breath formed small clouds of steam in the cold morning air as he exhaled the smell of dead meat. His tail *swish-swish-swished* behind him and the hair on his large brown mane drooped limply, clumped and matted in places. When Lillian looked into his brown eyes, she saw the flame of the candle flicker its reflection and noticed how his eyes had watered and dried in crusty lumps in the corners. His head hung as if defeated.

She shuddered and shook her head. "Oh, Leonidas," she said and felt around her neck for the lion's tooth Grady had given her so long ago. "It's time to leave, my love."

Lillian glanced at Charlie, then opened the door of the cage and slowly entered the den. She unhooked the specially made leather harness from where it hung on the wall. Kneeling down beside him, she picked up the brush she kept there and began to gently pass it across his fur, murmuring quietly, "Trust me, Leonidas. You'll have our own space. You'll be able to feel the ground beneath your feet at last."

Carefully she began to fasten the harness around his body and buckle it up. Leonidas replied with a shake of his mane, then opened his mouth wide as if to stretch his jaw but made no sound.

Her eyes filled with tears. She stuck out her hand and the lion licked it, the feeling of the rasp of his tongue lingering with the drying saliva.

"You . . . you will be a king's lion again," she stammered.

Lillian blinked and wiped away tears with the back of her hand. She looked over at Charlie. "Ready?"

Charlie nodded.

She opened the cage door and led Leonidas out, holding tightly onto his harness. Leonidas paused and stretched his body like a giant cat and gave a quiet growl of weary acceptance.

Woman and lion walked together side by side, Charlie bringing up the rear, towards the light at the end of the Great Hall.

Those who were there that day would say how they remembered Lillian standing in the doorway, the lion by her side, and how he had allowed himself to be guided into his cage on wheels where he lay down, put his head between his paws, and closed his eyes.

EVENTUALLY ALL THE animals marked for transportation were in their wheeled cages, or on the back of the carts, and were ready to go.

"Come on, come on," Grady said. "I want this lot on the move in the next hour or it will never get to Brighton before nightfall."

The crowd had continued to grow as, one by one, the animals were led out of the Exchange to take their place on the convoy. It seemed that every lavender girl, knife grinder, fruit seller, and market trader had stopped what they were doing to watch the preparations. Various musicians, recruited far and wide from the streets of London, now removed instruments from their cases and began a discordant tune-up. As the procession made ready to leave, two pie men appeared with their tin boxes on leather harnesses around their necks.

"Hot pies. Hot penny pies!" they cried, serving the meat-filled pastries on a sheet of newspaper, gravy ready to be poured into the hole made by the purchaser's finger.

Grady clapped his hands and for a moment there was silence. Then he opened his arms wide and with a sweep of his hand sent the pageant on its way. The musicians started up their instruments, the animals joined in with their familiar cry of yips and barks and howls, and the balladeer began to sing.

> *It was a glorious sight to see, you see,*
> *When the animals went to sea, you see*
> *No one in London but Polly and me*
> *All left Grady's Menagerie.*
> *The day the animals went to sea*
> *There were llamas and wolf cubs—one-two-three*
> *A foolish hyena too crazy for thee . . .*

AND SO IT went on. Grady stuck his chin in the air and puffed himself up with pride. "Now everyone will know the name of Grady's Menagerie," he said. "Purveyors of the finest animals to His Majesty. When all those fat culls in Brighton see the quality of our stock, they will be flocking to this place with open pocketbooks."

INDEED, IT WAS an occasion talked about in the public houses from Charing Cross, down the Strand and Fleet Street, and up to St. Pauls and beyond. And when the ale started to flow, the refrain of "What a glorious sight to see, when the animals went to sea" was accompanied by much flagon thumping and banging.

The story appeared in many newspapers, along with drawings of the caravan as it departed from the Exchange illustrated from both the front and their swaying disappearing behinds. Horses led the cages on wheels, with llamas trotting behind, tied to the cages. Grady's tokens were produced and admired and exchanged for as yet uncollected items.

BY THE TIME of the fire there were few in London who had not heard of the name Grady's Menagerie.

Twenty-Three

"WHERE IS HE?" LILLIAN DEMANDED OF Mrs. Ogden, about a month after the animals had departed.

Grady's oldest employee still opened the admission booth each morning, even though the beefeaters had abandoned their positions a week or so ago. Their red and gold-braided coats hung lifeless on the back of the door.

"Where do you think?" Mrs. Ogden replied without looking up, instead picking at a thread on her sleeve. "He's with that bloody elephant."

Lillian sighed. Since the flood and the departure of the animals, Grady's only interest seemed to be Bertha and the booze. True to his word, he spent his nights in the elephant's enclosure. Drinks would be set up on the table, beer for the elephant and the harder stuff for Grady, and every evening would end with a tired Grady falling into a stupor as he steadily drank his way through the proceeds of the animal sale.

"You're going to have to tell him," Mrs. Ogden insisted, her hands fluttering. "He'll listen to you. We've got no visitors. They've nothing to see and if he goes out of business then who will employ a poor old widow like me?"

"He told me yesterday that he was going down the docks last night."

"I doubt if he made it. He was already drunk by the time I left."

EACH DAY GRADY took personal care of Bertha's cleaning. He had acquired a special brush to scrub in between her toes—and heaven help any of the boys if it couldn't be found or they used it for something else. Patiently he would check that her nails and cuticles were of a suitable length and made sure that any buildup of rough skin was gently filed down and away. A separate brush was used to scrub the elephant's hide with soapy water, particular attention being paid to the bits Bertha couldn't reach herself, such as where the trunk joined the head.

As Lillian approached the elephant's enclosure, she could hear Grady crooning to Bertha.

"Don't you worry about that old rhino. We don't need anyone else, do we, gel?"

One of the boys ran past Lillian carrying a bucket of water into the enclosure, and she watched as Bertha put in her trunk, filled it with water, and sprayed it over her back—followed by a victorious *harrumph*.

Grady stepped back, rubbed his hands together, and said to Bertha, "Just the two of us, eh?"

"There's more than just you two, Grady," said Lillian.

"Ah, there you are, Lillian," he said, without taking his eyes off Bertha, who seemed to preen herself in his admiration. "Have you ever seen such a beautifully clean elephant?"

"It's the only one I've *ever* seen, Grady," said Lillian wearily. "But what about the rest of us? Mrs. Ogden is going out of her mind."

"Pah!" he said, waving away her concerns.

"Please listen," she insisted. "The best we had to offer has left for Brighton. Only the dullest of birds and the creatures visitors usually ignore are left. There's nothing to sell and we can't even count on the admission money anymore. When your rich customers arrive, they will want to see new and different creatures, but we have nothing."

She paused to see if he was listening. Putting a hand on his sleeve, she continued, "The beefeaters got wind there's no money and have left. Grady, we are all worried."

Grady shook off her hand. "Don't you worry, Lillian. I am sorting it. I told you." He walked away.

LILLIAN HAD QUICKLY settled back into her old quarters. Life at Neal Street with her husband had belonged to someone else, long ago. The Exchange was the only home she'd ever had. There had been no word from her husband since she left; she was starting to believe there never would be. She looked down at Samson curled in her lap while she stroked behind his ears and remembered Button's voice shouting at her to choose between himself and Samson. She knew she had made the right choice but still . . .

With so few animals to take care of, Lillian spent hour after hour sitting with her chimp, developing even more signs for basic words. By combining simple hand gestures and actions, Samson could communicate a wide range of desires and emotions, such as being tired or hungry, or wanting to climb on Lillian's back.

The bond between Samson and Teddy Diamond also grew deeper. Samson enjoyed grooming—and being groomed—and he and Teddy Diamond would often sit together, the chimp searching his way through the dog's fur, picking out the fleas which he would pop in his mouth, and in return the dog would lick and lick the chimp clean. If the dog dared to stop before Samson was ready, he would thump his chest and make an urgent screeching sound which Teddy Diamond understood immediately to mean "Don't stop!" But if the dog got bored, he would simply stand up and trot off. Samson might give chase or look around for Lillian, making the sign to jump into her arms.

Bertha was tolerant of Samson and did not complain if he ran into her enclosure. Instead, she joined in the play, letting him climb up on her back where Samson would balance, jumping from one leg to the other with Teddy Diamond barking up at him, the noise more often than not waking Grady from a drunken slumber. Bertha would reach behind with her trunk and grab the chimp, who would use the trunk as a makeshift swing, as if on a branch in a tree.

And so, as the summer drew to a close, Lillian's family passed their days, as if waiting for something to happen.

ONE EVENING AS Lillian was closing up, and Teddy Diamond and Samson were engaged in their mutual grooming, she heard a voice say, "So this is where you live?" She looked up to see a blonde-haired woman about a foot shorter than herself, carrying a selection of books under her arm, clad in the familiar green velvet with gold braid Lillian had come to know and love in Brighton.

"Miss Emily Lovetrue!" Lillian declared, standing to greet the visitor with a smile. "How wonderful to see you!"

Samson gave a screech of recognition at the visitor and Teddy Diamond, seeing that she was a friend, barked his delight, jumping up to say hello.

"Down, Teddy, down boy," said Lillian, sweeping Samson up onto her hip and indicating a chair for her to sit on. Miss Lovetrue removed her gloves.

Taking her friend's hands in her own, Lillian beamed at her with great delight. "What are you doing here?" she asked.

"I was on my way to attend a lecture at the Cheshire Cheese on Fleet Street and then remembered you were close by. I thought I simply could not be near without seeing this marvellous menagerie you told me so much about."

"And so you have found me," said Lillian with glee.

"Also, I came across a *very* interesting leaflet the last time I was at the theatre and couldn't wait to show it to you," Miss Lovetrue added with a smile, hooking a loose strand of hair behind her ear.

"How exciting! Look, Samson. Do you remember Miss Lovetrue?"

Samson replied by holding out his arms to the visitor and giving an excited screech.

"Let me take him," said Miss Lovetrue, and the chimp immediately jumped into her arms and started to cover her with kisses. "My, hasn't he grown?"

"Enough, Samson!" said Lillian. "Tell me how is Brighton and how is Mrs. Fortescue? And have you visited the new menagerie yet?"

"Oh my dear, so many questions! But first let me show you this leaflet, which I think you will find most curious indeed."

Miss Lovetrue put Samson on the floor while she fumbled in her handbag and produced a piece of paper folded into quarters.

She grinned as she handed it over. "I remember you telling me your story one evening in Brighton, and as soon as I saw this pamphlet I thought for sure it must be the person you described."

"What on earth can it be?" said Lillian, glancing up at her friend and unfolding the paper to reveal a picture of a man in a mask balancing on a white horse, its tail blowing out behind him as they rode around an auditorium of some sort. Other costumed characters, including one holding a burning hoop of fire, surrounded man and horse, all watched by a huge crowd.

"It's written in French," said Lillian, handing the leaflet back to Miss Lovetrue.

"Ah yes, let me translate. It says POPPIE'S PARISIAN PERFORMERS — COME SEE ACROBATS! JUGGLERS! TRICK RIDERS! FIRE EATERS! But never mind that. Look a little closer at the man on the horse."

Lillian looked again at the central figure in the leaflet and saw rosy cheeks and a curl in the middle of his forehead.

"Babyface Boothroyd!" she gasped.

"Yes, I thought it might be," her friend replied.

"Well, I never," said Lillian. "Where on earth did you get this?"

"I found it inside a French novel I picked up at the bookshop last week. Someone must have been using it as a marker."

Lillian's eyes gleamed. "I always wondered what happened to him after that brazen escape. So he's in Paris! Let's hope he stays well clear of London, lest anyone else should recognise him!"

She folded the leaflet once more and tucked it safely inside her apron. "Now come. You must tell me all the news." A few minutes later the two women were sitting in a quiet corner of the Exchange, Samson on Miss Lovetrue's lap and Teddy Diamond by Lillian's feet.

"Brighton remains very much as you left it, all the poorer for your absence, of course. Mrs. Fortescue said to be sure to pass on her regards if I saw you."

"And the animals? What news of them?"

"I have visited the Prince's menagerie and can confirm it is a very fine place indeed."

"Really?" said Lillian with some relief.

"For sure, it has become quite the place to visit on a Sunday afternoon following a walk in the gardens. All the people of quality make it their business to take a stroll and be seen there."

"And the lion? Leonidas? Is he well?" Lillian asked, fondling the tooth that still hung around her neck.

Miss Lovetrue clapped her hands with joy. "The lion is the most glorious and noble of creatures, just as you told me. He seems to spend most of his time in the outside pen, walking and pacing. He has to be coaxed to come in at night, I understand."

Lillian's heart grew tight. She swallowed hard, then allowed herself to smile. She knew she had done the right thing in not objecting to the lion leaving for Brighton. But she still missed the sound of his roar at night.

"And the rhinoceros?"

"Rhinoceros?" Miss Lovetrue queried.

"The large creature with a horn?"

Miss Lovetrue shook her head. "I am afraid I did not see a rhinoceros, my dear. Should there have been one?"

Lillian frowned. "Yes, most certainly! He came here when he was just a baby and was part of the contingent Grady sold to the new place. Got quite a price for it, I understand. There was a huge fuss when they left. Maybe you read about it in the newspapers? A wagon reinforced with bars, a cage on wheels? It took six horses to pull it."

Miss Lovetrue looked away and thought for a moment. "Well, I would most certainly have seen him and I am afraid that I did not. Too big a creature to remain hidden, I'm sure!"

Lillian drew in a deep breath and frowned.

Miss Lovetrue leaned forwards and took her hands in hers. "And now I have upset you. I would not hurt thee for the world. I am so sorry."

Lillian shook her head. "No, no. I am just surprised, and a little concerned as to his welfare. I am sure there is an explanation."

But instinct told her something was wrong.

"I am glad to hear so. Now, I must take my leave or I shall be late," Miss Lovetrue said, standing and pulling on her gloves once more, taking time to fasten the two calf leather-covered buttons at her wrist. "I am attending a talk by Miss Wollstonecraft, who is giving a lecture about the girls' school she opened in Newington Green. As you know, the education of women is a subject most dear to my heart."

"I do, and in your absence I have enjoyed reading your letters in *The Lady* magazine. So passionate!" Lillian replied, trying to sound as bright as she had when they first began talking.

"Then come, my dear," said Miss Lovetrue, giving a slight pull on Lillian's hand. "We shall go together?"

"I cannot," said Lillian, shaking her head, although in truth she would love to have gone. "There is too much to do today." She was anxious now to be rid of her visitor and talk to Grady.

"Another time, then," said her friend, gathering her books and tucking them under her arm. She gave Lillian her warmest smile. "*Au revoir, ma cherie*. It was wonderful to see you."

And then she was gone.

LILLIAN WENT STRAIGHT to the elephant's pen, where she found Grady slumped in the same chair, legs askew, his food-spattered waistcoat hanging open and his chin resting on his chest, which rose and fell with each breath. His wig sat at an awkward angle. Teddy Diamond padded over and sat down beside him, resting his head on his knee, whilst Samson clambered onto Bertha's back as she continued to munch her way through the pile of hay in the corner. Lillian stood and watched him as a thin dribble of saliva made its silent escape from the corner of his mouth. How could she ever have been so in thrall to this man?

The elephant signalled Lillian's arrival with a quiet bellow. Grady woke abruptly.

"Bertha? Bertha?" he said, wiping his mouth with the back of the hand.

"It's me, Grady," said Lillian, barely able to keep the disgust out of her voice.

"Ah, Lillian," he said, closing his eyes again and clasping his hands in front of his belly, which strained under his shirt. "Just another few minutes' kip before we open up."

"We've been open for hours, Grady. You've slept through it all. No one wants to come in when you're like this," she said, standing with her hands on her hips, looking down at the drink-sodden menagerie owner. "I don't know who smells worse, you or the elephant."

"What?" said Grady, sitting up and rubbing his eyes, running his tongue around his lips, then wiping the corners of his mouth with his thumb. "Bertha don't smell."

"Why didn't you tell me about Keebar, Grady?"

"Keebar?"

"Our rhino."

"Tell you what about the rhino?" he replied, squeezing his eyes shut.

"I have just had a visitor from Brighton. She says she's visited the Prince's new menagerie and there was no sign of a rhinoceros."

"No rhinoceros? Why, I—"

"And don't try lying to me, Grady. I've had enough of your lies."

"Aw, Lillian . . . darlin' . . ."

"Don't 'darling' me. Just tell me. Where has he gone?"

"I didn't tell you because I knew you'd be upset."

"Upset?"

Grady sighed, took off his wig, and scratched his head. "Keebar did not quite finish the journey to Brighton, Lillian."

"Did not finish?" she asked, squinting at him.

"All I can tell you is what was reported back to me."

"I want to know what happened," she said urgently.

Grady sat up and took a deep breath. He leaned over to pick up the heavy stone jar of liquor that was never far from his side these days. Lillian kicked it from his hand and it lay on its side. Nothing trickled out.

"Tell me!" she demanded.

"They said they were leading the wagons over some small bridge or other, across a stream outside the fields of Fulham. One of the horses became agitated by the noise of the rhino. It rose up on his haunches and the other horses panicked, then the wagon toppled over and . . ."

"And?" said Lillian.

"And the rhino wagon ended up in the stream. Too big to get out," Grady concluded, glancing up at Lillian then back down at his hands.

"You mean he—"

"Drowned. Yes." Grady looked away. "Not my fault, gel."

Angry tears appeared in Lillian's eyes, which Bertha tried to wipe away with her trunk.

"What did they do with him?"

Grady looked sheepish. "We got word to that friend of mine. You know, you've met him . . . John Hunter."

Lillian scoffed. "That surgeon ghoul?"

Grady nodded. "He sent his men down and they took the body away."

"And for your trouble you pocketed . . . how much?"

"Now, Lill, that's unfair. I've lost a lot of money with that rhino."

"And drunk the rest," said Lillian, shaking her head and looking away from the creature she had once respected.

The silence hung between them as Lillian appeared to reach a conclusion. "You've deceived me for the last time, Grady."

"What do you mean?" he said, his voice trembling.

"I'm leaving."

"Leaving? Leaving what?"

"Leaving you. The menagerie. The animals. There's nothing here for me now."

Grady made as if to stand up, but his brains were so addled with the drink that he immediately fell back in his chair. Lillian stood looking down at him.

"Goodbye, Grady. Come on, Samson," she said and walked out.

Grady turned to Bertha and said, "Bah! She'd never leave here. Where would she go? I'll speak to her later."

He looked around for the jug. "Now, where were we? Another drop, Bertha, my love?"

Settling back down in his chair, he patted his body for his pipe and baccy, mumbling to himself all the while. He filled the bowl with tobacco and after three attempts finally managed to get it alight. Taking in a deep breath of smoke, he choked as he let it out.

"She'd never leave here . . . *cough, cough* . . . never leave me . . ."

The hand holding the pipe fell to his side and he gave another little cough.

"I'll talk to her later . . . later . . ." he mumbled as the drink overcame him once more and the pipe fell from his hand. The burning tobacco fell out of the bowl and onto the dry straw, which caught quickly and began to burn.

Lillian was still angry as she walked upstairs to her room. *That is it! I have had enough,* she thought. Enough of Grady's lies and duplicitous dealings. He had driven a wedge between her and her husband, treated the animals appallingly, bought and sold as he saw fit—and had actually told someone she had given birth to a monkey in order to make a profit. He had never shown a jot of shame or remorse for any of it.

"That man," she said aloud through gritted teeth as she bent down to drag out her trunk from under the bed. Lillian pulled at the top handle on her chest of drawers and took out the few clothes she owned—a change of shirt, an apron, some undergarments— and threw them in. She wrapped her hand mirror in her camisole, then carefully placed the hairbrush, toothbrush, and teeth-cleaning powder on top of the clothes. She shook the bottle of lavender and held it to the light to see how much remained, relieved to see a few drops left.

At the bottom of the drawer lay the copy of *Wealth of Nations* that John had given her so long ago. She flicked through the pages, then looked around her as she thought back to the terrible night eight months ago when her baby had been born and died. She gave her head a small shake as she pushed the thought to the back of her mind. "Where will we go now, Samson?" she wondered aloud. The clock ticked steadily in the background and the small window rattled. *They never got round to fixing that,* she thought, and walked around the bed to close it.

Something tickled her nostrils. Her nose itched. She sniffed. She inhaled again.

"Oh my god," she said, as she realised her worst nightmare had become real.

"FIRE!" she screamed.

Lillian opened the door of her bedroom and could see wisps of smoke rising up the staircase. She searched the room, spied the pillowcase, and quickly dropped it into her washbowl, mercifully unemptied from her morning's ablutions, squeezed it out, and tied it around her nose and face. She did the same with her handkerchief and went to tie it around Samson's face, but he shook his head with a screech, pushing her away. "Samson, please!" she urged, but the chimp continued to shriek and shake his head. With time running out, she abandoned the trunk. Shooing Samson in front of her, she ran downstairs.

The Grand Hall was already starting to fill with smoke and noises of panic from both human and beasts. The pitiful bleatings, gruntings, brayings, and growlings of the trapped animals combined with urgent cries of "Fire!" seemed to come from every corner of the Exchange. Having lost sight of Samson, Lillian stood holding the damp pillowcase to her mouth, attempting to assess the situation, not knowing which way to turn or who to help first. Fleeing rats ran over her feet, which made an awful crunching sound as she ran through the debris of dead creatures accumulating on the floor as the flames claimed whatever hung above. Her eyes filled with tears from the smoke and she could hear the sound of timbers starting to creak under the strain. Boys ran this way and that, carrying bundles of possessions and random items such as spades and pickaxes. Everyone was coughing and trying to hold a cloth of some sort to their mouths.

As Charlie ran past, Lillian grabbed him by the shirt. Other boys stopped when they saw her familiar figure and clustered around her, clutching at her apron.

"Where's the fire? Where's Grady?" she demanded.

"Don't know, Miss. What should we do, Miss?" came the replies.

Lillian took charge. "Jack! Open all the pens and let the animals loose. Nick! Get the boys to gather as many pails of water as they can. Form a chain. Pass them along. Tom! Run down to the river and get the watermen. And send someone over to Somerset House to get the guards."

Her instructions were interrupted by a noise from the room above the Great Hall. The sound of a panicking elephant, trammelling the floor with her feet and bellowing and harrumphing, rose above the panic below. She could hear Teddy Diamond barking.

"Has anyone checked Bertha upstairs?"

The boys looked at each other, all shaking their heads. "No, Miss."

Lillian and Charlie looked at each other. "Charlie. Come with me."

Quickly they made their way up the wooden staircase as fast as they could and came face to face with the sight of the elephant mad with fear, her trunk waving wildly, ears flapping and eyes open so wide the whites were visible. A large hole had appeared where the fire had started and fallen through into the Great Hall below, taking the burning straw with it. Bertha was backed into a corner of the room where the floor still held. Teddy Diamond, tail singed and smoking, stood at the top of the stairs barking at Bertha whilst Grady, the fear in his eyes matching that of his beloved elephant, held onto the back of the window on the other side of the room, standing on a ledge that was already smaller than his feet and rapidly disappearing.

The flames leapt up through the hole. Grady glanced down at the fire below, then over at Bertha and back at his would-be rescuers, all the time coughing and eyes watering. Smoke was fast filling the room and the elephant was becoming increasingly agitated. Checking behind her, Lillian saw the flames had reached the stairs. She glanced at Charlie and gave a small shake of the head. Charlie looked away. Both had reached the same conclusion. There could be no way back down for the elephant except through the hole.

She shouted across at Grady. "Can you make your way around the edge?"

"I can't. The floor's all gone," he yelled back. Another part of the floor gave way and fell into the fire below.

"There's no other way down!"

"I'm not leaving Bertha!" A note of panic had entered his voice.

"You've got no choice, Grady!"

A man's voice came from below. "Grady! Can you hear me? The watermen are here. If you can't get out, you're going to have to jump. Can you hear me, Grady?"

"I can't leave Bertha," he yelled back at them.

"Come on," shouted Lillian over her shoulder at Charlie. "There's nothing else we can do. The stairs are already on fire."

Charlie hesitated, looking over at Grady. Then, pulling Teddy Diamond by the collar, all three ran down the stairs which collapsed behind them into the fire below.

Outside the cold night air hit her immediately and she bent double with coughing. A small crowd had gathered on the Strand and were running around trying to catch the stampeding animals with ropes and nets. The zebra was managing to elude both people and wolves, although one of the ostriches had been netted and a porcupine had been caught and tied up. The peacock was a pitiful sight, lying broken on the floor. Lillian could still hear the elephant bellowing from inside the burning building behind her, its voice getting higher and higher with fear. Pandemonium surrounded her. Men and boys ran back and forth carrying buckets of water or passing them along a line. Small animals and dead birds lay scattered everywhere, their once bright plumage now covered in water, soot, and dirt as their carcasses became mixed up with the dead rats and were trodden on and or kicked out of the way by the rescuers. The smell of smoke and singed meat was overwhelming. Teddy Diamond stood barking at the carnage and chaos.

Wiping the smoke from her eyes, she straightened up and found her husband standing in front of her.

"John," she said, eyes widening in surprise.

Button pulled his wife towards him in an embrace, then pushed her away, still holding onto her forearms, while inspecting her for signs of injury. "Are you hurt? What happened? I came just as soon as I heard."

"I'm fine but—poor Bertha . . ." she replied between coughs, cocking her head at the burning building behind them. Then she realised something was missing. "Oh my god. Samson! Where's Samson?"

But Samson was nowhere to be seen.

"Lillian!" shouted Button, as she slipped through his arms and began desperately searching for the lost chimp, grabbing boys and onlookers, asking them all the same question, "Have you seen him? Have you seen Samson? Do you know where's Samson?" only to be greeted by silent shaking heads, as they continued to pass buckets of water along the line.

Panting, Button caught up with her. "I'm going inside," he said, taking off his coat and thrusting it at Lillian. "Wait here. Do not move."

"No John, you mustn't," she shouted, but he had already disappeared into the building.

Then one of the boys pulled at her sleeve. "Miss! Miss!" he said, pointing upwards.

There at the window she could see Samson, his arms wrapped around Grady's neck, mouth open and screeching in fear. Both terrified.

"Samson!" she cried.

From where she was standing, she could see back inside the Great Hall. Six big river workers, employed by the insurance companies as part-time firefighters, were quickly unpacking a large tarpaulin, having succeeded in extinguishing the fire underneath the room where Grady and Bertha were trapped. Men and boys now formed a circle, each gripping an edge of the tarpaulin in their hands and positioning it directly below the hole above.

"Jump, Grady! Jump! We'll catch you," they shouted, flapping the tarpaulin in encouragement.

Lillian joined in their calls. "Jump, Grady! Jump!"

Grady held on tightly to Samson. He looked over at Bertha, who had retreated as far as she could from the fire, and their eyes met. For a brief second the elephant was silent. "I love you," Grady whispered, then closed his eyes and took a step off the ledge into the air, falling hard into the tarpaulin the men were holding. Before he could check if anything was broken, Samson had wriggled out of his arms and run back into the building. Grady scrambled to his feet, then looked up through the hole and roared, "Bertha!"

"Can't be catching no elephant, Grady," said one of the watermen, coughing and making ready to run from the fire, which blazed on inside the building.

Grady grabbed him by the lapels of his coat, "I'm begging you," he said, his eyes bulging and wild, spitting the words in the man's face.

"Not with that. It just ain't possible," the waterman said, shrugging him off. "I'm sorry."

The boys gathered around Grady and began pulling at him. "Come on, Mr. Grady. We got to go." They dragged him away as he continued to shout after his beloved elephant.

The watermen surged out of the burning building just as Lillian was trying to get back in.

"Let me in. Let me in," she screamed. "My husband's in there. He's got my baby. I know he has."

"Don't be stupid, Miss. That floor's about to come down any minute and that great bloody elephant is going to go with it."

Lillian shook off his hand and prepared to enter the building.

"That's suicide," he said, seizing the other arm and pushing her back. "Can't let you do it."

Before Lillian could argue with him, the world seemed to explode as two tons of elephant fell through the burning floor and hit the ground below with a crash and a final bellow. Silence descended for just a second or two before a cyclone ball of dust and dirt burst through the entrance of the Exchange.

And when the air cleared there stood Button, Samson in his arms, dishevelled and soiled by smoke and soot. As Lillian ran forwards to embrace them, the crowd broke into loud clapping and cheers and the family hugged each other until one of the watermen told them that there was nothing more that could be done to save the Exchange and they needed to move out of the way.

Two weeks later, Lillian and John stood hand in hand in the street, staring up at the blackened carcass of the Exchange. Samson was on Lillian's hip and Teddy Diamond leaned against John's leg. The rain fell steadily. Those who had to walk past could still catch the smell of cooked meat, mingled with the foetid smell of the animal stalls and the whiff of dead fire, but no one would tarry there, as if superstitious about the death of so many animals inside. It had taken many more hours for the watermen to get the fire under control and by that time there was very little left. The remains of the elephant were spirited away by someone who thought there was money to be made from the carcass, and now the floor was littered with charred bones, twisted bits of metal, and broken glass. Luckily no people had been lost and all the boys were accounted for. But Grady had not been seen since. Teddy Diamond had found a new home at Neal Street with Lillian, Button, and Samson.

Lillian looked up at the charred pictures of the creatures above the main door, once advertising the delights that could be found inside but their colours now faded by the smoke, the windows glassless and their frames more charcoal than wood. The entrance was empty. No crowds pushing their way past liveried doormen. No children pleading with their mothers for a ride on the zebra. No modern-day Noah enticing Londoners to come and see what was inside.

Nothing. Just silence.

Lillian turned her head towards her husband, who nodded. They walked away.

Epilogue

SHE COULD HEAR THE ROAR OF the lion as soon as she awoke and thought, it will soon be time for his feed. A further rumble followed, a lighter sound with a different tone. Lillian smiled. Since she had successfully persuaded Mr. Barclay to buy a second lion for the Prince's menagerie Leonidas had taken on a new lease of life. That companionship, as well the better quality food and open spaces, had transformed his coat, his skin. And if she was right in her suspicions, they would soon be welcoming a new addition to his family. She could not keep her husband away from the lion's enclosure, so obsessed was he with ensuring the successful delivery of the lioness's offspring. "Much more challenging than Lady Beauchamp's peacock," he had told her. Nowadays Button was more inclined to reach first for the potions that filled his medicine bag, liniments of tar, sulphur and turpentine, and powders such as Epsom or Glauber's salts, in preference to the instruments he had for a time been partial to.

He had agreed to join her when she accepted the position of Head Keeper to the Prince's menagerie and together they made a formidable team. Now she was free to put into practise all the ideas she had held for so long about how best to keep and display the

animals, how good food and space could make such a difference
to their well-being. She was particularly proud of the piped warm
water which heated the lions' den, as well as that of the llamas and
kangaroos, and had plans for a huge monkey house with swings
and shelter.

The caw of the seagulls interrupted her thoughts and she reached
out with her hand to feel Samson secure in his cot. She stretched,
then rolled over and pulled the blanket up around her chin as she
nestled down further against her husband's body. Lillian hugged
her swollen belly and smiled to herself at the thought of the coming spring and the promised new life.

Acknowledgments

I was inspired to write *The Candlelit Menagerie* following a chance purchase of Christopher Plumb's *The Georgian Menagerie*. His descriptions of The Exeter Exchange on The Strand, and the story of the cassowary bird in particular, inspired me to wonder what life might have been like in such a place.

My story originally intended to focus on the adventures of the young vet but as the character of Lillian evolved, I became increasingly intrigued as to how a misfit such as she might find a natural home amongst the animals stolen from their natural habitats. And how far could she go as a woman and a mother?

Ultimately, however, this novel is a work of fiction set in a time of great change in England, and whilst the settings may have been real, the events are entirely the work of my imagination.

I'd like to thank Beth Miller on the New Writing South team (in Brighton) who encouraged and nurtured me through the entire process of producing my story. "Just get it written," she would say, and taught me to ignore Imposter Syndrome.

Major thanks are also due to everyone in my writing group who read, listened, commented and contributed to the story. Your support has been invaluable and I don't think I could have done it without you.

And thanks also to my daughter, Poppie, who never fails to inspire me with her positivity.

My editor, Lilly Golden, at Skyhorse, has given invaluable help with her wise insights and finally, big love to Brad (Toastie) Taylor who initially introduced my novel to Skyhorse.